MW00629913

THE GHOST
AND THE
CHRISTMAS SPIRIT

HAUNTING DANIELLE

THE GHOST
AND THE
CHRISTMAS SPIRIT

USA TODAY BESTSELLING AUTHOR
BOBBI HOLMES

The Ghost and the Christmas Spirit
(Haunting Danielle, Book 23)
A Novel
By Bobbi Holmes
Cover Design: Elizabeth Mackey

Copyright © 2019 Bobbi Holmes
Robeth Publishing, LLC
All Rights Reserved.
robeth.net

ISBN: 978-1-949977-56-1

To Dorothy Burke, my grandma Hilda's friend,
who created the original Bridal Shoe for my sister and me,
and who inspired our family's Christmas Shoe tradition.

And to all those grandmothers out
there who lovingly create gifts from the heart.

ONE

The attractive thirtysomething couple strolled leisurely down the Astoria sidewalk, with the man's right arm wrapped around the woman's shoulders. She leaned against him as they made their way from the restaurant where they had just eaten breakfast to their parked car. It wasn't just any car. It was a black 1924 Packard Coupe, which the man had originally purchased over ninety years earlier—in his first life.

An elderly-looking man who called himself Colin Bari watched the couple from the other side of the street. Cane in hand, Colin observed the pair, noting they had dressed for the cooler weather, with the man wearing dress slacks and a shirt with a sharp overcoat and a cockily placed fedora hat, making him look as if he came from an earlier era—which he had.

The woman wore denims, knee-high boots, and a faux-fur jacket over her red cowl-neck sweater, with a matching knit cap. The red cap covered the top of her head and her ears, while dark curls slipped out from under its brim, almost touching her shoulders. She carried a purse, its strap draped over one shoulder. Colin suspected she was leaning close to the man not so much for his warmth, but because she wanted to be close to him.

Colin already knew who they were—Walt and Danielle Marlow. By the easy laughter and smiles the pair exchanged, it was obvious they were in love. Colin glanced to his watch and frowned. The curio shop would be opening in just a few minutes.

"IT'S GOING to be such a quiet Christmas, with just you and me in the house," Danielle said with a sigh.

Walt tightened his arm around Danielle. "Are you forgetting our Christmas Eve open house and the fact we're hosting Christmas dinner? Not exactly just you and me—which I wouldn't mind, by the way."

Danielle let out another sigh and pressed against Walt as she continued with him down the street. "I know. I just like having people around during the holidays. I rather miss the B and B at this time of year."

"If you will recall, having certain houseguests last Christmas almost got you killed," Walt reminded her.

Before Danielle had a chance to respond, the strap of the purse she was carrying broke, sending the handbag to the sidewalk, its contents spilling out.

"Drat!" Danielle cursed, coming to an abrupt stop. She leaned down to retrieve her purse.

Walt knelt down beside her, helping Danielle gather up her things.

"How did that happen?" Danielle grumbled as she shoved her wallet and a package of tissues back into her handbag.

"Is everything okay?" a man's voice called out.

Walt and Danielle had just tucked the last item back into the purse when they heard the voice. Standing back up, they looked to the nearby curio shop. Its door was now ajar as a man stood inside peeking out while turning the closed sign to open as he looked with concern to Walt and Danielle.

Hugging her handbag to her side, Danielle smiled at the man. "Aside from needing a new purse, we're fine."

"I wish I could help you. But I don't think I have any in stock— aside from a vintage pearl clutch," the man told her.

Danielle glanced up to the store sign hanging above its front door and window. It read *Mermaid Curio—unique treasures from the sea and around the world*. The man gave them both a parting nod, went back into his shop, and let the front door shut.

She looked to Walt with a hopeful expression. "Let's go inside and see what they have. We still need to find a couple of things for the white elephant gift exchange."

Walt tucked one hand in his pocket and placed his other hand on her lower back. He nodded to the store and said, "Let's go in."

FROM ACROSS THE street Colin watched as Walt and Danielle disappeared inside the curio shop. Stepping up to the edge of the sidewalk, he glanced to the right and then the left, looking for any oncoming traffic. Satisfied the road was clear, he hurried across the street, heading toward Mermaid Curio.

When he opened its door a moment later, it sent a bell overhead jingling, reminding him of sleigh bells. Stepping into the poorly lit gift shop, he spied Walt and Danielle standing by one of the counters, talking to the shop owner.

The man glanced up upon hearing the bell and saw Colin. He gave him a smile and called out, "I will be with you in a minute."

"No hurry," Colin called back, his accent barely discernible. "I'm just browsing."

Neither Walt nor Danielle paid any notice to the new arrival, nor had they heard him call out to the shop owner. Instead they chatted amongst themselves while studying a curious item in Danielle's hand. She turned it from side to side, trying to figure out what it was exactly. As best she could tell, it was a large gold high-heel shoe that someone had enthusiastically embellished with snippets of artificial poinsettia, tiny glass balls, and a multitude of what she assumed were fake gemstones.

"What exactly are you looking for?" the shop owner asked as he stood behind the counter, watching Danielle examine the curious item.

Still holding the gaudy shoe, she looked up to him with a smile. "I'm looking for a couple of things to buy for a white elephant gift exchange."

The man nodded to the unusual object in Danielle's hand and said, "I would think that Christmas shoe might be just the right thing. Assuming this is a gift exchange for Christmas."

Danielle arched her brow and looked back at the shoe in her hand. "Is this what this is, a Christmas shoe?" If anyone had ever worn the lone shoe, it was unwearable now, as the artificial flowers and other bobbles weren't just glued onto its exterior but inside.

The shop owner reached out and turned the shoe over in Danielle's hand, revealing the Christmas paper glued on its sole. "Considering the poinsettias and Christmas paper, that's what I'm calling it."

Danielle ran several fingertips over the bottom of the shoe, noting its roughness, suggesting many layers of wrapping paper had been decoupaged on its sole. "Yes, it's for Christmas," she said.

"Then this would be perfect," the man said with a mischievous grin.

Danielle looked up to him and extended her free hand. "I'm Danielle Marlow, and this is my husband, Walt. We're from Frederickport."

"Marlow? That wouldn't be Marlow House B and B, would it?" the man asked as he shook her hand.

"It used to be a B and B." After taking back her hand, she dug it into her purse and pulled out a business card.

"I'm Bud Darrel. You can call me Bud. I own this shop," the man explained. He accepted the business card after shaking Walt's hand.

"Nice to meet you," Danielle said, turning her attention back to the shoe.

"What exactly does one do with that?" Walt asked with a frown, glancing from the shoe to Bud.

Bud shrugged. "I suppose it's some sort of Christmas decoration. It was one of the items in a trunk I purchased from the Winterborne auction. I was just unpacking it. In fact, I haven't even had a chance to price any of the items. The trunk arrived last night, right after closing. I was just going through it before I went to unlock the door and turn the open sign around."

"Winterborne auction?" Danielle asked with a frown.

"Eloise Winterborne owned one of the oldest and largest houses in town. She passed away about six months ago. The estate recently auctioned off most of her personal items. I picked up this trunk." He pointed to an antique trunk several feet away. "After looking inside, I have a feeling they just shoved a bunch of junk in there that should have been tossed out or taken to the thrift store. But I was bidding on the trunk, not its contents."

Danielle set the shoe on the counter and walked over to the

trunk. She ran her hand over its intricate carving. "No, I imagine you didn't. This is quite exquisite."

Bud perked up. "You interested in it?"

Danielle shook her head and walked back to the counter with Walt. "No. Not really our style. But it is lovely. However, I am sort of interested in this shoe." She picked it up again and grinned at Walt.

Bud shrugged. "I suppose it would make a good white elephant gift."

"How much do you want for it?" Walt asked.

"Umm...how does five dollars sound?" Bud asked hopefully.

"Deal," Danielle said, setting the shoe back on the counter and looking around. "I need to find something else." She glanced at the other items strewn across the counter and then looked back up to Bud. "Is all this stuff from the trunk?"

"Yes. Just what's on the counter. Why don't you go look around the store? I'm sure you'll be able to find something else. There are more Christmas items over there." Bud pointed to the front of the shop.

Danielle was about to check out the suggested Christmas items when Walt reached in front of her and flipped over an upside-down picture frame. When he turned it over, it revealed an old black-and-white photograph behind the glass.

"I don't believe it," Walt murmured under his breath, picking up the frame for a closer look.

"What is it?" Danielle asked, looking at the photograph in the frame. It was a picture of two men standing on a dock. One held up a large fish while grinning proudly.

"It's George," Walt whispered under his breath. He looked to the shop owner and asked, "How much do you want for this?"

Bud, who had not heard Walt's whisper, glanced over to the framed picture. "I don't think the frame is an antique. The picture looks a little water damaged around the edges. What would you say to five dollars for that too?"

"Sold," Walt said, looking to Danielle. "You want to pay the man?"

After Danielle paid for the purchase, Bud walked to the cash register. Once he was out of earshot, Danielle asked Walt in a whisper, "Did you say George?"

"The man holding the fish. That's George Hemming. Marie's

5

father."

"Are you sure?" Danielle asked.

Walt nodded. "Absolutely. I suspect that might be the perfect white elephant gift for Adam. After all, George was his great-grandfather."

"That's a little better than a normal white elephant gift. I wouldn't mind putting it in a nice frame."

Walt shook his head. "I'm afraid you might destroy the photograph if you try to remove it. That water damage he mentioned—the photograph appears to be stuck to the glass."

"I suppose you're right. Anyway, I can't be giving Adam something too nice for a white elephant gift." Danielle chuckled and asked, "But how did this Winterborne woman get a picture of Marie's father?"

"I suppose we'll have to show Marie when we get home and ask her if she recognizes the other man in the picture. Perhaps it's someone from the Winterborne family, and they were friends with the Hemmings."

"Did you know any Winterbornes?" Danielle asked.

Walt shook his head. "No. The name's not familiar. But I know that's George holding the fish. I would recognize him anywhere."

Asking Marie Hemming Nichols about the man in the photograph would sound impossible to Marie's grandson Adam Nichols, if he had heard Walt's suggestion. After all, Marie had been dead for over two years. But what Adam didn't know, his grandmother's spirit wasn't ready to move on, and instead she had stuck around—as a ghost.

Adam would also not understand how Walt could have possibly recognized his great-grandfather, a man who had died years before Walt's birth. But what Adam didn't know—what most people didn't know—George Hemming had been one of Walt Marlow's best friends. That was before Walt had married Danielle, before he had been a ghost, before he had died in 1925.

Most people—the non-mediums of Walt and Danielle's acquaintance—believed the Walt Marlow who was now standing in the curio shop was simply a distant cousin of that other Walt, one who shared his name, lived in the house he once lived in, and was a bestselling author.

One thing Walt and Danielle had learned, life—and death—could sometimes be complicated.

TWO

Visitors to Mermaid Curio showed little interest in the antique crystal and china lining the shelves on aisle two. It seemed no one wanted great-grandma's fine china these days. In spite of the fact Colin Bari had remained in aisle two during Walt and Danielle's entire visit to the shop, he was no more interested in china and crystal than the others. His motive for being there was to eavesdrop without being seen.

The moment Walt and Danielle walked out the front door of Mermaid Curio—Danielle carrying the paper sack holding her purchase—Colin stepped out from the second aisle and made his way to the front window. The end of his cane tapped along the wooden floor as he hurried to see where the Marlows were now heading. For a man who appeared to be in his seventies, the use of the cane seemed more a fashion statement than function for Mr. Bari.

Bud started to say something to him, but the phone rang. As he answered the call, Colin moved closer to the window, the palm of his right hand resting on the pane of glass. Colin continued to watch Walt and Danielle as they headed for the Packard. The next moment a car pulled up alongside the vintage vehicle and parked. He watched as Danielle, who had just opened the passenger door to the Packard, seemed to recognize the driver of the other car. She hastily tossed the sack with her purchase into the Packard, shut the car door, and then went to greet the driver as he got out of his vehi-cle. She gave him an exuberant hug and then appeared to be intro-ducing him to Walt. The two men shook hands. Colin stood silently and watched them chat for a few minutes before they parted ways. The tall dark man turned and walked toward the front door of the curio shop while Walt and Danielle got into the Packard and drove away.

"What can I help you with, Mr. Bari?" Bud asked after he ended his phone call.

Colin turned from the window and smiled at the man. "I'm just doing a little browsing—getting some ideas for Christmas gifts."

"If you tell me who you're shopping for, maybe I can give you some suggestions," Bud offered.

"I appreciate that, but for the moment, I prefer to just browse." Colin gave the man a friendly smile.

In the next moment the man who had been talking to Walt and Danielle outside walked into the shop. Once again, the bell over the door jingled.

Recognizing the newcomer, the shop owner called out, "Mr. Jackson, you're still here."

"Please, call me Mathew. Yes. I'm hoping to get out of here tomorrow." Mathew Jackson stepped up to the counter and shook Bud's hand.

From his place at the window, Colin studied Mathew Jackson for a moment, trying to place him. Jackson was tall, stocky, with closely cropped black hair and skin the shade of coffee with just a touch of cream. It was then he remembered. *Ahh, he is Emma Jackson's grandson,* Colin thought.

"I am still interested in your grandmother's oak dresser," Bud told Mathew.

"I was hoping you would say that."

Mathew and Bud continued their negotiations while Colin looked back out the front window. He spied a middle-aged couple scurrying across the street from a parked car that hadn't been there a few minutes earlier. As they got closer, recognition dawned.

"Oh…this is going to be interesting," Colin muttered. He walked back over to the second aisle, losing himself amongst the crystal and china, listening to what was going to happen next.

BUD GLANCED up when the bell over the front door jingled again, and a couple he recognized walked in—Forrest and Marcella Hooper. The couple glanced around the shop as if just browsing. A moment later Marcella spied the Winterborne antique trunk. She gave her husband a little shove with her elbow and then nodded toward it.

"I'll send someone to pick it up in the morning," Bud told Mathew a few minutes later. The two men shook hands again in a parting gesture. It wasn't until Mathew had left the shop that the Hoopers stepped closer to the counter.

"Nice seeing you both again," Bud greeted the Hoopers.

"After all the rain we've had the last few weeks, we thought we'd take advantage of this morning's sunshine. Who knows how long it will last," Forrest told him. "Seemed like a good morning to take a walk through town."

"I see it arrived," Marcella said, reaching out and running a hand over the Winterborne trunk.

"It came in last night, right after closing," Bud said.

Forrest glanced at the items littering the counter. "I see you've been going through the trunk."

Marcella grinned sheepishly at the shop owner. "It was kind of disappointing, wasn't it?"

"You mean what was inside?" Bud asked with a laugh.

"I imagine you're just going to send the stuff over to the thrift shop," Forrest said.

"I was going to when I first unloaded it, but I've already sold two items from the trunk."

The smile vanished from Marcella's face. Her eyes quickly surveyed the cluttered counter, taking a silent inventory.

Forrest stepped up next to Marcella and began frantically sorting through the items.

Bud frowned. "Is there a problem? Are you looking for something?"

"It's not here," Forrest muttered.

"What did you sell?" Marcella demanded.

Confused, Bud looked from Marcella to Forrest. "I don't understand. What is the problem?"

"What did you sell?" Marcella repeated.

"Umm...some ugly shoe with a bunch of flowers glued on it

and an old picture frame with a black-and-white photograph. Did you want those for some reason?" he asked.

Forrest patted his wife's shoulder and was greeted by her glare. He looked to Bud and said, "We were just a little sentimental about a couple of the things they put in the trunk. We were hoping to buy them from you. I suppose I'm shocked anyone else was interested in them. They are only worth something to us, for sentimental reasons."

Bud frowned. "I don't understand. If you wanted any of those things, why did they add them to the trunk?"

"They didn't belong to us," Marcella reminded him. "It's not like they would let us just keep them."

"Considering what they're worth, I'm sure you could have just asked the estate lawyer if you could have them. Or at the very least, offer to buy them. We're not talking any significant money here," Bud said. "Typically those types of items never make it to auction, they get sent to the thrift shop or tossed out.

Forrest shook his head. "No. Mrs. Winterborne made very explicit instructions regarding the distribution of her estate. She wanted everything inventoried and sold. Nothing was to be thrown out."

"We were told if we wanted anything, we would have to bid on it at auction, like everyone else," Marcella added.

"Can I ask who bought the items?" Forrest inquired.

Bud picked up the business card Danielle had given him. He handed it to Forrest. "Have you ever heard of Marlow House?"

"Isn't it that bed and breakfast in Frederickport?" Marcella asked, snatching the card from her husband's hand.

"It used to be," Bud explained.

Marcella studied the card. It said *Marlow House, established 1871, Walt and Danielle Marlow,* with an address on Beach Drive and phone number. She glanced up from the card. "This is who bought it? Why in the world were they interested in that junk?"

Bud shrugged. "They said something about a Christmas gift exchange."

"They're giving those things as Christmas gifts?" Marcella asked in surprise.

"They said something about it being a white elephant gift exchange. You know, sort of like gag gifts," Bud explained.

"What did they pay for them?" Forrest asked.

After Bud told them the price, he said, "I have all the other stuff they put in the trunk. If you want to look through that, you're welcome to any of it, considering all that you've done."

Marcella looked down at the scattered items and shook her head. "No. We have to go." Still clutching Danielle's business card in her hand, she headed for the door. When she reached it, she paused and looked back at Forrest, who continued to stand by the counter, looking somewhat confused.

"Forrest!" she snapped. "Are you coming?"

Forrest jumped slightly as if jerked from a trance. He said a quick goodbye to the shop owner and hurried to his wife. After they walked out the front door, Colin once again moved out from aisle two and made his way back to the window. He looked outside and watched as the couple stood on the sidewalk in front of the store. Whatever Marcella was saying to her husband, she was doing it while making wild hand gestures and waving her arms, while Forrest stood quietly.

Bud walked over to the window and joined Colin. The two men silently watched the Hoopers.

"I wonder what that is all about," Bud asked. "She seems pretty upset."

"Yes...she does..." Colin agreed.

"I TOLD YOU, didn't I tell you?" Marcella repeated, this time punctuating the words with a quick sock to her husband's shoulder.

"Ouch! That hurt! Settle down!" He rubbed his injured shoulder and took a step back from his wife.

"Didn't I tell you we needed to get over here before the store opened this morning? We should have been the first customers through that door!" Marcella ranted.

"I had no idea someone would buy those ugly things," Forrest explained. "And I thought if we rushed over here right when he opened, it would look suspicious. We both agreed we needed to act casual about the whole thing."

"Yeah, well, and what good did that do us?"

"All is not lost. We know who has them," Forrest reminded her. "I'm sure we can convince the Marlows to sell it to us."

"And if they refuse?" Marcella asked.

"Everything has a price," he reminded her.

Marcella rolled her eyes. "Yeah, right. And just how would that look? It would look suspicious, that's how it would look."

"Then we appeal to their generosity. We can tell them what we told Bud, that it's sentimental. Who knows, maybe they'll just give it to us. From what I hear, those Marlows are loaded."

"And rich people aren't rich from generosity," Marcella snapped. "If they refuse to let us buy it back, we're not going to be able to entice them with money—considering who they are."

"Then we break in and take it," Forrest declared.

Marcella paused and asked in a calmer voice, "Are you serious?"

"Certainly. I didn't come all this way to give up now. If they don't accept our offer, then we come back and figure out some way to take it."

Marcella shook her head. "No. Don't be foolish. If they refuse to sell it to us and then it goes missing, they'll know who took it. I say we steal it and don't even ask them if they will sell it to us."

"You don't even want to try asking them if we can buy it?" he asked. "I can't believe they wouldn't just give it to us if we explained we wanted it for sentimental reasons. They just bought it to use as some punchline in a joke."

"Tell me, Forrest, if we had asked Eloise to give us something that she had picked up at a yard sale, because we had some sentimental attachment to it, would she have given it—or even sold it to us for the same price that she bought it for?"

"No."

Marcella nodded stubbornly. "Exactly. I think we should go over to Frederickport, stake out the place. We need to get in there and out—before they give the items away."

THREE

M arcella absently twisted a long strand of her gray hair as she
looked out the passenger window and watched the ocean
scenery roll by. They drove down the highway, heading for Frederickport. She hadn't exchanged a single word with her husband since
leaving Astoria, lost in her own private thoughts.

Glancing briefly over her shoulder into the back seat, Marcella
noted the suitcases and then looked back out the side window. Their
bags had been packed and in the car even before going to the
Mermaid Curio that morning. They had checked out of the room
they had been renting for the past week—renting since they had
been forced to move out of the Winterborne estate. Of course, they
could not very well stay there now, it was up for sale and the
executor felt it would show better without the Hoopers underfoot.
The Winterborne estate had sucked all it needed from them and
had practically kicked them to the curb. So much for loyalty,
Marcella thought.

Forrest broke the silence. "We need a plan."

Marcella released her lock of hair. It fell to her shoulder and
began to untwist. She looked at her husband and frowned. "I
thought we had a plan. Steal what we want."

"Have you ever broken into a house before?" Forrest asked.

"Of course not. Don't be ridiculous."

"Exactly. Which is why we can't rush this. It sounds like we have a few days. Which means we have time to come up with a plan. I don't want to find myself in jail."

"Even if we get caught, I seriously doubt we will actually get thrown into jail. For one thing, neither of us has a record. And as far as anyone knows, it's practically worthless—five dollars at best. After all, isn't that what Bud said he got for it? The most we would get is a slap on the wrist."

"Maybe that is true, but if we get arrested, it also means we failed to get it back. We need to succeed and then leave Oregon, like we initially planned."

Marcella silently studied Forrest as he looked down the highway, his hands firmly on the steering wheel. After a moment she nodded and said, "Yeah, you're right. Do you have any ideas?"

"First, I say we find Marlow House, get the lay of the land— figure out the best way to get in and out," Forrest began. "Then we should probably find someplace to stay for a few days."

"It's really too bad Marlow House is no longer a bed and breakfast. We could just check in there. It would make everything so much easier."

WITH THE HELP of the GPS on Marcella's cellphone, they were able to drive straight to Marlow House. Forrest pulled up in front of the property and parked a moment, the motor still running. They looked up to the impressive Second Empire–style Victorian house with its mansard roofline. No blinds were drawn on the dormer windows on what appeared to be the attic or third floor. A black cat sat on the windowsill, looking down at the street. Blinds were also open on one of the windows on the first floor, revealing a towering Christmas tree, its limbs heavy with shiny red and gold balls. An old-fashioned red-bowed Christmas wreath hung on the front door, while Christmas lights draped festively below the roofline.

"That's obviously it," Marcella said, nodding to the large sign in front of the house saying *Marlow House*, along with the date it was founded.

"It doesn't look like anyone is home," Forrest said.

"They probably aren't back from Astoria yet," Marcella suggested. "But then again, according to the map, an alley runs behind the house, and I wouldn't be surprised if there is a garage back there. Just because there are no cars parked out front or in that side driveway doesn't mean no one is in the house."

Forrest put the car in gear. "Let's go park at the pier and walk back." He pulled out in the street and turned the car around, heading south.

"Why the pier?" Marcella asked.

"Time to play tourist. Park down at the pier, walk back up to Marlow House, look around."

"Okay. But I want to lock our suitcases in the trunk. Everything we own is in them," Marcella said.

PEARL HUCKABEE STOOD in front of her house, looking up at the Christmas lights she'd hired a handyman to hang several weeks earlier. She pulled the brim of her cloche hat outward to screen out some of the sun while she looked up to one section of her roofline, where some of the hooks appeared to have come out, leaving a section of the strand dangling.

She cursed under her breath. "He's just going to have to come back and fix it," she muttered. "And he'd better not think I'm going to pay him another dime!"

If she were a younger woman, she would have hung the lights herself, but considering she was past middle age, she couldn't afford to break something; after all, she lived alone. While she was in fairly good shape for a woman her age, trim and fit, she didn't want to be careless. But fixing a few hooks was not the same as hanging the entire strand, and if he expected to be paid for coming back, then she would just fix it herself, Pearl thought.

She readjusted the hat on her head of gray hair and walked up to her front porch and sat down on a patio chair. Leaning back, she glanced up and down her street. She knew many of her neighbors on Beach Drive considered her a newcomer. Her next-door neighbor on the north side was Danielle Marlow, who Pearl believed was treated like Frederickport royalty. But Danielle Marlow hadn't even lived on Beach Drive for four years—or even in Oregon for that matter. She was only a Marlow due to the fact she had married a distant cousin of Walt Marlow, whose grandfather had founded the town in 1870.

According to what Pearl had heard around town, Walt Marlow

didn't have two nickels to rub together when he had married Danielle. Perhaps the two strutted around the neighborhood like theirs was some great romance, but Pearl knew the truth. Walt Marlow married Danielle for the money—as a way to get his hands on some of the family fortune she had managed to cheat from its rightful heirs. At least, that was what Pearl believed.

Of course, Pearl suspected Walt had some money now, although she didn't believe he had as much as people claimed. Sure, he had written a book and it made it to the New York Times bestseller list. But it was only one book. While people talked about how it was being made into a movie, she certainly hadn't heard anything of the movie actually getting made. Pearl was fairly certain the only reason Walt Marlow managed to get the book published in the first place was due to the friendship his wife had with Jon Altar. It was probably another reason Walt married the woman.

Jon Altar was actually the pen name for Ian Bartley. Ian and his wife, Lily, lived in the house across the street. From what Pearl knew, Ian had moved into the house around the same time Danielle had moved to town. When Danielle moved to Frederickport, she had brought along her best friend, Lily, who eventually married Ian. The pair had recently had a baby, and Pearl did not look forward to the child causing mischief in the neighborhood when it got older, as children tended to do.

The neighbor to the south of Pearl was Heather Donovan, a snotty little thirtysomething who reminded Pearl of Wednesday from *The Addams Family*. She was thick as thieves with the Marlow and Bartley bunch, along with that other fellow, Chris Johnson, who lived up the street and had that vicious pit bull. As far as Pearl was concerned, pit bulls should be outlawed. Pearl didn't know when Chris and Heather had moved to Frederickport, but she had heard it was sometime after Danielle had moved to town.

Pearl believed this place of the world belonged more to her than any of the others. Years before she bought her house, it had belonged to her grandmother. She had spent her childhood visiting her grandmother at the beach house, and for her it had always been home. As far as she was concerned, all the others were outsiders —interlopers.

She sat quietly on the porch, letting her mind wander, when she realized she had forgotten to latch her front gate. With a sigh, she reluctantly stood up and started down her walkway toward the street. Just as she reached the sidewalk, she spied a couple coming from the direction of the pier.

They appeared to be about her age. Pearl thought the woman wore her hair entirely too long for someone her age. Not that Pearl felt old, but she was no teenager. The man by her side wore glasses, a mustache and a baseball cap on his head. He was a slender man and Pearl wondered if the hat concealed a bald or balding head. She believed most men who wore hats did so to conceal a lack of hair. Of course, Walt Marlow was the exception. He had a healthy head of dark hair, but always seemed to be wearing a fedora when out and about.

"Good day," the man said cheerfully as they approached.

"Hello," Pearl returned. "You aren't from around here, are you?"

The man and woman stopped in front of Pearl's gate.

"No, we're just visiting for the holidays," the woman said. "You have such a lovely street."

"Thank you. I think so." Pearl smiled broadly.

The woman motioned to the house next door. "I read that house used to be a bed and breakfast."

"Well, it's not anymore," Pearl snapped.

"That's too bad," the man said. "It looks like a nice place to stay."

Pearl shook her head. "You can't be running a business in a residential area."

"I guess not," the woman muttered.

"My wife was reading a little about the local history on our drive this morning. Is it really true there's a tunnel that runs under your street?"

"Where did you hear that?" Pearl asked with a frown.

"From one of the websites I found," the woman explained.

"It's true, but you can't get to it. The only access is through Marlow House and a house across the street."

"That's very interesting," the man said.

"It is a nuisance, that's what it is," Pearl snapped.

"So who lives in Marlow House now that it isn't a bed and breakfast?" the woman asked.

"Walt and Danielle Marlow." Pearl craned her neck and looked over at the house. "Although, I don't think they're home right now. I saw them leave early this morning in that Packard of theirs. It hasn't come back."

"Packard?" the man asked with interest.

Pearl shrugged. "One of those old cars people like to drive around to show off. But who knows, maybe they are home. They usually park their cars behind their house in the garage."

"THAT WOMAN certainly did not seem to like the Marlows," Forrest said as he drove into the parking lot of the Seahorse Motel an hour later.

"You mean the Marlows' busybody neighbor? No, she didn't. We need to watch out for that one when we break into the house. Which, by the way, I think I know how we might be able to do."

"How is that?" Forrest asked.

"There was a doggy door in that side entrance at the Marlows'. I noticed it when we were talking to that woman. I didn't want to say anything to you about it with her standing there. But I bet I could climb through it."

"The only problem, if you have a doggie door, it means you have a dog. Something I didn't really count on."

Marcella grinned at Forrest. "Didn't you hear what that woman said? When she was complaining about her neighbor's menacing cat, she didn't say anything about a dog, but she did mention the other dogs in the neighborhood, like a golden retriever across the street and a pit bull a few doors down. No, I think she would have mentioned if they had a dog. It would have given her more to complain about. I bet that doggy door is really a cat door."

"A cat is definitely less threatening than a dog," Forrest said as they got out of the vehicle. Together he and Marcella walked to the front office of the Seahorse Motel, hoping there would be a vacancy.

When they walked into the office a few minutes later, a tall elderly gentleman with a neatly trimmed beard and a cane in hand stood at the counter, checking in. They waited quietly behind him for their turn.

"And how long will you be staying with us, Mr. Bari?" the man at the front desk asked.

FOUR

After leaving Mathew Jackson at Mermaid Curio, Walt and Danielle drove down the street to pick up a package for the Frederickport Museum. They then went on to do a little more Christmas shopping. Several hours later they finally returned to their car. As Danielle opened the passenger door to the Packard, she glanced at her watch and then looked over at Walt.

"We have a little time to kill before we meet Mathew for lunch. Why don't we try to find that Winterborne house? I'm curious to see what it looks like. I wouldn't mind taking a picture of it since that's where our two white elephant gifts came from."

"Do you know where it is?" Walt asked as he climbed into the car, closing the door behind him.

"I'll try doing a search for it, and if I can't find anything, I'll pull up the real estate website. The way Bud was talking sounds like they have it for sale." Danielle got into the car and flippantly added, "You should know all about that. After all, didn't you used to be a real estate agent?"

"Cute," Walt said dryly as he inserted the key in the ignition. The spirit who had occupied Walt's body before him—a distant cousin who shared his name—had been a real estate agent.

Danielle fished her cellphone from her purse and began searching for the property.

"Do we still need to stop at Adam's office after we get back into Frederickport?" Walt asked.

"Yes, and the museum, to drop off that package. But we should have plenty of time. I just assumed we'd head back to Frederickport after we have lunch with Mathew, unless you have something else you want to do."

"No. That works for me."

WALT PULLED up in front of what appeared to be a mansion—a somewhat dilapidated mansion—with three floors, an attic, and a large for sale sign posted out front. Walt turned off the ignition and remained in the car with Danielle, looking up at the house.

"I remember it now," Walt said.

"You know this house?" Danielle asked.

"Yes. But it looked much better back then. It's rather run-down."

"Do you remember who lived here?" Danielle asked.

"Vaguely. I came here a couple of times with George. It was before he was married. They had a daughter he was interested in. But her last name was not Winterborne."

"He wasn't going with Marie's mother yet, I assume."

Walt shook his head. "No. This was a few years before they started seeing each other. George and I were just teenagers at the time. He was rather smitten with the girl, from what I recall."

"Whoever buys this house is going to have their work cut out for them. I got the impression it has been occupied all this time, until the last owner died six months ago, yet it seems to be ready to fall down. In comparison, Marlow House, empty for almost ninety years, was in relatively good shape when I moved in."

"It wasn't empty. I was there," Walt reminded her.

"As a ghost, Walt. That doesn't count." Danielle glanced at her watch. "It's almost time to meet Mathew. Let me take a picture before we go."

WHEN WALT and Danielle arrived at the restaurant, they found it decked out for the holidays, with an abundance of potted poinsettia plants, stockings hanging on the fireplace in the waiting area, and random decorations shoved in every nook and corner. Before they had a chance to give their name to the hostess, Danielle spied Mathew already sitting at a table.

"I'm so glad we were able to do this," Mathew said a few minutes later after Walt and Danielle joined him.

"So am I. I'm also glad you were finally able to meet Walt," Danielle said as she took a seat.

"I've heard so much about you," Walt chimed in. What he didn't tell Mathew was that he had known his grandmother Emma, along with his grandfather.

"I'm sorry I wasn't able to meet you for breakfast, like you initially suggested. But I had so much to do this morning," Mathew said.

"No problem." Danielle picked up a menu and opened it. "I was surprised to see you over at Mermaid Curio."

"One of my cousins wanted Grandma's oak dresser, but then decided it wasn't going to work. No one else in the family seemed to want it," Mathew explained. "And the owner of the store had approached me about Grandmother's antiques."

"While I appreciate antiques, most of my friends aren't that interested," Danielle said. "They prefer something more modern."

"Danielle tells me you finally decided to sell your grandmother's house," Walt said.

"Yes. Grandma has been gone for almost three years now. After she passed away, we planned to sell her house, but then we decided to keep it as a vacation home we could all enjoy. But the fact is everyone is so busy, it barely got used. It just seemed foolish to keep it, considering the upkeep."

"And Astoria real estate, especially something as nice as your grandmother's, I imagine you won't have a problem selling it," Danielle said.

"Whatever happened to my grandmother's rocking chair?" Mathew asked. He had given Marie the rocking chair after Emma had passed away.

Danielle smiled softly. "Marie loved that chair. After she died, it bounced around for a while but eventually ended up with Lily."

"Ahh, Lily had a baby, didn't she?" Mathew grinned.

"She did. A little boy named Connor."

"Grandma would have liked that, knowing her rocking chair

was in a home with a baby. I suppose Emma and Marie are together now. They became pretty close friends that last year."

Walt and Danielle exchanged glances but were spared having to comment when the server walked up to the table. The fact was, while Emma had moved on to be with her husband after she had died, Marie had decided to stick around. She simply was not ready to move on—and she wasn't especially anxious to see her husband. As she had reminded Danielle, wedding vows said *until death do us part*. There was nothing in the contract that stated she owed her husband anything in the hereafter.

The server left to get their drink orders, and the three looked over their menus. When the server returned with their beverages, she took their food order and then left the table again.

"I feel a little spoiled today," Danielle said with a chuckle. "Both breakfast and lunch out."

"Since I've been here, I've been eating out every day. There is no food in Grandma's house, and I really didn't want to mess up the kitchen, not when we're listing it."

"Do you have it on the market yet?" Danielle asked.

"The real estate agent is coming over this afternoon, and we'll be finalizing the listing contract, and he'll be taking some pictures. Tomorrow I'm heading back home after Bud picks up the dresser."

"If you ever come back this way, remember you always have a place to stay at Marlow House," Danielle reminded him.

"Thank you. I appreciate the offer. And I'll probably take you up on it."

They continued to talk for another ten or fifteen minutes before the server brought their food. When they were alone at the table again, Mathew asked, "So what did you buy at Mermaid Curio? I noticed you put a sack in your car when I pulled up."

Danielle told him about the shoe and the framed picture. While she described the shoe in detail, she didn't mention Marie's father was the man in the photograph.

"Grandma knew Eloise Winterborne; she went to her church. Grandma was far more patient with the woman than I would have been," Mathew explained before tasting his clam chowder.

"How do you mean?" Danielle asked.

"I went to church with Grandma a few times when I'd visit, and I met Mrs. Winterborne. She made a point of telling me she had no problem with coloreds going to her church. Insisted she was quite liberal."

Danielle cringed.

Walt reserved comment. At one time he had used the term *colored*, unaware that a term from the 1920s was inappropriate for the current era. In retrospect, he suspected it was probably inappropriate for the 1920s.

"Grandma would remind me that Eloise was an old woman and didn't know any better, and that she had used the term herself," Mathew said.

"I read Ian's article about your grandmother and her life," Walt interjected. "It was a fascinating read."

"It was a beautiful tribute to my grandparents, and it showed a raw glimpse into what life was like back then. They were the grandchildren of slaves, freed but not welcome in the state of their birth," Mathew explained.

"But your grandma stayed," Danielle reminded him.

"Yes, but it wasn't easy."

"No, it wasn't. Especially considering how active the Klan was in Oregon back then," Walt added.

Mathew looked up to Walt and smiled. "I read your book. You might write fiction, but I think you did an amazing job depicting life back then. Of course, I didn't live back then," Mathew added with a laugh. "But it just seemed so real."

Walt grinned at Mathew. "I hope you enjoyed it."

They chatted a few more minutes about Walt's and Ian's writing before the conversation was brought back to the Winterbornes.

"So tell me about this Christmas shoe. Sounds quite horrid," Mathew teased. "What are you supposed to do with it?"

"I assume it's a decoration," Danielle said with a shrug.

"It sounds like something Eloise would make. I remember once Grandma told me she was into all that arts and craft stuff, would take classes over at the community center. She tried to get Grandma to go with her. My grandmother found it rather amusing."

"Amusing how?" Danielle asked.

"My grandparents worked hard all of their lives. For many years, they couldn't afford extras. Grandma always made her children's clothes. And at Christmastime the gifts were homemade," Mathew explained.

"I like homemade gifts," Danielle said. "They come from the heart."

Mathew nodded. "I understand that. But Grandma saw it a little differently. Eloise wasn't making homemade gifts, she was making junk to decorate her house with—like crocheted tissue boxes and embroidered dish towels. She never gave any of the stuff away."

"That might have been kind of her," Walt joked.

"Good point." Mathew gave Walt a nod. "According to Grandma, Eloise Winterborne was a woman who could afford to shop wherever she wanted. Grandma just found it peculiar she preferred to make things that looked—as Grandma called them —*junky*. Plus, Mrs. Winterborne was quite the garage-sale addict."

"Garage-sale addict?" Walt asked with a frown.

"Yes. Richer than Croesus, but every week she would go to all the garage sales in the area and buy up everyone's junk. According to Grandma, she repurposed a lot of it for her craft projects."

"So who gets her money?" Danielle asked. "I assume she still had the family fortune when she died, considering it sounds like she wasn't out spending it at expensive stores. Unless, of course, she spent it all at garage sales and on craft supplies."

"From what I heard, it all goes to charity. She was the last in her family, and she didn't have anyone to leave it to. Grandma used to say that couple who took care of her would probably get the bulk of the estate. After all, they were with her for over twenty years. But from what I heard, they weren't left a penny in the will."

"Maybe they took care of her, but we drove by the house today," Danielle said. "I don't think they did a very good job of taking care of that house."

FIVE

When Walt and Danielle arrived back in Frederickport on Saturday afternoon, their first stop was Frederickport Vacation Properties to see Adam Nichols. Neighbor, good friend, and wealthy philanthropist Chris Glandon, who went by the alias Chris Johnson, had gone out of town several days earlier, and he needed Danielle to sign some legal documents in his absence. The papers were at Adam's office.

Adam's assistant, Leslie, had taken Saturday off, so when they walked in the front door, they found Adam sitting at Leslie's desk with Melony Carmichael sitting across from him. The two lounged casually, leaning back in the chairs, feet on the desk, while they each held a paper plate holding a liberal slice of chocolate cake. Neither attempted to stand when Walt and Danielle walked through the doorway. Instead, Adam took another bite of cake while Melony waved her fork at them in greeting before digging the utensil back into chocolate frosting.

Surveying the situation, Danielle shook her head in mock rebuke as she tossed her purse on an empty chair. "Goofing off. Is this what you do when Leslie is gone?"

"It's double fudge chocolate cake—from Old Salts," Melony said in a conspiratorial tone. Respected attorney Melony Carmichael, looked more fashion model than lawyer, with her naturally long blond hair, stunning blue eyes, and shapely figure.

"Danielle's recipe?" Walt asked hopefully.

Melony nodded. "And I think they have mastered it." She pointed to a table on the other side of the office. "There is more."

"Hey," Adam said with a scowl. "They can't have any!"

"I bought it," Melony reminded him as she took another bite.

"Fine," Adam said in mock outrage before turning a smile on the pair. "Help yourself."

Walt didn't have to be told twice, but Danielle declined the offer. She was still full from lunch.

"I suppose I should have called you," Adam said as he took his feet off the desk and sat up straighter.

"You don't need me to sign those papers?" Danielle asked. She picked up the purse she had set on the chair a moment earlier and moved it to the floor before sitting down.

"Chris came back early," Melony explained. "He stopped in about an hour ago and signed the papers himself."

"No problem," Walt said, taking a bite of the cake.

"Of course not, you got cake," Danielle teased.

The four friends sat around the front office desk while three of them ate double fudge chocolate cake.

"So how was your visit with Mathew?" Adam asked.

"It was nice. But I'm a little sad to think they're selling Emma's house. Do you know the Realtor he's using?"

"Of course, I referred him," Adam said with a Cheshire cat grin.

"Ahh, so you'll get a commission," Danielle said.

Adam only smiled in response and took another bite of cake.

"Did you get any Christmas shopping done?" Melony asked.

"We did. In fact, we picked up our white elephant gifts," Danielle told them.

"What did you get? I haven't gotten mine yet," Adam said.

"They can't tell us," Melony told him. "That would spoil it."

Adam shrugged. "It's just going to be something no one wants anyway."

"Scrooge," Melony teased.

"Do either of you know anything about the Winterbornes from Astoria?" Danielle asked impulsively.

Melony had just finished her last bite of cake. She wiped her mouth with a napkin and then asked, "You mean Eloise Winterborne?"

"So you knew her?" Danielle asked.

Melony nodded. "Yeah. Sort of. My father's law firm used to represent her. But after Dad died, I don't think she cared much for Clarence. She changed lawyers, according to what my mother told me back then. Why do you ask?"

"She died about six months ago, and one of the shops that we went into had an old trunk of hers that they bought at auction. We were curious and went by her house. From what I heard, she had money, but the condition of that property, she obviously didn't spend it on house maintenance," Danielle explained.

After tossing her napkin and paper plate in the trash can, Melony leaned back in the chair again, yet this time kept her feet on the floor. "I remember when she hired the people who took care of her."

"You mean the ones she didn't even mention in her will?" Adam asked. "In spite of how long they had taken care of her."

Melony gave Adam a nod. "Yeah, I can't help but feel sorry for them, considering they took care of her for about twenty years and won't see any retirement other than some Social Security."

"According to Mathew, she didn't spend much money aside from visiting yard sales and buying craft supplies," Danielle said.

"What I remember," Melony began, "she was in her sixties when her husband died. She had never driven a car, and her husband had always handled things like the grocery shopping and running errands. One of the first things she did after he died was look for a live-in couple to take care of her. But before she hired anyone, she had my father find a company to completely inventory the estate—down to the last pencil."

"Why did she want an inventory?" Danielle asked.

"She didn't want anyone to steal from her. Every year, she insisted the company inventory the estate again—to see if anything was missing. It was her way of keeping the couple honest, I guess. From what I heard, she was quite obsessive about it."

Danielle shrugged. "In all fairness, when someone is alone and getting older, that happens all too often—caretakers steal from the elderly."

"True," Melony said with a nod. "And as I recall, the couple they hired was actually pretty good-natured about it all. At least, from what I heard. Which, considering everything, I do think it was pretty sucky when they were not even mentioned in her will. All those years of loyalty. Nothing."

"From what I understand, it's not like she had anything worth stealing," Adam added. "Not unless they got ahold of her bank account."

"From what my mother told me, Eloise Winterborne was always a frugal woman. She married into money, but hadn't grown up with it. Of course, the Winterbornes might have had a nice house back then and had money in the bank, but they were never known for being extravagant," Melony explained.

"They did have one notable treasure—the Winterborne engagement ring," Adam reminded her. He looked at Danielle and said, "It was probably not as valuable as your Missing Thorndike, but I suspect it was close."

"I heard about that, but I never saw it," Melony noted.

"Grandma told me about it," Adam said.

"What was the Winterborne engagement ring?" Danielle asked.

"It was handed down in the Winterborne family. It was Eloise's engagement ring. An antique ring with perfect diamonds. Quite exquisite. From what I heard, she sold it a few years before she died," Melony said.

The next minute the conversation was interrupted when Adam's grandmother suddenly appeared and called out cheerfully, "You are all here!"

The only people in the office who knew of the spirit's arrival were Walt and Danielle. They briefly glanced Marie's way while pretending nothing unusual had just happened. Marie, the spirit of a ninety-something woman who had died—yet who preferred to assume the appearance of an eighty-something woman—stood in the middle of the office, wearing a floral sundress and floppy straw hat. She glanced around for somewhere to sit, but when she saw all the nearby chairs were taken, she opted to float in midair on what appeared to be an invisible chair.

"So what are we all talking about?" Marie asked. "Did you have a nice visit with Mathew? I would have gone with you, but Eva wants me to go with her to Astoria tomorrow, something going on at the Film Museum she wants to attend. I didn't see any reason to go twice in one week."

Unable to answer Marie's question without sounding like a crazy person to Adam and Melony, Walt asked Melony, "If Eloise

Winterborne had plenty of money, and if she was as frugal as you say, why would she sell something like her engagement ring?"

"Ahh, we are talking about Eloise Winterborne," Marie chirped.

"I don't really know," Melony said.

"Well, I do," Marie answered. "Emma told me about the woman; she went to her church. Eloise Winterborne was always complaining about those people who worked for her, claimed they were stealing things. She couldn't prove it. But she knew they were. Or so she told Emma. But if they were stealing things, then why not just fire them? According to what she told Emma, she pulled a fast one and sold the ring so they couldn't get to it. She had already stopped wearing it because of the arthritis in her hands."

Adam had been speculating on why he thought Eloise had sold the ring while Marie told what she knew. Danielle found it difficult to keep up with both conversations, but managed to hear Adam say, "It's not like she had any family left to hand it down to anyway. I guess she figured she might as well sell it now and get the money."

"SO WHY WERE you talking about Eloise Winterborne?" Marie asked after they left Adam's office. The ghost hovered behind Walt's and Danielle's seats in the Packard.

"We bought some items that had been auctioned off from her estate," Danielle told her. "Have a look in that small blue paper bag back there. There is one Walt thinks Adam might like."

Marie glanced down at the sack. It floated up to her, hovering in midair. The next moment the Christmas shoe floated from the bag. The spirit laughed. "I'm not sure why you imagine Adam would want this."

Danielle glanced to the back seat and smiled. "No, the other thing in the sack."

The gaudy shoe floated back into the bag, and up floated the framed photo. It hovered in front of Marie's face.

"Is that my father?" Marie squealed in delight.

"It certainly is," Walt said.

"He looks so young there. Where was this taken?" Marie asked.

"I don't know. That came from the Winterborne estate," Walt told her. "We thought you might know who that other man is."

"No, I don't recognize him. How odd," Marie said. "I didn't

know those people, and from what Emma told me, they moved to Astoria years after my father died."

"The Winterbornes weren't the first people to live in that house?" Danielle asked.

"No. I wonder how my father's photograph ended up at the Winterborne estate," Marie asked.

"There are several logical possibilities," Walt suggested.

"Which are?" Marie asked.

"You might not be aware of the fact, but your father was a bit smitten with the young lady who lived in that house—which I know now was before the Winterbornes purchased the property. Perhaps the picture was taken back then when he was seeing her, and it somehow got left in the house when it sold—like a box of items forgotten in the attic. But I believe the second possibility is more plausible," Walt explained.

"And what is that?" Marie asked.

"That Eloise Winterborne, who Mathew claimed had a penchant for picking up things at yard sales, purchased it at some yard sale in Astoria—maybe even from some family member related to that other fellow in the photograph."

"I do believe Adam will love this picture," Marie said happily as the framed photograph settled back into the sack.

"You were saying back at Adam's office that Eloise sold the ring because she was afraid her employees were going to take it?" Danielle asked.

"That's what she told Emma. Both Emma and I never understood why anyone would keep someone in their employ—especially one who lived in your home—that you didn't trust. But I suppose she must have felt she needed someone and didn't know how to go about hiring a replacement. After all, this was probably about five years ago or less, according to what Emma told me. Eloise Winterborne was in her eighties back then, and unlike me, who had a grandson I could rely on, she had no one."

"I wonder if she had her attorney find a buyer for the ring. I know when I tried to find a buyer for the Missing Thorndike, I didn't know how to go about it. Which is why I still have it," Danielle said.

"No, she didn't. You will never guess who bought it. From what she told Emma, she sold it to Samuel Hayman."

"Samuel?" Danielle asked in surprise. Samuel Hayman had

owned the jewelry store in Frederickport, which had been founded by his grandfather decades earlier. He had also made an unsuccessful attempt to abscond with the diamonds and emeralds from Danielle's Missing Thorndike, which had earned him some prison time.

"Yes. Although, I don't believe he was the one who actually bought it. We all know Samuel didn't have that kind of money," Marie said.

"No. If anything, he probably found her a buyer and then kept some sort of commission," Danielle suggested.

SIX

The next stop for Walt and Danielle, before heading home, was the Frederickport Museum. When they pulled up to park, Marie said her goodbyes and vanished. Together Walt and Danielle walked up to the entrance of the museum, Walt carrying the large package they had brought back from Astoria. When they walked inside, they were greeted by someone they hadn't expected to see— Elizabeth Sparks.

Elizabeth, a talented art teacher with the Frederickport school district, also gave private art lessons and classes, as well as occasionally working for the area law enforcement when they needed a police sketch done. She had also worked with Danielle on a local fundraiser to raise money for the art department.

"Elizabeth, nice to see you," Danielle greeted the other woman. They quickly exchanged hugs. "Do they have you doing docent duty today?"

Elizabeth laughed at the idea. "No. I gave a craft class today. A lot of people showed up. We were making tree ornaments."

"Sounds fun," Danielle said.

Elizabeth eyed the package Walt carried. "What do you have there?"

"Millie sent out an email last night, asking if anyone was going to Astoria in the next week," Danielle began.

"Ahh…I got that email too. So you were the one who responded, volunteered to pick it up?" Elizabeth asked.

Danielle shrugged. "We were going to be there anyway."

"Where would you like me to put it?" Walt asked.

"Probably in the back office. I'm the only one here—everyone else left a few minutes ago." Elizabeth glanced at her watch. "Let me lock the front door first. We're due to close in a couple of minutes anyway, and I would rather no one walk in while no one is up front."

Walt and Danielle waited patiently while Elizabeth locked the front door. They then followed her through the museum, to the back office.

"Now with the Bonnet paintings here, they are super careful about not leaving the front unlocked unless someone is up there," Elizabeth explained. "Although the Bonnet section is already locked down for the night with the alarm on."

"I'm just glad I don't have to worry about that anymore," Danielle said. Two of the Bonnet paintings had belonged to Danielle—and the third had belonged to the museum. After their true value had been discovered, the paintings had been sold to the Glandon Foundation, which had in turn put them on display at the Frederickport Museum, with added security.

When they reached the back of the museum, Danielle spied a banquet table filled with handmade ornaments. She stopped to look at them while Elizabeth showed Walt where he could set the heavy package. When the two returned to Danielle, they found her sitting at the table, looking at the ornaments.

"These are wonderful," Danielle told Elizabeth.

"Thank you. But I didn't make them all. That's what my class made today. I have to leave them here to dry." Elizabeth took a seat at the table with Danielle.

"I sort of wish I had taken your class today," Danielle said, still inspecting the ornaments.

Walt joined them at the table. "I think these are much nicer than the Christmas shoe."

Elizabeth looked up. "Christmas shoe?"

Danielle chuckled. "Today when we were in Astoria, we stopped at a little curio shop and picked up a couple of items that came from a recent estate sale up there. I don't know if you have heard of the Winterborne estate?"

"You mean Eloise Winterborne?" Elizabeth asked.

"You knew her?" Danielle asked.

"Sure. Sweet little lady. She was a regular at my craft classes. I always made sure to send her a flyer if I was having one. She was quite creative."

"Danielle bought one of her creations—the shop owner called it a Christmas shoe. Frankly, I don't really understand it, a high-heel shoe with Christmas wrapping paper glued all over its sole and fake flowers glued inside."

Elizabeth laughed. "While Eloise never made anything like that in any of my classes, I have a feeling I may have given her the idea. I believe I once told her the story of my family's Christmas shoe."

"Your family has a Christmas shoe?" Danielle asked.

Elizabeth smiled. "It was more a family tradition—or maybe a family joke? Perhaps a little of both."

"I have to hear this," Danielle insisted.

Fifteen minutes later, Walt and Danielle sat with Elizabeth in the museum office, each sipping a cup of hot tea.

"It all began when my aunt got married," Elizabeth told them. "One of my grandmother's close friends was a little like Eloise. She loved doing arts and crafts. After finding out my aunt's bridesmaids were wearing blue, she spray-painted a high-heel shoe blue. And we are talking a large shoe—size twelve at least. She covered it with countless little fake gems and glittery bobbles. I imagine much of it came from old costume jewelry."

"What did she intend to do with it?" Walt asked.

"She gave it to my aunt as a wedding gift. Fortunately my grand-mother's friend was not there when my aunt opened it. I understand the reaction was quite comical. I think most assumed it was some elaborate joke. But from the pictures I saw of it, it was no joke to that dear little lady. She must have spent hours making that shoe for my aunt—and I'm sure she believed it was truly beautiful."

"What did your aunt do with it?" Danielle asked.

"Probably shoved it in some closet. I don't think my aunt displayed it in her home. But when my parents married, my aunt wrapped it up and gave it to my mother as a shower gift. After all, Mom had relentlessly teased her sister about the shoe."

Danielle laughed.

"The funny thing, the same little lady made my mother a shoe. Mom's was painted lavender to match the color of her bridesmaid dresses. It was actually my mother's second marriage. The first time, she had eloped when she was very young. When she married Dad, my grandmother insisted she have a big wedding like her sister."

"So your mom had a pair of them?" Danielle said.

Elizabeth grinned. "Yes, but only until my aunt and uncle moved into their new house. My mother gave her the pair of wedding shoes as a housewarming gift."

Danielle laughed. "I bet they loved that."

"From what I heard, my aunt thought it was hilarious—my uncle not so much."

"So what is a Christmas shoe?" Walt asked.

"The wedding shoes were passed back and forth between Mom and my aunt until my uncle made them disappear. I don't think he thought the whole thing was very funny."

"That's too bad," Danielle said.

"Years later, when I was in grade school, my mother told my brother and me the story of the wedding shoes. I was in third grade at the time. It was right before Christmas. My grandfather was very ill. We were staying with them, helping my grandmother take care of him. We decided it would be fun to bring back the shoe—this time as a Christmas shoe. The idea was to add some laughter to the holiday. While Grandpa was pretty ill, he always had a great sense of humor, and I think he liked the idea of us making another shoe and then springing it on my aunt and her husband that Christmas, when we were all opening our gifts."

"So you made a Christmas shoe?" Danielle asked.

"Yes. We found an inexpensive pair of high-heel shoes at a discount store. Then we brought them home and had fun decorating one—trying to make it as gaudy as possible. I remember how much fun Grandpa had watching us and giving us suggestions on what to glue on next."

"So how did your aunt like her gift?" Walt asked.

"Everyone got a good laugh. For the next ten years or so that shoe bounced from family member to family member. The trick was figuring out how to wrap it so the recipient wouldn't know they were getting it. We had a lot of fun with that shoe. My grandfather passed away the next year, but we kept it going in his honor. Sort of a tangible family joke—something that may seem rather silly to others but had meaning to us."

"So who is getting the shoe this year?" Danielle asked.

Elizabeth shrugged. "Our family's Christmas shoe went the way of the wedding shoes."

"Your uncle got rid of it too?" Danielle asked.

Elizabeth laughed. "No—at least I don't think so. Anyway, I remember telling Eloise about our Christmas shoe, and I wouldn't be surprised if that's what gave her the idea to make her own. But in Eloise's case, I imagine she used it as a Christmas decoration; she really did not have anyone to give it to."

They finished their tea and Danielle asked, "What plans do you have for Christmas? Any more craft classes?"

Elizabeth shook her head. "No, today was my last class. I'm going to enjoy the rest of my Christmas break, catching up on sleep and visiting with family."

"Do your parents live in town?" Walt asked.

"They used to. They moved to Portland a few years back. But they're coming to spend Christmas with me. I'm really excited they're going to be here. It just seems as the years go by, our family gets scattered farther and farther apart. When we were kids, we would spend every Christmas with my aunt and uncle's family. But they live in California now, and their one son lives in Colorado, and the other lives in Tennessee. It has been years since I've seen them. And my brother, well, I haven't spent Christmas with him for ages."

"I'm glad you're going to be able to spend Christmas with your parents," Danielle said.

When Danielle got into the Packard with Walt fifteen minutes later, she sat quietly in the passenger seat, thinking about her conversation with Elizabeth.

"What's wrong?" Walt asked, noting her serious expression.

"I was just thinking about how I always feel sorry for myself at this time of year, because my parents are gone—I don't have any siblings or cousins. But the fact is, even people who have a big family, it's not a guarantee they'll be with them for the holidays. I may not have any family beyond you, but that doesn't mean I won't be surrounded by people—and spirits—I love this Christmas. And for that, I am sincerely blessed."

SEVEN

Chris Johnson's friend, neighbor and employee—Heather Donovan—called him stupidly good looking. When she said it, it never sounded like a compliment, and it wasn't a lie. When Lily had first met him, she thought he looked like one of those models used on the covers of romance novels, with his vivid blue eyes, sandy-colored hair and hunky physique. When discussing his appearance with Danielle in the early stages of their friendship with Chris, Lily had also called him an underwear model. But to some—especially on those days Chris dressed down—he looked like a surfer bum.

Exhausted from that morning's flight and the long drive from the Portland airport, Chris made no attempt to unpack the suitcase he had tossed on his bed along with his cellphone. When he had arrived back in Frederickport that afternoon, his first stop was to sign some real estate papers Adam had ready for him. The next stop was Heather's house to pick up his dog, Hunny.

The moment he had walked in Heather's front door and made some offhanded remark about being exhausted, she immediately reminded him it was entirely his own fault. Had he taken her suggestion—a suggestion she had made on countless occasions—he would have hired a driver and a private plane, and then the trip would have been less tiring. After all, he could easily afford it, considering the Glandon fortune.

However, he had already tried the private-plane route—with disastrous results; plus there was another reason for not chartering a plane or buying his own. Chris enjoyed meeting people, and he found it possible to meet the most interesting people on flights—each with their own story, often coming from faraway places or perhaps from his own town. He had initially met Melony Carmichael on a flight back from New York, and they had since become good friends. The reason for not buying a limousine and hiring a driver had more to do with the discomfort he felt when someone else was behind the wheel.

Glandon was his real surname, yet he chose to go by his adopted mother's maiden name—Johnson—a more common name, making it easier for him to conceal his real identity. Most people believed he was simply an employee of the philanthropist Chris Glandon, founder of the Glandon Foundation.

Many people in Frederickport had already figured out Chris's true identity, but they had chosen to keep that information to themselves and not share it with outsiders. They rather enjoyed having such a wealthy philanthropist living amongst them, especially when he frequently made generous donations to local causes.

Happy to have her human home, Hunny seemed unable to contain her energy. So instead of unpacking, Chris took the dog out the back door for a run along the beach. They were gone for almost an hour.

Chris hadn't eaten anything since leaving the airport, and his stomach growled in protest. When he and Hunny returned from their walk, he went to the kitchen in search of food. Hunny sat quietly on the kitchen floor and watched as Chris searched his refrigerator for something edible. He pulled out a package of steak and gave it a sniff. Satisfied it was not going to kill him, he tossed it on the kitchen counter and then grabbed a cold beer. The dog plopped down on the floor, no longer sitting but now stretched out leisurely, watching Chris's every move.

After opening the can of beer, Chris took a swig and set it on the counter. He picked up the package of meat and ripped it open, giving it another sniff just to be safe. He grabbed the bottle of olive oil sitting on the counter and poured a generous amount of it into the clean frying pan already sitting on his stove. He set the now open bottle of olive oil back on the counter and turned on the burner under the frying pan.

He watched the oil, waiting for it to heat up. When confident it was sufficiently hot, he tossed in the slab of steak, making the oil sizzle and pop. Hunny's ears perked up at the sound. Chris absently tossed the now empty meat package on one of the unlit burners on the stove and grabbed a dishtowel off the counter and wiped off his hands.

The next moment, his cellphone began to ring from the bedroom. He tossed the dishcloth down and started to leave the kitchen to retrieve the phone and then remembered the sizzling pan. With a quick jaunt back to the stove, he hastily turned one of the control knobs before racing to his bedroom. When he got to the bedroom, Hunny was at his side. Chris picked up the phone and looked at the caller ID. It was Heather.

"Hey, Heather," Chris answered, sitting on the edge of the bed. He reached down and stroked the top of Hunny's head as the dog leaned against his legs.

"I forgot to ask you when you picked up Hunny, but when is your brother going to be here?" she asked.

"Tomorrow afternoon. I get to drive back to the airport to get him. Lucky me."

"Do you need me to do anything for you? Help you get ready? Maybe run to the store and stock your fridge?"

Moving his cellphone away from his ear, he frowned at it briefly and then returned it to his ear. "That is a rather nice offer."

"Oh, don't take it personally. I just don't want the poor guy to starve when he visits. I've seen what you keep in your refrigerator."

Chris laughed. "Thanks. I'm planning to go to the store in the morning and pick up a few things before I head out to the airport. But I appreciate the offer."

"Not going to offer to clean your place, but please tell me you at least vacuumed?" Heather asked.

"Now you're making me feel like some helpless guy who can't take care of himself."

"Did you vacuum?" she pressed.

"If you must know, I hired Joanne to come over and clean this place while I was gone."

"And did you get that smoke detector fixed? You can't have your brother staying there if the smoke detectors don't work."

"Yes, I had them fixed," Chris lied. He silently reminded himself to call the electrician on Monday.

Hunny suddenly jumped up and raced from the room. She started barking.

"What's with Hunny?" Heather asked.

Chris glanced to the doorway and sniffed the air. *What is that I smell?* Phone in hand, still talking to Heather, he went to find out what Hunny was barking at. The moment he stepped into the hallway, he saw it—smoke.

Still holding the phone, he raced down to the kitchen and found not only the package he had tossed on the stove had been engulfed in flames, fire raged from the now charred steak. Yet what he found most troubling, the flames were currently feeding on his overhead cabinets and quickly racing toward his living room.

"Call the fire department. My kitchen's on fire!" Chris yelled into the phone.

STANDING WITH HEATHER, Hunny by his side, Chris looked up hopelessly at his house as he watched the firemen put out the last of the flames. His first priority had been getting Hunny safely outside. He had tried to go back into the house and use a fire extinguisher on the kitchen before the flames spread and did more damage, but each time he tried to go back inside, his protective dog insisted on following him. While Hunny normally obeyed Chris's command to stay, this time she refused to leave his side.

By the time one of his neighbors had arrived to hold onto Hunny's collar so he could go back inside his house, the fire had taken on a life of its own. Angry flames engulfed his home.

"Reminds me of Presley House," Heather said dully. She watched as the beach house collapsed into itself while dark smoke billowed from its remains. Fortunately the fire had not touched any of the neighboring houses.

Presley House, located in a nearby neighborhood, had once belonged to Heather's family. It had burned down three years earlier on Halloween night. Heather, Danielle and Lily had barely escaped that fire, and the house—like Chris's now—had been destroyed.

Chris groaned. "I can't believe this happened."

"What did happen?" Heather asked. "We were talking on the phone one minute, and then next you're yelling for me to call the fire department."

"I thought I turned the burner off when I went to answer the phone. But I must have turned the wrong one."

Chris's next-door neighbors to the north, the Crawfords, stood some distance away with some of the other neighbors, talking amongst themselves, watching the commotion, and expressing relief that none of their houses had caught on fire. Lily and Ian hurried up the street to Chris and Heather, with baby Connor wrapped in a warm blanket, held securely in Lily's arms.

MARCELLA AND FORREST had checked into the Seahorse Motel and had returned to the pier to get something to eat at Pier Café. They had just parked their car and were starting to walk down the pier when they heard the sirens. Curious, they took a detour and started up Beach Drive.

One of the first things they noticed—aside from the house fire down the street—there was a black Packard parked in front of Marlow House. Noticing how the neighbors on this street seemed to be all rushing outside and heading north to see the fire, they decided it might be an opportunity to take a closer look at Marlow House while everyone else's attention would be focused elsewhere.

Just as they were one door down from the woman they had talked to earlier, they noticed her rushing out her front gate and heading up the street to the gathering crowd. Before they reached the Packard, a man and woman walked out the front door of Marlow House and hurried down the front walk, their attention on the commotion up the street.

Marcella and Forrest stopped walking and watched the couple. "That must be Walt and Danielle Marlow," Marcella whispered to her husband. They started walking again, and when they reached the Packard, Marcella peeked inside, hoping the Marlows had carelessly left their purchase in the car, but she didn't see anything.

"Let's try that side gate," Marcella whispered.

"With all these people?" Forrest asked.

"They're all down the street. No one is going to look up here while all that is going on."

"Looks like they have the fire about out."

"Then we need to hurry!" She walked to the side gate and found it unlocked. Looking over her shoulder, she waved for her husband to follow. A moment later they entered the side yard of Marlow House. To Marcella's delight, she discovered the back door was unlocked, so there was no need for her to climb through the pet door.

Marcella opened her purse and pulled out a pair of gloves. She looked at her husband and said, "I put these in my purse when we unpacked at the motel. I thought I might need them. I don't want to leave fingerprints." She handed her husband her purse and slipped on the gloves.

"I don't have any gloves," he said.

"You don't need any. I'll go inside. Stand guard out here. Warn me if you see anyone coming."

EIGHT

B y the time Danielle and Walt reached Chris's house—or what was left of it—they found Chris in a conversation with Officer Brian Henderson. Heather stood silently to his right, with Hunny standing between them. The dog panted heavily as if she had just finished running. On the other side of Chris stood Lily and Ian, with Ian now holding a sleeping Connor while they listened to what Brian had to say. Nearby stood many of the other neighbors, including Pearl Huckabee, who glared at Hunny while calling out, "That dog is off a leash! Officer Henderson! That dog should be on a leash!"

Brian stopped talking to Chris for a moment and turned a frown to Pearl while Danielle greeted Chris with a comforting hug, and Walt patted his shoulder reassuringly.

"Mrs. Huckabee, your neighbor just lost his home," Brian reminded her.

"Well, I am sorry about that. But there are laws, you know, and a dog like that should be restrained at all times before someone gets hurt!"

"I'm afraid Hunny's leash was burned up in the fire," Chris snapped.

"Then lock him up in your car until you can properly restrain him!" she shouted back.

Brian walked over to Hunny, leaned down, and said in a loud voice, "Do you intend to attack anyone?"

The next moment the dog jumped up and licked Brian's face repeatedly, her butt wagging with what little tail she possessed. Brian laughed and scratched the dog under her ears, telling her to sit. She sat. Without a word Brian walked to his squad car, retrieved a small piece of rope, and handed it to Chris.

"You can use this for now to restrain that vicious dog of yours," Brian told him.

Pearl glared at Brian but relaxed slightly when Chris looped one end of the rope under the collar, securing it by holding both ends in his hand. Hunny, unfazed by the rope, sat down by Chris's feet.

"You and Hunny can stay with us tonight," Danielle told him.

"There is no reason for that!" Pearl called out.

Chris's friends turned to face Pearl.

"Excuse me?" Danielle said.

"He works for that foundation, doesn't he?" Pearl answered. "I don't see why he can't just stay there. That place must have a hundred rooms, it's so big. It used to be a house; surely there is a bedroom he can use."

"For one thing, there are no beds in the building," Heather snapped. "And for another, it really is none of your business."

"It certainly is. Marlow House is no longer a boardinghouse," Pearl reminded her. "They can't be taking in boarders," Pearl insisted.

"It was never a boardinghouse," Lily corrected.

"Then Chris can stay with me," Heather said stubbornly.

"That would be totally improper!" Pearl sputtered. "Do you really wish to have your reputation in shreds? You, as a single woman, living with your boss? You don't want to do that."

"I have a reputation?" Heather smirked.

"Okay, then Chris can stay in a motel, and Hunny can stay with us, since I doubt the hotel would allow the dog," Danielle suggested. Walt flashed her a questioning look and then realized she was baiting their neighbor.

"No!" Pearl shouted. "Absolutely not. I do not want that pit bull next door to me! It is bad enough I've had to put up with it being down the street!"

Danielle chuckled and said, "Yes, I rather thought that was the real issue."

"Mrs. Huckabee, we have had this conversation before; there is nothing illegal about the Marlows taking in a houseguest," Brian reminded her. "And there are no regulations against pit bulls in Frederickport. Plus, Hunny is an extremely well-behaved dog, and I have never witnessed her displaying any aggression."

They were interrupted when one of the firemen came out of the house and walked up to Chris with news on what they had found inside.

"It looks like the fire started at the stove, as you suspected," the fireman told Chris. "There were two burners all the way on. When you left the room, it must have overheated and—"

"You walked out of your kitchen with the stove on!" Pearl shrieked.

The fireman stopped talking and with the others turned to face Pearl.

"You could have burned down the entire neighborhood! You could have killed someone! You careless man! I don't want you living next door to me!" Pearl ranted.

Brian rolled his eyes and walked to Pearl, taking her by an elbow and ushering her away from the other neighbors. He began whispering to her, but what he was saying, Chris and his friends could not hear.

"I'm sorry about that," the fireman said. "Considering all that you've been through today, you certainly don't need someone screaming at you right now. I need to go back inside and finish up. We can talk later."

When the fireman walked away, Lily whispered, "Who would have thought Brian Henderson would end up being Chris's champion?"

Danielle chuckled. "Yeah, I like him a lot better these days now that he's no longer trying to throw one of us in jail."

Heather looked over at Pearl, who now looked as if she had just eaten a lemon as Brian continued to talk to her.

"Times like this I wish I had Walt's gift," Heather told her friends in a whisper. "I'd give her a good swift kick in the butt about now."

"I can't be manhandling women—especially an older woman," Walt told her. "It simply is not very gentlemanly."

"Well, I am no gentleman," Heather reminded him.

"Sometimes your violent tendencies are endearing," Chris told Heather. "As long as you aren't punching me in the arm."

"I told you," Heather said primly, "I am not going to do that anymore. I realized that if I were a guy and you were a woman, and I punched you in the arm when you irritated me, well, I would probably get arrested. So, if it is not right for a man to hit a woman, then I suppose it is just as wrong for a woman to punch a man."

"I thought you just said you wanted me to kick Pearl?" Walt asked with a laugh.

Heather shrugged. "You can't expect me to change overnight, can you? I am a work in progress."

They all laughed and Lily said, "I have to say, I sort of agree with Heather. Wish I could give that woman a good smack. She is annoying."

"There is one thing I can do," Walt said as he looked over to Pearl and Brian. The other friends looked over too, waiting to see Walt's intentions. A moment later Brian gave Pearl a parting nod and started to walk back to them while Pearl turned abruptly and angrily headed to her own house. The next moment Pearl's cloche hat flew off her head; it spiraled in front of her as if leading the way home. She broke into a run, chasing the hat down the street.

"I just hope she doesn't have a heart attack running like that," Walt said under his breath. "Or I am going to feel guilty."

NOT LONG AFTER Pearl started chasing her hat, Connor woke up and began to fuss. Lily announced he needed to be fed, so she and Ian headed back home with their son, telling the others they would meet them over at Marlow House later.

The other neighbors eventually went home, and after partitioning off Chris's property to keep the curious from poking around and getting hurt, the firemen finally began packing up to leave. By the time Brian drove off, the only ones standing in front of the burnt remains of Chris's house were Chris, Heather, Walt, Danielle and Hunny.

"While this really sucks, I'm grateful no one was hurt," Chris said, taking a final look at what had been his house.

"On a positive note, you can now build that dream beach house you always wanted," Danielle said. "You already have the lot."

Walt chuckled and wrapped one arm casually around Danielle. "I married Pollyanna."

"Let's go back to Marlow House, and I'll fix us all something to eat," Danielle suggested. "You too, Heather."

"That's what I was doing when I burned my freaking house down, fixing myself something to eat."

"And then I called…oh no, it was my fault? I am the reason your house burned down! If I hadn't called, you would never have left that pan on the stove unattended!" Heather moaned.

Chris flashed Heather a smile and gave her a gentle sock to the arm. The mild assault caught her by surprise and she stopped talking. Her eyes wide, she looked at Chris and rubbed her arm even though the slight poke hadn't hurt. Finally she asked, "What was that for?"

"You did burn my house down," he teased.

Heather punched Chris's arm, but not as gently as he had tapped hers. "And you lied to me. You never got that smoke detector fixed, did you?"

DANIELLE AND WALT led the way up their front walk, with Hunny trailing behind, followed by Chris and Heather.

"I am really sorry about calling," Heather apologized.

"Don't be silly. This was not your fault," Chris insisted. "I just wasn't paying attention, and instead of turning the burner off, I must have turned another one on. And you're right, I didn't get the smoke detectors fixed. I forgot."

"I thought you have a fire extinguisher in your kitchen?" she asked.

"I do. But Hunny was acting so erratic around the fire. I just wanted to get her out of the house, and then I intended to go right back in and put the fire out, but she just wouldn't leave my side."

"Poor thing, it probably freaked her out, and then our crazy neighbor started yelling at her," Heather said as they followed Walt, Danielle and Hunny up to the front porch.

"Fortunately, Hunny didn't realize she was being yelled at," Chris said as he stopped a moment, waiting for Danielle to open the front door.

Walt and Danielle entered the house first, followed by Hunny and then Heather and Chris, with Chris shutting the door behind them. Emotionally drained, Chris followed the others toward the kitchen, but right when Danielle passed the open doorway to the downstairs bedroom, she stopped abruptly and let out a scream. She stood looking into the room. Everything that had been in the bedroom closet was now spread out on the floor, while every dresser drawer was pulled open.

"What the…" Danielle stammered.

The others rushed to her side and looked into the bedroom.

"Gee, Danielle, did you fire Joanne?" Chris asked dryly, looking into the ransacked room.

NINE

Marcella sat quietly in the booth as the waitress with the purple hair set the two plates of food on the table.

"Can I get you anything else?" the server asked.

Forrest shook his head. "I don't need anything. Marcella?"

Marcella looked over the food on her plate and then glanced up at the server. "No, this is fine."

Just as the waitress left the table, Marcella picked up a French fry and began absently nibbling on one end while going over in her mind all that had happened that day.

"You were in the house forever. I can't believe you didn't find it. Could it have been in the car after all?" Forrest asked.

Marcella picked up her burger. "I doubt it. Like I told you, I was only able to go through the rooms on the first floor. It's a big house!"

"If that neighbor hadn't come back, you could have looked longer. But she has a clear view into that side yard from her house, and I didn't think we should risk you staying longer."

"No, you did the right thing." Marcella took a bite of her burger.

"What are we going to do now? I'm almost tempted to knock on their door and offer to buy it."

Marcella looked up from her burger. "Are you nuts? I didn't exactly leave the place as I found it. Not that I broke anything, but I was trying to get through there as quickly as possible, so I just opened drawers, cabinets, moved things."

"What really sucks—assume they did take the package upstairs to their bedroom with them when they got home—I doubt they will leave it up there. So if we manage to get in the house again, it's like starting the search all over—it could be downstairs or upstairs."

"I'm thinking maybe under the tree," Marcella said before taking another bite of her burger.

Forrest frowned. "What do you mean?"

"According to Bud, they bought those things as Christmas gifts. And what do people do with Christmas gifts? They wrap them and put them under the tree."

"What are you saying?"

"Maybe next time we will be lucky. Maybe the next time I won't have to look any farther than the Christmas tree in their living room." Marcella set the partially eaten burger on her plate and picked up her glass of soda and took a sip.

"I'm not sure how we're going to get back in. I don't want to break any windows. They'll obviously know someone was in their house; I don't imagine they'll leave the door conveniently unlocked again. And they might even lock that pet door."

"Oh, didn't I tell you?" Marcella grinned and then stood up partially as she shoved one hand into the pocket of her pants. She pulled out a key, set it on the table, and sat down again.

Forrest frowned at the key. "What is that to?"

"A key to Marlow House. So we don't have to rely on them leaving a door unlocked, climb through the pet door, or break any windows."

"Are you sure it's a key to the house?"

"Yes. I tried it on the front door. And you will be proud of me, because I don't think they'll miss it. I found it on a key ring that was shoved in the back of a desk drawer in the front room. There must have been a dozen keys on the ring, and I didn't want to take the whole thing and chance them noticing it missing and then change the locks. I got lucky, and the second key I tried was the one to the front door. I took it off and then put the key ring back where I found it and shut the drawer."

"I'm impressed." Forrest beamed.

"Had I found the key sooner, I would have taken my time and put everything back exactly as it was so they wouldn't know someone had been there. But before I found the key, I thought it was my one shot to search the house, and I was just trying to blast through the place as fast as possible."

"So what now, stake out the house, and when they leave go inside and do another search?" Forrest asked.

"That's about all we can do. But I'm hoping they make it easy to find and put it under the tree."

COLIN BARI STOOD outside his room at the Seahorse Motel. He watched as the Hoopers' car drove into the parking lot. They were staying in the room next to his, on the north side. The room on the south side of his was currently empty. But Bari was fairly certain that room would be rented out within the hour. He didn't think Owen would want to spend another night in his car, and from what Colin knew, the vacant room next to his was the last vacancy in Frederickport.

Of course, there was another option—which would save Colin significant time and effort. For a brief moment yesterday he had imagined it might go that way. But then Owen ended up sleeping in his car, and Colin decided it was time to go to Astoria and retrieve the one thing that might give Owen the necessary nudge. But time was slipping away, and he didn't want Owen to disappear.

Colin thumbed through the tourist magazine he had picked up in the front office, listing local restaurants and sights of interest. He flipped through its pages, pretending to read it as the Hoopers' parked their car nearby. He peeked over the magazine and watched as the couple got out of their vehicle and began walking his way.

"Good afternoon," Colin greeted them when they got closer. He closed the magazine and smiled at the couple. "You wouldn't happen to be able to recommend a good local restaurant?"

Marcella and Forrest stopped by Colin, and Marcella asked, "Aren't you cold out here?"

"I enjoy the brisk air," Colin explained.

"We just ate at the Pier Café and the food was pretty good. It's right on the pier. We also noticed an ice cream shop next to it," Forrest told him.

"Thank you. Are you two staying through Christmas?" Colin asked.

Marcella glanced to her husband and back to Colin. "We're just taking one day at a time. But we'll probably be here a few more days. Just enjoying a little holiday."

"How nice," Colin returned.

They exchanged a few more pleasantries before Marcella and Forrest excused themselves and went into their room, closing and locking the door behind them.

Now standing alone in front of his room, Colin whispered to himself, "That must mean you didn't find it. When you do—if you do—I certainly hope you don't complicate matters for me."

Rolling up the magazine, he tucked it under one arm and made his way to the front office, his cane in hand.

DARK SUNGLASSES CONCEALED Owen Gardener's eyes, while his thick dark beard covered much of his face. On his head he wore a baseball cap. It covered his shortly cut hair. A younger Owen had once thought men who wore full beards did so because they were losing their hair, and if they couldn't grow hair on the top of their head, they would do it on their chin. He had since learned that was not necessarily true. Owen had a healthy head of hair. Until the gray streaks, its color had once matched his beard. While gray had recently been sneaking into his beard, as it had taken over the hair on his head, he had managed to pluck out each gray whisker, but soon—if he didn't wish to have a thin beard—he would need to shave it off or let it go gray. He was not fond of gray beards. The last thing he wanted was for people to start calling him Santa Claus, especially since he wasn't even forty yet.

Owen sat alone in his car, trying to decide what to do next. He had pulled into the Seahorse Motel parking lot on impulse, just minutes earlier, and had parked in front of the registration office. By the number of cars in the motel parking lot, he wondered if they even had any vacancies. This entire trip had been spur of the moment, and now that he was in Frederickport, he wasn't sure what he was going to do—or if he was going to stay. But it had been a long drive, followed by an uncomfortable night sleeping in his car, and now he was exhausted. If he could get a room—at least for tonight—then he could figure out his next move.

With a weary sigh, Owen climbed out of his car, slammed its

door shut, and started for the registration office. Right before reaching the building, a tall, thin, bearded, elderly man, who had come from the direction of one of the rooms, reached the office entrance first. The man opened the door wide and motioned with his cane for Owen to enter before him, while saying, "Good afternoon. Lovely day, isn't it?"

"Yes, it is." Owen gave the man a nod and added, "Thank you." While walking through the open doorway, Owen got a closer look of the older man's face. There was something familiar about him. *Who is he?* Owen wondered. The man had a slight accent, yet Owen couldn't place it.

Once inside, the older man took a seat at a sofa in the waiting area and began reading a magazine. Owen headed for the front counter, relieved to see the young woman at the registration desk was an unfamiliar face.

"How can I help you?" the woman greeted Owen.

"I would like to get a room, please," Owen told her.

"You are in luck. We have one room left. We've been crazy busy. How long are you planning to stay?" she asked.

"Through Christmas." The moment the words left his mouth, he was momentarily stunned. *Where did that come from?* he asked himself. Five minutes earlier his intention was to just get a room for the night and then figure out what he wanted to do after getting a good night's sleep. Perhaps it had been because of what she had said —that it was the last room they had available. While somewhat surprised at his own words, Owen didn't correct himself.

COLIN SAT QUIETLY on the sofa, pretending to read. He had heard what Owen said to the woman at the registration desk —*through Christmas*. He smiled. Things were moving along as planned. His only concern was the Hoopers. They needed to stay out of his way and not muck things up.

TEN

Hunny followed Brian and Danielle as they walked from room to room on the first floor of Marlow House. When Brian walked up the stairs to take a brief look at the second and third floors, Hunny stayed with him, yet Danielle returned to the living room.

"I just remembered—Max. Maybe he saw something," Heather suggested. Max was Danielle's cat.

"I already talked to him. He was upstairs in our room, sitting on the windowsill. He didn't see anyone come into the house. He was watching all the activity down the street. Which is why I'm fairly certain whoever came in, came in through the kitchen door. I already explained to him Hunny would be staying with us." Walt hadn't actually talked to the cat—it was more a telepathic communication, a gift that had come to him while in the spirit realm. His ability to converse with some animals—like his telekinetic powers, which he had developed when being a ghost—he had somehow managed to bring with him when he moved back over to the living world.

DANIELLE, Walt, Heather and Chris sat in the living room of Marlow House, watching as Brian Henderson jotted something

54

down in his notepad. He stood near the sofa, where Walt and Danielle were, across from where Heather and Chris sat on the matching chairs.

"And it doesn't look like anything was taken?" Brian asked.

"It's entirely possible something is missing, and we just haven't noticed," Danielle said. "In the big scheme of things—" she glanced over to Chris, who had just lost his house "—it is not that big a deal. But we figured we needed to report it."

"There is no sign of forced entry," Brian said.

"No. Like I mentioned earlier, they probably came through the kitchen door. I don't think I locked it when we got home from Astoria," Danielle told him. "And when we went up to Chris's, we left through the front door. That door was locked when we got home."

Brian closed his notepad and glanced briefly up toward the ceiling. "I have to agree with you. I don't think they made it to the second floor."

Hunny, who had been sitting by Brian's side, made a growling sound.

Surprised, Brian looked down at the pit bull. "Did she just growl at me?"

Heather chuckled. "No. That's Hunny's way of talking. Freaks some people out. But it's not a growl."

"Sounded like a growl," Brian said, still looking down at the dog.

Hunny stood up, her butt and tail going into a full wag as she wiggled closer to Brian and pressed her nose against his pant leg. He reached down and she licked his hand.

"She likes you," Danielle told him.

Brian chuckled and looked back to his notepad to review his notes. "Unless this is some prankster with an odd sense of humor, it looks like they were searching for something and got interrupted. Do you have any idea what that might be?"

Danielle shook her head. "Not really. And the strange thing, there was a twenty-dollar bill and some change in clear view in the parlor, and it wasn't touched. My iPad is still sitting on the desk in the library, and the credit card I used to pay a bill is still on the kitchen counter by the phone."

"Most of your neighbors were outside, watching the fire. I'll talk to them and see if anyone saw anything," Brian said.

"Aren't you going to take fingerprints?" Heather asked.

"I could, but considering most of Frederickport came through here less than two months ago for the haunted house, I doubt it would do much good," Brian explained.

"Joanne is a good housekeeper, but I don't think she has wiped down every inch of this house since then. I have to agree with Brian, it would be impossible to rule out prints that were here before the break-in," Walt said.

"I guess we need to go back to being more careful about keeping our doors locked," Danielle said with a sigh.

Heather frowned. "I'd like to know what they were looking for."

"Whoever it is obviously didn't consider you might have security cameras. Everyone has security cameras these days," Chris said.

"Or they are familiar with Marlow House," Brian suggested.

"Are you saying someone we know did this?" Danielle asked.

"Not necessarily someone who is a friend. But someone who has been here before." Brian snapped his pen closed and slipped it in his pocket. He looked from Walt to Danielle. "If you find something that is missing—or you figure out what they were looking for—let me know. But for now, the only thing I can do is talk to your neighbors."

BRIAN WAS JUST DRIVING AWAY when Lily and Ian walked into Marlow House with baby Connor, and Sadie their golden retriever trailing behind them. In spite of the recent break-in, Danielle had not bothered to lock the front door after she had walked Brian out. The Bartleys walked in without knocking, seeing nothing unusual about the door being unlocked. They were just heading to the living room when they walked by the open doorway to the downstairs bedroom and spied Danielle in the room, returning boxes to the closet, while all the dresser drawers were pulled out.

"Did you lose something?" Lily asked, stepping into the room with her wiggling bundle.

"No. I'm just trying to put things back in order," Danielle explained, now closing the dresser drawers.

"What's going on?" Ian asked from the doorway.

"While we were up at Chris's, someone broke in Marlow House, ransacked the downstairs. They went through every room on the first floor, like they were looking for something, but nothing seems to have been touched on the second floor or in our room."

"What's missing?" Ian asked.

Danielle shrugged. "That's just it. We haven't noticed anything yet. I have no clue what they were looking for. Walt, Heather and I are putting the rooms back in order. Chris is in the living room, drowning his sorrows. Why don't you go on in there and keep him company. I'll just be a minute. Have you eaten yet?"

"No, we were wondering if you wanted us to pick up some take-out," Lily asked.

"I was going to make something, but considering how this day is going, I think takeout might be a better option." Danielle walked over to Lily and gave Connor a quick kiss. The baby giggled.

<hr/>

CHRIS SAT on one of the chairs facing the sofa, sipping the brandy Walt had given him. His friends discussed what they wanted to eat while he questioned his own good sense drinking the brandy, considering he hadn't eaten in hours. Emotionally drained, he unintentionally tuned out the others while his mind sorted all that needed to be done now that he was technically homeless.

"I said give me your credit card," Heather demanded for the second time.

Jolted out of his fog, Chris looked up and found Heather standing over him, her hand out, waiting for him to comply with her demand.

"My credit card?" He frowned. "Oh, for the food, of course." He stood briefly and removed his wallet.

"No, silly. Not for the food. Ian said he was treating," Heather said with an impatient eye roll.

"Then what do you need my credit card for?" Chris asked while handing her the card. He tucked his wallet back in his pocket and sat back down.

"Weren't you listening?" Heather asked.

"I guess not."

"I said, while they get the food, I'll run out and get you some things you're going to need. You are obviously going to need clothes and basic toiletries until you have time to shop. I imagine you are going to want to take a shower tonight and will want something clean to put on. While you might like to sleep in the buff—which I have no idea if you do or not—I don't imagine Walt will appreciate you prancing around his house naked."

"I do not prance," Chris argued.

"Yes, please spare me the prancing nude Chris," Walt called out.

"You'll need something to wear in the morning," Heather added.

"You don't have to do that," Chris said, starting to stand up. "I should go get some clothes before all the stores close."

Heather pushed him back in the chair. "Don't be silly. You are having a bad day as it is, and you just downed a glass of brandy and are on your second; I don't think you want to be pulled over for a DUI."

"Heather has a point," Ian chimed in.

"Anyway, I am your assistant. Isn't this the kind of thing an assistant does?" Heather asked.

"I don't know..." Chris murmured.

"Anyway, however long it takes me, I was planning to add it to my timecard." Heather slipped the credit card in her purse.

"You don't have a timecard," Chris reminded her. "I pay you a salary."

"There is always the Christmas bonus," Heather reminded him with a smile. From her purse she pulled out a pen and small pad of paper and handed them to Chris.

"What is this for?" Chris asked.

"Write down your sizes—and anything you need that I might not think of."

After Heather left a few minutes later, Danielle told Chris, "When she gets back, I'll throw your new clothes in the wash."

"Why? Is Heather going to buy me dirty clothes?" Chris asked.

"Eww, you have to wash your new clothes," Lily said. "You never know who might have tried them on."

———

LILY WENT with Ian to pick up the food, leaving Connor behind with Danielle. Connor napped on the sofa between Walt and Danielle, stretched out on a baby blanket. Sadie and Hunny dozed nearby on the floor. Max had come down from the attic bedroom and now perched on the back of the sofa, looking down at Connor, while Walt silently warned him not to wake the baby.

Chris sat in one of the chairs across from them, sipping his second brandy. He looked up at Walt and Danielle and said, "I just thought of something. My brother is coming tomorrow for Christmas, and I don't have a house. I suppose I should call Adam and see if he has something for me to rent. After all, I'm going to need to find something anyway."

"Why don't you just stay here?" Walt suggested. "At least through Christmas, while your brother is here. It will give you time to figure out what you want to do."

"Stay here?" Chris asked.

"I think that's a great idea," Danielle said. "It's not like we don't have plenty of room. Hunny would be happy here. And maybe having a pit bull might discourage future break-ins."

"Because we all know what a ferocious guard dog Hunny is," Walt said with a snort.

"I have to admit, the idea of moving into a vacation rental for Christmas does not really appeal to me, especially since my brother is going to be here. But staying at Marlow House for the holidays—I kind of like that idea. If it really is okay," Chris said.

"For some reason the idea of you moving back in here for a while does not annoy me near as much as it once would have," Walt said dryly.

"Perhaps that's because you got the girl?" Chris teased.

"That and the fact it will drive Pearl Huckabee insane knowing you are living here with Hunny," Walt said.

ELEVEN

Onetime silent screen star Eva Thorndike had been dead for a little over a century. One thing that she had learned since moving over to the other side was that she was something of an anomaly. After death, most spirits chose to move on to the next level, leaving behind their earthly constraints. It was typically the confused souls, the ones who hadn't come to terms with their deaths, who lingered. Yet even in those cases, Eva found, long-term lingerers were rare.

Death had never confused Eva. She had expected it, considering her debilitating illness had struck at such a young age. At first she had railed against it—determined to live her dream, which in many ways she had—rising to the top in her chosen profession. It was her anger at such an early death, one that had prevented her from reaching her full potential—a transition to talkies—that kept her from moving on.

Her life now—or more accurately her death—had become much more amusing the last few years. Beach Drive had become something of a magnet for mediums, giving her more than the lingering dead to communicate with. And then there was Marie, someone she had met in her early days as a ghost. Of course, back then Marie had been a baby and had no idea the beautiful woman who would visit her in the nursery and sing her lullabies was a ghost.

Then one day Marie—just like that—could no longer see or hear her.

Years went by, Marie got older, and one day at the age of ninety-one, Marie found herself murdered and then a ghost. Like Eva, she decided to stick around, which gave the two spirits an opportunity to reconnect.

Eva had just left Marie, who was heading over to Marlow House, while Eva went on to check in on Chris. Eva rather adored Chris—what was there not to like? Had he been alive back during her heyday as an actress, she could easily imagine him as her leading man. Women would have adored him—women did adore him.

Many of Chris's close Frederickport friends assumed he had been so busy with his foundation that he had little time for a social life. Some even speculated he might still be pining over Danielle. Yet Eva knew the truth. Chris often escorted beautiful women out to dinner and the theater when traveling for the foundation—and sometimes he would drive into Portland for a date with some young woman he had met. However, he had not found anyone whom he cared enough about to share his real identity with. Eva was beginning to wonder if he ever would.

It took her a moment to comprehend what she was seeing. Chris's house—it was virtually gone, a sad heap of scorched timber and ash. Ignoring the *'no trespassing'* signs someone had erected, she moved through what had once been Chris's home. As dismal as it seemed, she didn't imagine he had been killed in the fire—if that was the case, then she would have expected to see his spirit. She couldn't imagine him moving on without first saying goodbye to his friends. Although, maybe that was exactly what he was doing right now, over at Marlow House saying goodbye. Another possibility, he had been injured and was at the hospital.

The next moment Eva found herself standing in the kitchen of Marlow House. Sitting at the kitchen table were Walt, Danielle and Marie.

"Where is Chris?" Eva demanded.

"They were just telling me what happened," Marie told her.

"He's still sleeping. We put him in the downstairs bedroom last night," Danielle explained as she sipped her morning coffee.

The next moment Marie moved the empty chair out from the table so Eva could sit down without the tabletop cutting her image in half. Eva accepted the silent invitation.

"What happened?" Eva asked.

Danielle went on to tell about yesterday's series of events.

When Danielle finished with the telling, Eva asked, "What is he going to do?"

"For now he's staying here, at least through Christmas. His brother is coming this afternoon. I'm fairly certain he'll decide to rebuild on his lot," Danielle explained.

Danielle's cellphone began to ring. She picked it up off the table and looked to see who was calling—it was Joanne, their housekeeper.

"Hi, Joanne," Danielle said the next moment, holding her cellphone to her ear. The others at the kitchen table sat quietly and listened.

"Is it true what I heard? Did Chris's house burn down?" Joanne asked.

"Unfortunately. But he is okay. No one was hurt. We put him in the downstairs bedroom."

"Oh dear, I didn't have any sheets on that bed," Joanne fretted.

"No problem. I gave Chris some clean sheets and helped him put them on the bed," Danielle explained. "But I guess I'll need to put some sheets on one of the beds upstairs. His brother is coming for Christmas, and they'll be staying here now."

"I'm coming over there. I'll get the room ready for Chris's brother. I'd like to run the vacuum before he arrives. And why don't you text me a grocery list. I'm sure you're going to need some more food."

"But today is your day off," Danielle argued.

"Don't be silly. I want to do this. What about that list?"

Danielle smiled. "Okay, I'll get Walt to help me make a list, and I'll send it to you. You are wonderful, Joanne. We're going to Pearl Cove in about thirty minutes for brunch. Would you like to join us? My treat."

"I need to get the house ready for guests! You all go and have fun, but don't forget to text me what you need."

Danielle hung up the phone a few minutes later and chuckled. "I think Joanne was rather excited at the prospect of having guests here."

"I believe she misses the B and B," Walt said.

MARCELLA PUSHED her now empty breakfast plate to the middle of the table. She sat with her husband at a booth in Pier Café. Glancing over at the lunch counter, she spied the elderly man from the room next to theirs at the Seahorse Motel. He sat alone with just a cup of coffee. An empty chair separated him from a bearded man she was fairly certain was also staying at their motel. Like the elderly gentleman, he appeared to be alone.

"Should we walk over to the house? Maybe we'll be lucky and they won't be home," Forrest suggested.

Before Marcella answered, she spied a woman entering the diner. She watched the woman take a seat across the room before saying, "I think this might be an excellent time to go over. Look who just walked in."

Forrest glanced to where Marcella was looking. It was the Marlows' grouchy neighbor.

"Hopefully she came for breakfast and will be here a while. If so, I know exactly what we need to do," Marcella said.

Forrest glanced from the woman back to his wife. "What's that?"

"We should be able to look up the street and see if any cars are parked in front of Marlow House. If not, we can walk up through the alley and look in the window of their garage. If their car is gone, then we can safely assume we can go in the house."

"What happens if one of them took the car—and the other one stayed home?" he asked.

Marcella considered the question a moment. "If both of their cars are there, then we know for sure we can't go in. But if one of them is gone, you can walk around to the front door and ring the bell. If someone answers, you can ask them some lame tourist question. But if no one answers, then we can go right in. But we should go now, while the old busybody is here."

COLIN FIDGETED with his coffee cup as he watched the Hoopers hurriedly pay their bill and rush from the diner. He glanced over his shoulder at Pearl Huckabee and muttered under his breath, "Going for another try?"

"Excuse me?" the man next to him said.

Colin looked up at Owen and smiled. "Sorry, I was just talking to myself."

Owen flashed him a smile and said, "I've been doing a bit of that myself lately." Owen stood up, pulled some money from his pocket, and tossed it on the counter. He gave Colin a parting nod.

Still fidgeting with his coffee cup, Colin watched Owen leave the restaurant. He shook his head. "Still in conflict, are you, boy? I guess you're going to need me."

THE HOOPERS HAD GLANCED up the street after stepping off the pier, but saw no cars parked by Marlow House. They continued to the alleyway. When they reached the back of Marlow House, Marcella was about to go peek in the garage window when they noticed the garage door opening. Forrest grabbed hold of his wife's wrist and dragged her into some nearby bushes.

Hidden among the foliage, the Hoopers watched as the black Packard backed out of the garage. After the vehicle was completely outside, the door closed. A moment later the Packard drove by Marcella and Forrest, who continued to crouch in the bushes.

"Did you see that!" Marcella whispered. "They were both in the car."

"Now what?" he asked.

"Let's go through the backyard. Doesn't look like the gate is locked. With the neighbor gone, there's no one to see us. If we're lucky, that key will also work on the kitchen door. Otherwise, we're going to have to go around to the front door," Marcella told her husband.

"Let's hope it works," he whispered.

Marcella had slipped on her gloves after leaving the diner. Considering the weather, she doubted anyone would find it odd. To her delight the key worked on the back door, as it had on the front door.

"You want me to go in with you?" he asked.

"No. Stay out here and watch to see if anyone comes. If that neighbor returns, come in the house, and we can go out the front door. But keep an eye on the front of the house as well as the back."

"I hope I can watch everything," he said nervously.

"Just do it!" she snapped before slipping into the kitchen.

MARCELLA STOOD in Marlow House's kitchen and glanced around. The first thing she noticed, they had obviously put the house back to normal. All the drawers and cabinets were shut. Her plan was to go quickly through the first floor, see if there were any packages that hadn't been there yesterday—yet this time she didn't intend to go through all the cabinets. She would look under the tree to see if any packages had been added before going upstairs to look around.

From the kitchen she slipped out into the hallway and looked in the living room. There were no packages under the Christmas tree. From the living room she walked into the downstairs bedroom and looked around quickly. She was surprised to find a number of shopping bags piled in one corner. They hadn't been there yesterday.

Kneeling on the floor by the shopping bags, she started going through them when she heard what sounded like a low growl. She froze. The growling sound grew louder.

Swallowing nervously, Marcella slowly turned around to face the open doorway. To her utter horror she found herself looking into the menacing eyes of a brindle pit bull.

"Holy crap," Marcella said with a gulp.

The dog continued to stare at her, no longer making the ominous sound.

"Nice doggie," she said in a wavering voice, slowly standing up.

The pit bull cocked its head slightly, studying her.

"Hi, sweetheart." Marcella forced herself to speak in a soft, calm voice, one reserved for speaking to toddlers you were trying to win over. "Hi, sweet baby. You are a good doggie, aren't you?"

In the next moment the dog lunged, running full force at Marcella. Before she could move, its front paws landed on her chest, knocking her down. The terrified woman found herself sprawled out on the bedroom floor, looking up into the eyes of the pit bull, its face just inches from hers as the dog's heavy body kept her pinned to the floor.

TWELVE

M arcella had never been fond of a dog licking her, but she decided that was preferable to one sinking its teeth into her flesh. Still on the floor, flat on her back, she thought if her heart beat any faster, it would surely burst out of her chest. She opened her eyes and passively accepted the sloppy wet kisses covering every inch of her face. If she survived this pit bull attack, she would definitely need a good shower.

Finally managing to rein in her composure, she warily tried pushing the dog away as she sat up while talking baby talk in hopes of keeping the canine in his current mood. To her relief the dog remained in friendly mode and promptly sat down on his butt. *No—her butt.* Marcella silently corrected herself, noticing the dog was female.

"Nice doggy," Marcella said again, pulling herself up. She looked at the dog, which was no longer sitting, but wiggling its butt in an enthusiastic tail wag. "Umm…I think I need to go now."

Not wishing to press her luck, Marcella quickly exited the bedroom and headed toward the kitchen. Yet the dog was obviously not ready to say goodbye to her new friend and trailed closely behind her. As soon as Marcella reached the kitchen, she quickly entered and closed the door behind her, barricading the dog from the room.

With a sigh of relief, her heart still racing, Marcella flew out the kitchen door into the side yard, running into her husband, practically knocking him to the ground.

"Let's get the hell out of here!" she cried.

"What happened?" he asked.

"There's a pit bull in there!"

"Did it bite you?" he asked.

"No, but I thought it was going to lick me to death." She ran toward the gate leading to the street. She stopped suddenly when she spied a car pull up and park.

"Out through the alley!" she shouted, grabbing hold of her husband's hand. The two ran through the side yard and out the back gate into the alleyway.

JOANNE INTENDED to open the side gate so she could pull up in the driveway and park near the kitchen door. She had sacks of groceries to carry into the house. But she knew Hunny was inside, and she didn't want her to get out of the yard. Joanne was not concerned about Hunny getting out and hurting someone. She worried what Pearl Huckabee might do if the pit bull got out and into the neighbor's yard.

She entered through the front door and was greeted by Hunny. When she reached the kitchen door, she was surprised to find it already closed.

"That's odd," Joanne said. She glanced down at the dog, who stood by her side with her butt and tail wagging. "Did you close the door, girl?" She looked at the door again and frowned. "Although, I'm not sure how you could have done that, since it opens into the kitchen."

MELONY AND ADAM joined their friends for brunch at Pearl Cove. Seated at a table overlooking the ocean, the party included Walt, Danielle, Heather, Chris, Lily, Ian and Connor. Also in attendance were the spirits Marie and Eva, but only the mediums could see and hear them—and only those who lived on Beach Drive were aware of their existence. Both Melony and Adam remained utterly clueless about the ghostly members of their party.

"I am so sorry about your house," Melony told Chris for the second time.

"There are a couple of nice houses on the market," Adam told him.

Chris shook his head. "No. I'm going to rebuild. But I'll need you to find me something to rent while it's under construction. I'm guessing it's going to take me six months to a year to rebuild."

Adam cringed. "At the moment, I don't have any rentals. I should have something after Christmas. And most of my owners have restrictions on what kind of dogs they allow. Of course, for the right price you could probably get what you need."

"Or maybe buy something to live in while he builds, and sell it later?" Heather suggested. "Then pets aren't an issue."

"Only problem with that, there is still escrow to consider. Chris is going to need something he can move right into. That will be more challenging. Our local market is a little tight right now, and I can't think of any vacant houses currently on the market," Adam explained.

"He is welcome to stay with us while he figures out something," Danielle said.

Adam looked over to Danielle and then glanced to Walt to see his reaction.

Walt shrugged. "He has already moved into our downstairs bedroom. I told him he could stay as long as he agreed not to prance around the house naked."

Chris rolled his eyes at Walt and said, "Oh, shut up." He laughed.

Confused, Adam looked from Chris to Walt and then to Danielle.

"It's nothing," Danielle assured Adam. "They're just being silly."

Melony changed the subject. "Your brother is coming today?"

"He should be here this afternoon," Chris told her.

"I wonder how Pearl Huckabee is going to like Marlow House turning into a boardinghouse again," Adam teased.

"I hardly call two holiday guests a boardinghouse," Danielle scoffed.

Lily went on to tell Adam and Melony about the tantrum Pearl had thrown the previous day.

"That woman really is horrid," Melony said.

"Well, it is Christmas, so I guess we should try being more positive with her," Danielle suggested.

"Yeah, right," Heather said with a snort.

"Did you lose everything?" Melony asked.

"Just material things," Chris said. "All my photographs—pictures from when I was a kid—I digitalized them all a few years ago. I have them and copies of most of my important documents saved on the cloud. Of course, I have some things over at my office. The other stuff is all replaceable."

"The clothes you have on now, are those new?" Melony asked.

Chris nodded. "Yes. I have this amazing assistant. She picked up just about everything I needed to get by for a few weeks."

Melony looked over at Heather and smiled. "You went shopping for him?"

"Yeah. It was kind of fun. I've never been able to go clothes shopping and not worry about how much I was spending. It would have been more fun had I been shopping for myself."

They all laughed, and Chris said, "I'll tell you what. I'll give you back that credit card to use, and you can go on a shopping spree for yourself."

Heather perked up. "Really?"

Chris shrugged. "Sure."

Heather frowned. "Umm…does this mean I don't get a Christmas bonus?"

Chris laughed.

WHILE DANIELLE and her friends enjoyed their brunch at Pearl Cove, Joanne put the groceries away at Marlow House, and Marcella and Forrest walked back to the pier to retrieve their vehicle. Over on the main street, Sunday business was brisk with Christmas shoppers. One of those shoppers was Elizabeth Sparks, who leisurely window-shopped while searching for the perfect gift for her mother.

She stood outside one store window, checking out the winter jackets worn by the mannequins, when she had the eerie sensation someone was watching her. Instead of turning around, she glanced to the right and caught the reflection of a man in the store window. He stood not far from her, seemingly looking in her direction, yet with his sunglasses she could not see his eyes. A shiver traveled up her spine. This was not the first time she had seen the man. She knew he was watching her.

PEARL HUCKABEE STOOD at her upstairs bedroom window, looking down at her neighbor's yard. With a scowl she watched as the pit bull ran around the lawn, playing with a ball, periodically tossing it in the air before catching it. The dog was alone.

Parked in the side drive was the car that belonged to the woman who cleaned for the Marlows. Pearl was about to turn from the window when she noticed another car drive up the street. It belonged to her other neighbor, Heather Donovan. If she was not mistaken, the neighbor who had burned down his house was sitting in the passenger seat.

Curious, she remained at the window and watched. It looked as if Heather stopped down by Chris's house. She then turned the car around and came back down the street. Chris was no longer with her. Heather pulled into her own driveway, and a minute later, Chris Johnson came driving down in his car. He parked in front of Marlow House.

"Wonderful, we are going to be having all these cars parked over here," Pearl grumbled. She noticed motion from the backyard and spied Walt and Danielle Marlow entering their backyard from the alleyway. Pearl assumed they had just parked the Packard in their garage.

She watched as the pit bull greeted the Marlows. A moment later Danielle went inside the house while Walt sat down on the back porch, petting the dog.

"WHEN YOU LEFT, you locked poor Hunny out of the kitchen," Joanne told Danielle when she walked into the house. "She couldn't go outside."

"We did?" Danielle frowned. "I could swear we left the door open."

Joanne shrugged. "No big deal. I don't think she was locked out long."

Joanne left the kitchen to go upstairs to finish preparing the guest room.

"I guess we locked Hunny out of the kitchen when we went to brunch," Danielle told Walt when he walked into the house with Hunny a few minutes later.

Walt glanced toward the open doorway leading to the hall. "Where's Joanne?"

"She went upstairs. Why?"

Before Walt could explain, Chris walked into the kitchen. "I parked my car in front of your house. I hope that's okay." Chris leaned down and greeted his dog.

"When Joanne leaves, you can park in the side drive if you want," Danielle told him. "Walt and I usually park in the garage now."

"Chris, can you please shut that door? I need to tell you both something, and I don't want Joanne to overhear."

Curious, Chris shut the door and turned to face Walt, Hunny by his side.

"I guess we accidentally locked poor Hunny out of the kitchen when we went to brunch," Danielle began.

"No we didn't," Walt countered.

"Yes we did," Danielle argued. "Joanne told me Hunny was locked out of the kitchen when she got here, so she couldn't use the dog door and get outside."

"I know that door was open when we left. I checked it," Chris argued.

"But Joanne said—" Danielle began, only to be cut off by Walt.

"Danielle, I know what Joanne told you. Please, I need to tell you this before she comes down here," Walt said impatiently.

Both Chris and Danielle turned their full attention to Walt.

"What is it?" she asked.

"Someone was in the house again. According to Hunny, while we were gone, she found a lady in Chris's room, going through the things Heather just bought him."

"What lady?" Danielle asked.

"My guess, whoever went through the house yesterday."

"What exactly did Hunny say about it?" Chris asked. He then frowned and added, "That sounds like such a weird question."

"Technically speaking, Hunny didn't say anything. But she did tell me about the lady—who Hunny believes was a very nice lady. She gave her lots of kisses."

"This woman who broke in our house kissed Hunny?" Danielle asked.

Walt laughed. "No. Hunny kissed her. She said she tasted a little like bacon. I suspect whoever it was had just had breakfast."

"Are you saying the woman is the one who locked Hunny out of the kitchen?" Danielle asked.

"According to Hunny, yes. Which made Hunny rather sad. She believed she had just met a new friend," Walt told her.

"Who is this woman who keeps breaking into our house?" Danielle asked.

Walt shook his head. "I don't know. Hunny had never seen her before, and I'm afraid dogs are not terrific at giving good descriptions. I just know it's someone who tastes a little like bacon."

THIRTEEN

W rapped in warm jackets, Marcella and Forrest walked along the beach in front of the Seahorse Motel. It was not an easy task for either person, as walking in the sand had become progressively more difficult as the years went by. But they didn't want to be cooped up in their small motel room, and they needed to discuss what they should do next. Marcella wasn't crazy about sitting in some restaurant, going over their plans. One never knew who might overhear them.

"I've been thinking about that dog," Marcella began.

"You mean the dog that neighbor said the Marlows didn't have?" he asked.

"True. But she did mention a pit bull who lives down the street," Marcella reminded him.

"You think the Marlows were dog sitting for their neighbor?" he asked.

She shrugged. "That would explain why the dog was there. While I got out of there pretty quick, I don't think anyone else was in the house."

Forrest stopped walking, his breathing labored. "Let's go back to the motel. Walking in this sand is killing me."

Marcella nodded. "I was just going to suggest that."

When they reached the motel a few moments later, Marcella

nodded to the registration office and said, "Let's go in there for a minute. I want to find out more about that dog."

"How are you going to do that in there?" he asked.

"I have a hunch."

A MAN STOOD behind the registration desk instead of the woman who had checked them in the previous day. He wore a name tag; it read *Sam*. Sitting on the sofa was the elderly gentleman from the room next door, reading a newspaper, and Marcella wondered briefly if the man always hung out in the front office. Perhaps he was lonely, she thought.

"How can I help you?" the man behind the counter asked Marcella when she approached.

"Hello, we are staying here. And yesterday, when we were sight-seeing, we noticed there was a house fire down from the pier."

"Ahh, the fire over on Beach Drive, yes. I heard the house was destroyed." He shook his head in sympathy. "Right before Christmas. Poor Chris."

"He was a friend of yours?" Marcella asked.

"More an acquaintance. He works for the Glandon Foundation."

"Glandon Foundation?" She frowned.

"They do a lot of nonprofit work."

"I hope no one was hurt," she said.

"From what I understand, he managed to get outside with his dog."

"I hope his dog wasn't hurt," she said.

The man shook his head. "From what I heard, no one was."

"I'm curious, what kind of dog is it? I love dogs." Marcella smiled sweetly.

"A pit bull."

"Oh, those can be mean dogs," Marcella said with a shiver.

The man shrugged.

"I hope this Chris and his dog are able to find someplace to stay. So sad to lose your home, especially right before Christmas," Marcella said.

"From what I heard, he's staying over at Marlow House. He's a close friend of the Marlows."

"At least that explains where the pit bull came from," Marcella told her husband after they left the office and headed back to their motel room.

"Now what? We weren't counting on a dog being there."

"True. But as much as that dog about gave me a heart attack, she really wasn't much of a guard dog, unless licking excessively is some new way of trying to apprehend robbers. Next time I will take along some dog treats."

THE HOOPERS DIDN'T NOTICE Colin following them out of the motel office. He watched as they went into their room, shutting the door behind them. He took a seat outside, on one of the plastic beach chairs the motel had set up between their doors. Leaning back in the chair, he glanced over to the Hoopers' room and noticed someone inside opening the window blinds so they could look out.

"I just need to keep you two out of my way," he said under his breath before looking from their window and glancing out to the parking lot. A few moments later Owen drove up in his car and parked. Colin watched as his other neighbor got out of the vehicle and started walking up to his room.

"Good morning. Although, I suppose it is afternoon now," Colin greeted him when Owen was within earshot.

Owen nodded. "Afternoon. It's a little chilly out here, isn't it?" He glanced up at the sky and discovered the rain clouds that had been gathering earlier had vanished. He looked back to the man sitting in the plastic patio chair.

"I enjoy the brisk sea air. I don't believe I introduced myself earlier. I'm Colin Bari." He smiled at Owen and extended his hand. Colin had been fairly certain the young man had recognized him earlier, considering his expression. Colin didn't imagine Owen was quite ready to run into anyone he had once known—not yet. As soon as Colin said his name, he noticed Owen's subtle change of expression. It was obvious to him the name meant nothing to Owen, and Colin was certain his young motel neighbor was probably feeling a pang of relief, believing he had been wrong in thinking Colin was someone from his Frederickport past.

Owen accepted the handshake and said, "Nice to meet you. I'm Owen—Owen Gardener."

"Would you like to join me?" Colin motioned to the empty chair next to him. "The sun actually feels pretty good, especially since the breeze stopped."

"Maybe for a minute," Owen said with a smile as he sat down in the empty chair.

"Are you here visiting family for Christmas?" Colin asked.

Owen shrugged and said, "I'm just passing through. I don't really do much for Christmas anymore."

"Really? I love Christmas. It is my favorite time of year," Colin said.

"Are you here visiting family for Christmas?" Owen asked.

"Unfortunately, I don't have any family left. I never got married, so I never had children," Colin explained. "I never had any brothers and sisters, so there are no nieces or nephews. But that doesn't mean I still can't enjoy the spirit of Christmas."

"Spirit of Christmas?" Owen frowned.

Colin took a deep breath, closed his eyes briefly, and then looked at Owen and smiled. "Yes. Can't you feel it? A time when anything is possible?"

Owen stared at Colin, yet said nothing. After a moment he stood up and said, "It was nice chatting with you, but I'm tired. I didn't sleep very good last night. I think I'm going to go take a nap."

Colin said his goodbyes and watched the young man walk away. After Owen went into his motel room, Colin whispered, "Time for the next phase of my plan. Have fun washing your hands." Colin chuckled, leaned back in the chair, and waited.

ONCE INSIDE HIS MOTEL ROOM, Owen pulled his wallet and cellphone out of his pocket. He tossed them on the dresser and then removed his jacket. Dropping the jacket on a chair, he sat on the end of the bed and removed his shoes. Several minutes later he went to use the bathroom before crashing for a nap. When he was done using the toilet, he went to wash his hands. After turning on the faucet, he started to put his hands under the running water when the water began to sputter. No longer flowing, the water came out of the faucet in several short bursts and then stopped altogether.

Frowning at the faucet, he turned its handle to the right and then left, but no matter which direction he turned it, nothing happened. He walked over to the tub and shower and tried turning on the water there—but again, nothing happened. Glancing at the toilet, he tried flushing it. It had flushed a moment ago, but this time it refused to flush.

Now irritated, he walked out of the bathroom and to the phone sitting on the nightstand. He called the front desk.

"The water is not working in my room," Owen told the person on the other side of the line a moment later.

"I'll be right over," the man from the office assured him.

Five minutes later, Sam knocked on Owen's door. After trying the faucets for himself, he excused himself a moment later and went outside.

"Excuse me, that's your room, right?" Sam asked Colin, pointing to the door of his motel room.

"Yes, it is. Is there a problem?" Colin asked.

"Can I get you to go inside and see if your sink and tub has water?"

"Certainly." Colin stood up, went inside his room for a moment, and then came back outside. "No, I'm afraid I don't have any water in there."

With a weary sigh, Sam said, "Okay. We'll get it fixed."

A few minutes later Sam went to the Hoopers' door and knocked.

"Yes?" Marcella said when she opened the door a moment later.

"I'm Sam from the front office. I'm sorry to disturb you, but this building seems to be experiencing some plumbing problems."

"Plumbing problems? What kind?" Marcella frowned.

"Is your water working?" Sam asked.

"It was a minute ago. Do you need to come in and look at it?" she asked.

"If you don't mind."

"Certainly." Marcella opened the door wider for Sam to enter. When he walked into the motel room, he found Forrest sitting on one of the chairs, watching television. He went straight to the bathroom. To his surprise their sink, tub and shower, and toilet seemed to be in perfect working order.

SOMEONE ONCE COMPARED Ruby Crabtree to an angry

Strawberry Shortcake doll, with her curly red short hair, round face, and pug nose. While Ruby was only five feet tall, the motel owner had proved to be a force to be reckoned with. It wasn't just that she had sent four husbands to the grave—but she seemed to have the ability to always get what she wanted. Over a year ago that had included maintaining ownership to the Seahorse Motel, in spite of the fact certain information had come to light that indicated Ruby's family might have illegally obtained the property where they had built the motel—property that had once belonged to the Marlow Family.

Ruby stood outside the motel office, ranting to Sam. "Did you have to call the plumber? You know they will charge me double time since it's Sunday. Can't you fix it? Isn't that what I pay you for?"

Sam groaned. "I tried. But I have no idea what's wrong. It's only those two rooms. And they both have guests. We need to get it fixed immediately."

"Move them to another room," she suggested.

"I told you. We're full."

"We're never full this time of year," she reminded him.

Sam shrugged. "I know. But yesterday the last three rooms were taken."

"Certainly someone is getting ready to check out?"

"No. It seems that almost all our guests have family in Frederick-port they're visiting for the holidays. I don't know about the three who arrived yesterday, I didn't check them in. But they're registered through Christmas. I double-checked, because two of the rooms that were rented out yesterday are the two with plumbing problems."

Before Ruby had a chance to respond, the plumber walked up to them.

"When can you get it fixed?" Ruby asked immediately. "And how much is this going to cost me?"

"The good news, it looks like the problem is confined to those two rooms. The bad news, it's going to take a while; we will have some parts to order. Plus, I can't get to it until after Christmas. We are slammed right now and a little shorthanded for the holidays."

"There is no way to get the water on for those rooms?" Ruby asked.

The plumber shook his head. "I'm afraid not." He went on to explain the problem in detail.

FOURTEEN

Originally, Chris had planned to pick his brother, Noah, up at the airport. But after the fire, Chris had called Noah and informed him they would be staying at Marlow House. Noah had insisted on renting a car and driving from the airport to Frederickport. Noah didn't believe his little brother needed to make that round-trip drive to Portland, especially after losing his home to a fire.

When Noah arrived at Marlow House Sunday afternoon, Danielle thought he hadn't changed much since she had met him the previous December. However, she did think he looked more rested—relaxed—happy—which was saying a great deal since the man had just fought holiday traffic at two airports and had driven a couple of hours before reaching Frederickport.

Danielle noticed the resemblance between the two brothers more this time than when she had first met Noah. The brothers shared more than a physical resemblance. Noah, like Chris, was a medium. He too could see ghosts—just as their mother had been able to do.

Danielle stood in the entry hall with Walt, Chris and Hunny while they all greeted Noah.

"Thank you so much for letting me stay here," Noah said after giving Danielle a hug in greeting.

"We're happy to have you. I just wish we hadn't had to burn Chris's house down in order to do it," she said with a smile.

"If anyone burned my house down, it was me," Chris grumbled and then flashed a smile to Danielle before giving his brother an exuberant bear hug.

Until the previous Christmas, Chris hadn't seen his older brother since he was a toddler. In fact, he hadn't even remembered he had an older brother. They had been put in foster care after losing both parents, yet unlike Noah, Chris had eventually been adopted.

A friend of Noah's had helped track Chris down, and last Christmas they had reunited. After the holiday, Noah went back to his teaching job, and Chris stayed in Frederickport, running the foundation from the money he had inherited from his adopted parents. Yet he and Noah had kept in touch, often talking daily.

After the hug between brothers ended, Walt shook Noah's hand, and then he motioned down the hallway and said, "Why don't we take this in the living room. Joanne made some sandwiches. She thought Noah might be hungry after all his traveling this morning."

Chris glanced down at Hunny. "I hope those sandwiches are still there."

"I had a talk with Hunny. I told her not to touch them," Walt said.

"It's rather nice to be with people who find nothing unusual about talking to spirits or having meaningful conversations with pit bulls," Noah said.

THEY HAD JUST WALKED into the living room when the front doorbell rang. Danielle glanced out the window and noticed an unfamiliar vehicle parked in front of Noah's rental car.

"I'll go get that. You guys start on the food," Danielle said.

A few minutes later Danielle opened the front door and found Ruby Crabtree standing on her porch.

"Ruby? Wow, this is a surprise," Danielle greeted her.

"I'm sorry for just barging in," Ruby said. "But I need to talk to you, and I didn't think I should do this over the phone."

"Umm, sure. Come on in." She opened the door wider and stepped to one side, letting Ruby enter. "Walt is in the living room with Chris and Chris's brother. They're having some sandwiches. Would you like some? We have plenty."

"No. I would just like to talk to you—alone if that is possible," Ruby told her.

"Sure." Danielle led Ruby into the parlor, shutting the door behind them. Danielle took a seat on the sofa while Ruby sat on one of the chairs facing her.

"How is Chris, by the way? I heard what happened to his house. That's horrible," Ruby said.

"He's okay. Just grateful no one got hurt. He plans to rebuild. For the time being, he'll be staying here."

"And you said his brother is here?"

Danielle nodded. "Yes. He came to spend Christmas with Chris. Now that Chris no longer has a home, we told them they could stay here."

"That's very generous of you. But then, you enjoyed running the B and B, didn't you?"

"Actually, I did. But we're okay with how things are now."

"I was rather hoping you might be willing to take in two more guests."

Danielle frowned. "Excuse me?"

"I don't know if you are aware of how busy all the local motels are in town. In fact, there is not a single vacancy."

"That's kind of unusual for this time of year," Danielle said.

Ruby nodded. "Yes, it is. Winter is usually pretty slow, but it does pick up a little around Christmas—mostly families of locals who need some place to stay. But this year…well, I guess everyone in town has relatives visiting for the holiday, and they apparently don't have room for all of them. Which is good for us, but…"

"But?"

"I have two guests who are checked in through Christmas. This morning the water stopped working in their rooms. And they certainly can't stay in those rooms if they can't take a shower or flush the toilet."

"What does the plumber say?" Danielle asked.

"The plumber promises us the other rooms are fine. Whatever the problem is, it's confined to those two rooms. But they can't fix it until after Christmas."

"Have you called another plumber?" Danielle asked.

"Yes. And no one can even come out until after Christmas."

"So what is it you want from me?" Danielle asked.

"Is there any way—please, please—that you will take my two guests? I'll pay for their rooms. And you don't even have to provide breakfast, because we don't provide breakfast anyway."

"Ruby, I would love to help you. But you know I can't rent out rooms anymore. We don't have a license."

"Just this one time," Ruby begged.

Danielle glanced to her south wall. "I'm afraid a relative of yours would be down to the city to complain in a heartbeat if she had any idea we were taking renters again."

"Pearl Huckabee? Please, don't remind me that woman is related to me," Ruby grumbled.

"You know how she is," Danielle reminded her.

"I know. But it is Christmas. And I have nowhere to put those two people."

"A couple? I thought you said you needed two rooms," Danielle asked.

"Not a couple. Two men, an older gentleman and a younger man, about your age. They aren't together. But their rooms are the ones where the water stopped working."

The next moment Walt walked into the parlor. He looked with surprise from Danielle to Ruby. "Is everything okay?" he asked.

"Walt, can you come in here a minute?" Danielle told him.

After Walt walked into the parlor and took a seat next to Danielle, she told him what Ruby had said. After she finished her telling, he looked at Ruby and asked, "You said they are both staying through Christmas. I assume they are here to visit with family. Maybe one of their family members can put them up?"

Ruby shook her head. "No. I talked to both men. I was hoping that might be the case. But it seems both men are just passing through, and for whatever reason they planned to spend Christmas in Frederickport, I'm assuming alone, since they both claimed they didn't know anyone in town."

"That's sad," Danielle said.

"I know. And I really hate having to tell them there's nowhere for them to stay in town, especially since they're already here."

"They could stay here," Walt suggested.

"Walt, like I told Ruby, we can't take in renters. I can't even imagine the fit Pearl would throw if she found out."

Walt laughed. "I wasn't suggesting we take in renters. I was simply suggesting we open our home to two travelers for Christmas. It's not like we haven't had strangers under our roof before, and we have plenty of room."

"You mean not charge them?" Danielle asked with a grin.

Walt responded with a smile.

"If you would do that, I'll donate the rent money to whatever charity you want!" Ruby vowed.

"It's a deal," Danielle said. "And tell them it includes breakfast. We'll be making it anyway."

"Thank you, thank you!" Ruby gushed.

Danielle stood up. "If you will excuse me, I have to talk to Joanne. I believe she is still in the kitchen. I need to tell her two more guests are coming."

"WHERE ARE THEY PUTTING YOU?" Marcella asked Owen as he carried his suitcase to his car as she followed along. A few minutes earlier she had overheard a conversation between him and the motel owner when she had gone to fill up her ice bucket.

"Marlow House. It used to be a bed and breakfast. I've always wanted to see inside that house," Owen said. They reached his car, and Marcella watched as he opened his trunk and tossed his suitcase in the back of his vehicle.

"So I guess that means they can't fix your water? I wonder if we're going to have a problem in our room," she asked.

Owen shrugged and slammed the trunk shut. "According to the plumber, the problem is confined to my room and Mr. Bari's."

"Mr. Bari?" She frowned.

"The man right next door to you. The room between us. You shouldn't have any problems with the water."

"And Mr. Bari, are they moving him too?" she asked.

"Apparently so. I guess they talked to him before they told me. Well, I need to get going. Nice to meet you. Enjoy your stay."

Marcella stood silently and watched Owen drive away. She turned abruptly and hurried back to her room. Just before she reached it, she made an abrupt right and headed for Mr. Bari's door. She knocked loudly. A moment later, he peeked outside.

"Yes? How can I help you?" he asked.

"I understand your room has some plumbing problems," Marcella said.

Opening his door wider, Colin stood in his doorway and smiled at Marcella. "Yes. In fact, I'm going to have to move."

"I am so sorry to hear that. What a pain. Just when you're all settled in," she said.

"No problem, I already packed."

"I was just thinking, if it would be easier for you, you could move into our room and we'll let the motel move us somewhere else. After all, it is Christmas, and I hate thinking of how inconvenient this is for you."

"I AM SO MAD!" Marcella shouted at Forrest after she entered their motel room ten minutes later, slamming the door closed behind her.

"What's wrong?" Forrest asked.

"Why couldn't we have plumbing problems like the rooms next door?"

"You don't want to be able to take a shower? Flush the toilet?"

"Don't be stupid," she snapped, throwing herself on the bed dejectedly.

"Then please tell me what you are talking about."

"Do you know where they are moving them?"

"Moving who?"

"The guys renting the rooms with no water. They're moving them to Marlow House. Marlow House! If we had just been checked into one of those two rooms now, we could have been the ones going over there, not them!"

"Are you serious?"

"Yes, I am serious. I tried to get that old guy next door to switch rooms with us—but he wouldn't budge."

FIFTEEN

"Mrs. Huckabee, I didn't expect to see you again today," Carla greeted her when Pearl took a seat at Pier Café's lunch counter, which she stood behind refilling the salt and pepper shakers.

"I'm hoping you have some of that apple pie I saw this morning," Pearl told her.

"We certainly do. Would you like me to warm it up?" Carla asked, as she rescrewed the lids on the salt and pepper shakers.

"Yes, and I'd like a scoop of vanilla ice cream on it and a cup of coffee. I'd like some water too."

"Certainly." Carla abandoned the salt and pepper shakers and then went to get Pearl a glass of ice water. After setting the water in front of Pearl and filling her coffee cup, she went to get the pie and ice cream.

"It sure was sad what happened to Chris's house," Carla said as she set the plate with the pie and ice cream in front of Pearl a few minutes later.

"He burned the house down himself," Pearl said as she picked up her fork.

"You certainly aren't suggesting he intentionally burned his house down?" Carla asked.

"I don't know if it was intentional or not. Although it's not unusual for someone to use arson to scam the insurance company. I

85

heard he was rebuilding, so perhaps he figured a fire would be an easy way to pay for a new house," Pearl said as she dug her fork in the ice cream atop the slice of pie.

Carla frowned at Pearl. "I don't see Chris doing something like that."

While Carla was not known for her discretion and had been the source of many rumors that had circulated in Frederickport, there was one bit of news she had mostly kept to herself—and it was a doozy. She had discovered Chris Johnson was, in fact, the philanthropist and billionaire Chris Glandon. While it would have been a delicious story to spread, even Carla understood it was to her advantage to do someone like Chris a favor in keeping the secret, as opposed to spreading it around for her five minutes of fame.

Instead of pointing out to Pearl that someone like Chris did not need to commit arson to raise money to build a new house, she left the sour woman to her pie. Fortunately for her, a new customer had just walked into the diner, giving Carla an excuse to cut short their conversation.

The new customer who had entered the diner was art teacher Elizabeth Sparks. She took a table by the door, some distance from the counter where Pearl sat.

"Afternoon, Elizabeth," Carla greeted her.

"Oh, hi, Carla," Elizabeth said absently as she glanced through the menu she had picked up from the end of the table.

Carla noted Elizabeth did not seem her normal cheerful self.

"Is everything okay?" Carla asked as she took a seat across from the young woman.

Elizabeth glanced up at Carla, who now sat at her table. She closed her menu. "I've been Christmas shopping all day."

"What's wrong, couldn't find what you wanted?"

Elizabeth shook her head. "No. It's not that. It's just…well…I've had the weirdest feeling the last couple of days. Like I'm being followed. Stalked even."

"Stalked?" Carla asked. "By who? Have you talked to the police?"

"I don't know who. And no, I haven't talked to anyone about it. In fact, you're the first person I've mentioned it to."

Resting her elbows on the tabletop, Carla leaned forward and said, "Tell me all about it."

"Friday, when I got up in the morning and opened my front

blinds, there was a car parked in front of my house. I didn't recognize it. There was a man sitting inside the car. When he looked up and saw me at the window, he just stared for a moment, and then he drove away real quick."

"Not that unusual to get nosey tourists who like to check out houses," Carla said. "Or one who is lost and looking for an address."

"That's kind of what I thought at first. But then, I kept running into him around town. I even noticed his reflection in a store window, and I swear he was watching me."

"And you don't know who he is?" Carla asked.

Elizabeth shook her head. "No. He wasn't familiar. The whole thing is creeping me out."

"You need to talk to the police about this," Carla insisted.

AFTER FINISHING her pie and ice cream, Pearl walked home from the pier. Just as she reached her front gate, she noticed a taxi driving slowly up the street. It passed her house and then slowed down in front of Marlow House and parked. The driver and a passenger got out of the car. Curious, Pearl kept walking. She reached the back of the taxi just as the driver was opening the trunk of the car. The passenger, an older gentleman, stood on the sidewalk, waiting for his suitcase.

"I think you may be at the wrong place," Pearl said as she approached the taxi.

The driver looked up at her and frowned. "Excuse me?"

Pearl looked at the passenger, who continued to stand on the nearby sidewalk, cane in hand.

"You aren't family or friend of the Marlows, are you? I am sure you're not family, since I heard they don't have any," Pearl asked.

The passenger cocked his head slightly and smiled at Pearl. "No, no relation. At least, none that I am aware of. And we haven't been formally introduced. But I do believe I am at the right place."

The taxi driver set the suitcase on the sidewalk and shut the trunk lid. "I'll carry it up for you."

"No need. It has wheels. I will be fine, and a little exercise does me good," the older man said cheerfully.

"But you are not at the right place," Pearl argued.

"Ma'am," the taxi driver interrupted, "I was told I was to bring him to Marlow House. And Marlow House B and B is the only Marlow House I know of in Frederickport."

"But it is no longer a B and B!" she argued.

The taxi driver shrugged and got back in his car after wishing his passenger a goodbye. He drove off before Pearl could continue her argument. She looked back to the elderly passenger and saw he had already gone through Marlow House's gate and was almost to the front door.

She would have followed him to see what was going on, when a second car pulled up and parked in front of Marlow House—that made three cars parked along the street in front of her neighbor's house. A bearded young man wearing sunglasses climbed out of the vehicle and walked to his trunk to retrieve his suitcases.

"Certainly you aren't staying here too?" Pearl demanded when she spied him taking suitcases from the trunk.

"Is there a problem?" he asked.

"Yes, there is a problem. Who are you?"

"I'm not sure it is any of your business. But I am a guest of Marlow House B and B, and you are?"

"I live next door, and Marlow House is no longer a B and B!"

The man shrugged. "Whatever." He picked up his suitcases and walked up to the front gate.

Fuming, Pearl turned around and stomped back to her house, planning to call the business licensing department and let them know Danielle Marlow was once again operating an illegal boardinghouse. Just as she reached her side gate, she remembered it was Sunday and the licensing department was closed.

WHEN DANIELLE OPENED the door for Colin Bari, she immediately noted his cane. While the elderly man looked fairly spry, considering he seemed to be managing his suitcase without a problem, she worried about the stairs. After brief introductions were made, she said, "I had planned to put you upstairs. We only have one bedroom on the first floor..."

"Upstairs will be fine," he said.

"I'm sure Chris—that's who is in the downstairs bedroom—will switch rooms with you."

Colin reached out and patted Danielle's arm. "Honestly, Mrs. Marlow, I have no problem with stairs. In fact, the extra exercise is good for me. Keeps me going."

"If you are sure?" she asked.

Walt, who had been standing in the background listening, stepped forward and introduced himself.

"I'll show Mr. Bari to his room," Walt said, taking the older man's suitcase from him. "I believe another one of our guests just pulled up."

A few minutes later, as Danielle watched Walt carry the suitcase up the stairs, Mr. Bari trailing behind him, the front doorbell rang. When she answered it a moment later, she found a bearded man in sunglasses standing on her porch, suitcases in hand.

"You must be Mr. Gardener?" Danielle asked.

"And you are Mrs. Marlow?" he asked with a smile.

Danielle opened the door wider and said, "Please call me Danielle."

"And you have to call me Owen," he said as he stepped inside the house and glanced around.

As Danielle closed the door behind him, he said, "You have a nosey neighbor out there trying to screen all your visitors."

"Thin, gray-haired woman?" she asked.

"I think that's the one." Owen set his suitcases on the floor.

Danielle let out a sigh. "That's our next-door neighbor, Pearl Huckabee. Marlow House used to be a B and B, which Mrs. Huckabee was never happy about. She didn't like living next door to a bed and breakfast."

Owen cringed as he removed his sunglasses. "I'm sorry. I might have referred to this place as a B and B. Mrs. Crabtree did explain that you were no longer a business, but that you had graciously agreed to put us up for the holidays. I'm really sorry if I caused more problems with your neighbor."

Danielle chuckled. "I wouldn't worry about it. I rather think she enjoys her outrage."

Owen slipped his glasses into his shirt pocket and smiled at Danielle.

Danielle looked into Owen's eyes and returned the smile. Just as she did, something caught her attention, and she paused a moment, still looking into Owen's face.

"Have we met before?" she asked.

He shrugged. "Not that I'm aware of."

"Your name is not familiar. But there is something about you. So familiar. You aren't on TV or something, are you?" she asked.

He laughed. "Hardly."

"Have you been to Frederickport before? Maybe I saw you then? I've lived here since 2014."

He shook his head. "No. I can practically guarantee this is the first time you have ever seen me in Frederickport."

WALT AND DANIELLE sat with Chris and Noah in the living room on Sunday evening, with Hunny sleeping by Chris's feet and Max dozing under the Christmas tree. Owen had left to get something for dinner, while Colin had retired to his room, telling them it had been a long day and he was turning in for the night.

"I was rather hoping Mr. Bari would join us this evening," Noah said. "I'm still trying to place him, and it is driving me crazy."

"Place him?" Danielle asked. "You think you know him?"

"Noah was telling me earlier he thought there was something familiar about him—and I was about to say the same thing," Walt said.

Danielle looked to Walt. "You think you've met him before?"

Walt shrugged. "I don't know. I don't recognize his name. But there is something so familiar about him. And then Noah said the same thing."

"It's going to come to me," Noah said, taking a sip of his wine.

"Odd, I was about to say one of our guests looked familiar to me too," Danielle said.

"You think you've seen Mr. Bari too?" Chris asked. "Maybe he's an actor."

Danielle shook her head. "No. Not Mr. Bari. Owen. He looks super familiar to me. Something about his eyes."

SIXTEEN

On Monday morning Marie's first stop was Marlow House to see how the guests had settled in. She found them gathered at the dining room table, enjoying breakfast and chatting. Growing bored with the conversation—since she could only listen—she headed across the street to check in on baby Connor.

Outside, rain fell in a drizzle, but it no longer bothered Marie now that she was a ghost. Moving through the outside wall to Connor's nursery, she found him nestled in his mother's arms as he greedily nursed at her breast. Marie smiled at the sweet sight, thinking how angelic Lily looked with her wisps of red hair gently framing her delicate features and the adoring look she gave her son —a ginger Madonna. With a sigh, Marie watched, understanding that Lily had no idea she had entered the room.

"We'll wait a little bit before we get you dressed," Lily whispered down to her son. "We're going to Pier Café this afternoon to have lunch with Walt and Danielle, and I need to find something warm and snuggly for you to wear."

"No!" Marie gasped. "You can't take him out in this weather! He will catch his death of cold."

Lily continued to talk to her son, oblivious to the ghost in the room.

"YOU NEED to do something for me," Marie announced when she popped into Heather's kitchen after leaving Lily and Connor.

Heather, who stood at her stove filling a cup with hot water for tea, made a jerking motion at the sudden appearance of the ghost, splashing hot water all over the stovetop.

"Marie, don't sneak up on me like that!" Heather snapped. Setting the teapot back on the stove, she grabbed a towel and began wiping up the spill.

"I'm sorry, dear. But the others are all having breakfast at Marlow House, and I can't just barge in there, not with the guests."

"What do you need?" Heather asked.

"I want you to tell Lily that I will happily babysit Connor this afternoon while she and Ian meet Walt and Danielle for lunch at Pier Café. It is miserable cold outside. Not fit for a baby."

Heather arched her brow. "How do you know it's miserable cold? You're a ghost. You don't have a real body. You can't feel heat or cold."

"Don't be snotty, young lady. I am perfectly aware of the weather without actually feeling it," Marie said primly.

"Okay. But do you honestly think Lily and Ian are going to leave you alone with Connor? Seriously? To babysit? What happens if someone stops by the house and finds the baby alone?"

"He won't be alone!"

"Uhh...yeah...tell that to the police...Well, not to Police Chief MacDonald, but if anyone else happens to stop by."

"Then you have to stay too. Don't you have the week off? It's not like you have to go to work," Marie insisted.

"But I planned to stay in my PJs all day and read a book," Heather fairly whined.

"And you can do that at Lily and Ian's house. I'll watch Connor. You won't have to do anything, just be there with me. Come on now, wouldn't it be nice for Lily and Ian to have some adult time?"

THE MORNING DRIZZLE HAD STOPPED, yet it remained damp and chilly outside, with gray skies overhead. The weather did not keep Walt and Danielle from walking down to the pier to meet Lily and Ian for lunch. Each wearing a warm jacket, gloves and a hat, they walked hand in hand down the street, discussing the guests currently staying at Marlow House.

Just as they walked by Pearl's front gate, Danielle paused a moment, tugging Walt to a stop as she looked up to the house. She noticed the Christmas lights decorating the eaves of Pearl's house were still on, and Danielle figured her neighbor had forgotten to turn them off the night before. She glanced over to Pearl's front door and noticed a pinecone Christmas wreath embellished with a large red bow. In the downstairs window she could see a large poinsettia sitting on a table.

Danielle looked to the second floor. The blinds to Pearl's bedroom window were open, and just as Danielle was going to turn and start down the street again, her neighbor appeared at the window. The older woman glared down at them. Without thought Danielle gave Pearl a quick wave and smile. Pearl responded by shutting her blinds.

"I think she likes you," Walt teased. The two started down the street again.

"You know what surprises me?" Danielle asked.

"No, what?"

"That she put up Christmas lights. I didn't expect her to decorate for Christmas. Maybe put up a black wreath on the front door."

"A wreath of mourning?" Walt asked with a chuckle.

Danielle shrugged. "A black wreath would seem more in character."

A moment later they noticed a police car driving up the street. Just as it reached them, it pulled over and stopped. Down went the passenger window. Brian Henderson sat in the driver's seat. He leaned over to the now open car window.

"Hello, Brian," Danielle greeted him, now standing with Walt on the sidewalk by the police car.

"I have you to blame for this," Brian grumbled.

"What did I do now?" Danielle asked.

"Your neighbor has been calling me since last night, complaining about you."

"Why is she calling you?" Walt asked.

"Because I foolishly gave her my card once, and since then she thinks I'm her personal cop. Please tell me you aren't renting rooms out."

"No, we're not renting rooms out," Danielle said with a laugh.

"But we do have guests." She went on to explain about the favor they were doing Ruby.

"At first I thought she was still trying to make something out of Chris and his brother staying with you. But then she said cars were arriving all day yesterday delivering guests to your door."

Danielle chuckled. "A slight exaggeration."

"Okay. I will go explain to her—*again*—that you are within your legal rights to take in nonpaying holiday guests," Brian said with a sigh.

WHEN WALT and Danielle arrived at Pier Café, they found Lily and Ian already sitting at a booth. They were surprised to discover the baby was not with them.

"Where is Connor? Is Kelly babysitting?" Danielle asked as she took a seat across from Lily.

"No. Marie is babysitting," Lily told her.

"Marie?" Danielle asked in surprised.

"More accurately, Marie and Heather," Ian told them. "But I think Marie is doing the actual babysitting, and Heather is just there so we don't get nailed by child protective services." They went on to tell them how Heather had come over that morning to speak for Marie—who, of course, they could not see or hear. Marie wanted to watch Connor while they went to lunch, and Heather had agreed to stay too, yet confessed she would probably spend her time reading her book and raiding their refrigerator.

"It kind of sucks you can't always use Marie to sit with Connor," Danielle said. "She would love that, and there is no way anything bad would happen to him under her watch."

"He also adores her," Lily added.

"But as Heather pointed out, leaving Marie alone with Connor could end up causing us real problems. Can you imagine if my sister stopped by and found her nephew alone?" Ian asked.

"Or stopped by with her boyfriend—the cop," Lily added.

"I'm actually a little surprised Heather has exhibited such common sense," Walt observed.

"I think it's sweet Heather agreed to hang around while Marie watched him," Lily said. "And while I love being a mom, I have to admit, sometimes it is nice to take a little break."

"DO we have to eat here again?" Forrest asked Marcella as they walked up the pier.

"It's close to Marlow House. We need to keep an eye on the place and look for our next opportunity," Marcella said as he opened the door to the café.

The moment Marcella stepped into Pier Café, she spied Walt and Danielle sitting at a booth with another couple. She gave Forrest a little nudge and motioned for him to follow her. He silently obeyed. A moment later they sat in the empty booth next to Walt and Danielle. Marcella picked up a menu and leaned closer to the next booth, listening.

"SO YOU'RE a B and B again?" Lily asked.

Danielle laughed and said, "Don't say that too loud. Pearl might overhear." Danielle then repeated their morning conversation with Brian.

"Are your guests in town visiting family?" Ian asked.

"Only Noah. Our Seahorse Motel refugees are just spending Christmas in Frederickport. Which sounds kind of sad to me. Checking into a motel all alone at Christmastime," Danielle said.

"You don't think they're serial killers, do you?" Lily asked.

"Not both of them," Danielle teased. "Nah, one is an older gentleman. He's probably in his late seventies. Seems in fairly good shape for his age. I don't think he has anyone left in his life, from what he said at breakfast. And the other one, I think he might be in his late thirties, maybe forties. Kind of a drifter, maybe. But I didn't get any negative vibes off him. He seems like a nice enough guy, but there is something really familiar about him."

"Both Noah and I thought there was something familiar about the other one—Mr. Bari," Walt added.

"It got me thinking, since they are both alone and staying with us through Christmas, I would like to invite them to Christmas dinner and to the white elephant gift exchange and, of course, the Christmas Eve open house. Is that okay with everyone? I'd like to buy the two gifts they would need to bring. I don't want to ask them to bring anything," Danielle said.

"I think that would be fine. I got our gifts already," Lily said.

"I thought I was done shopping for the party. But I think we're going to need to get another one anyway. So I guess I'll look for three more—providing they agree to come," Danielle said.

"You decided not to use one of the things you bought in Astoria?" Ian asked.

"One of those needs to go to Adam," Walt explained.

"Adam?" Lily asked.

"It's a framed picture of Adam's great-grandfather—George Hemming. Walt recognized him. I don't know what we were thinking. We both thought it would be a perfect gift for the white elephant game for Adam."

"But there is no guarantee he would get it," Lily reminded them.

"Exactly. We both zoned out and forgot that part. So we're going to give him the framed picture as a Christmas gift and give it to him on Christmas night. But we need to find something else for the game," Danielle said.

Carla walked up to their table and asked about Chris before taking their order. Later, when she removed their plates, she lingered a bit to chat some more.

"You're friends with Elizabeth Sparks, aren't you?" Carla asked Danielle.

"Yes, why?" Danielle asked.

"I think you need to talk her into going to the police about her stalker," Carla began.

"Stalker?" Lily gasped.

Carla went on to recount the conversation she'd had the previous day with Elizabeth Sparks.

FORREST AND MARCELLA ate their lunch in silence as they listened to every word said in the next booth over. Finally, the four diners finished eating, paid their bill, and stood up to leave. When they walked out of the diner, Forrest looked to Marcella and asked, "Did you hear what they were saying about Elizabeth Sparks?"

Marcella pushed her empty plate to the center of the table and looked at her husband. "I wonder who's stalking that little opportunist."

SEVENTEEN

When Walt and Danielle returned to Marlow House after having lunch with Lily and Ian on Monday morning, they found Chris in the living room with his brother, Noah. Hunny enthusiastically greeted them both when they entered the room.

"I rather like having a dog greet me when we come home," Danielle said as she petted Hunny.

"Doesn't Max greet you?" Chris teased from the sofa, not standing up when the couple walked into the room.

"Actually, Max can sometimes be very uncatlike and does greet us when we get home. But I have a feeling he's sleeping upstairs," Danielle said as she took a seat next to Chris.

"Have you seen our guests?" Walt asked as he sat on the chair next to Noah, facing the sofa.

"Owen left not long after you did," Chris told him. "And about five minutes later Mr. Bari left. I know he told us to call him Colin, but I feel odd calling him by his first name. He just seems like someone you should be more formal with."

"I sort of know what you mean. I feel the same way too. But he seems very nice," Danielle said.

"Not saying he isn't nice," Chris argued. "There is just something about him—I don't know, like a favorite teacher that you would never call by his first name."

"Did Owen come back and go upstairs?" Walt asked. "His car is parked out front. In fact, it doesn't look like it has moved."

"They both said they were going for a walk," Noah explained. "Surprised you didn't see them."

"Not a terrific day for a walk. It's cold out there," Danielle said with a shiver.

"Didn't you guys walk to the pier?" Chris asked.

"Exactly," Danielle said.

"So how was lunch?" Noah asked.

"We had a nice visit with Lily and Ian. They left Connor at home," Danielle explained.

"Who watched him?" Chris asked.

"Marie," Danielle said with a grin. She went on to explain how it was actually Heather and Marie.

When Danielle finished her story, Noah laughed and said, "One thing I love about being here—aside from getting to hang out with my baby brother—is talking about subjects I could never share before."

"Like babysitting ghosts?" Danielle teased.

"To be honest, I've rarely come across a spirit who is able to do what Marie does," Noah said. "A few have made doors slam, and of course, there is the old classic, lights flickering."

"Marie couldn't always do what she does. It's something she developed over time—the same for Walt. Back when he was a ghost," Danielle said.

"I like to think of myself back then more as a free spirit, not a ghost," Walt said with a grin.

"Whatever you were," Chris began, "ghost or spirit, I've often thought it would all make a fascinating study on paranormal activity. Can all spirits develop powers like Marie—is Eva right and some higher power limits what a spirit can do depending on intent—there is so much to learn. I would love to finance such a study."

"Are you serious?" Danielle asked in surprise.

"Serious about wanting to fund such a study? Yes. Serious about ever actually doing it? No. As it is, I find it difficult enough to keep flying under the radar these days. If a study like that leaked out—that I was funding it—no, instead of being known as the elusive philanthropist, I'd be labeled the crackpot rich kid, and I imagine even a greater target for people wanting to exploit me," Chris said.

"Crackpot rich kid?" Walt said with a grin. "I think that should be my new nickname for you."

"Oh, shut up," Chris returned with a laugh.

The next moment Max sauntered into the room. Hunny greeted the cat, her butt wiggling, yet she respectfully kept several inches between her and the cat, not wanting to be swatted. Max walked up to Walt, sat down, looked at him, and then meowed. He stood back up and walked over to the Christmas tree to find another sleeping place.

"Max tells me one of our guests is back. He must have come in through the kitchen door. He's upstairs in his room."

"Did he say which one?" Danielle asked.

"Sounds like Owen," Walt told her.

"He is not nearly as friendly as Colin," Noah said in a soft voice.

"I wouldn't call him unfriendly—more reserved," Danielle said.

"Isn't that about the same thing?" Chris asked.

Danielle shrugged. "Not necessarily. Someone who is unfriendly, well, I think of our neighbor Pearl."

"She's just mean," Chris corrected, reaching down to pet his dog.

"But a reserved person—I guess it is about the same as being shy," Danielle suggested.

"Not sure I would call Owen shy," Walt said. "He just seems like someone who likes to keep his business to himself. Not a bad quality."

Hunny jumped up and let out a bark. She ran to the open doorway, but instead of going to the hall, she stood with her butt and tail wagging.

"I think someone just came in the front door," Walt said. He looked at Hunny and silently conveyed for her to come back to the sofa and sit down. The dog reluctantly obeyed.

They all glanced to the doorway. A few moments later Colin walked into the living room, cane in hand.

"Did you have a nice walk?" Danielle asked Colin.

"Yes, I did, thank you."

Walt stood up and motioned for Colin to take his chair, and then he walked over and sat on the sofa with Chris and Danielle, with Danielle sitting in the middle.

"But it is a little chilly out there," Danielle noted.

"I found it exhilarating," Colin said. "I love the smell of the ocean."

"Chris told us you left not long after we did. Surprised we didn't see you," Danielle said.

"I saw you. You were almost to the pier when I started down the street," Colin explained.

"Did you go to the pier?" Walt asked.

"No. I walked to town," Colin told them.

As Colin sat down, Noah asked, "I've been trying to place your accent. You aren't from this country, are you?"

Colin grinned at Noah. "No. I was born in a little port village along the Mediterranean Sea. I suppose that's one reason I so love walking along the ocean."

"Really?" Danielle perked up. "So when did you come to America?"

"Seems like over a hundred years ago," he said with a laugh.

"Do you still have family back there?" Danielle asked.

He shook his head. "No. I was an only child. My parents died when I was young—I wasn't a child, but barely a man yet. I was fortunate though; financially, my parents left me well off. It allowed me to do what I wanted, which included travel."

"Sounds like you've had a fascinating life," Chris said.

"I've been blessed," Colin replied.

"So what brings you to Frederickport? You said yesterday you don't have family here," Danielle asked.

"No, I don't have family here. I never married, never had children. As for what brought me to Oregon—I just felt this is where I needed to be for Christmas. Christmas is such a magical time of year."

"It's always been my favorite holiday," Danielle said.

"Mine too. It's the one time of year that even the most closed hearts can open—when even the ungenerous can find themselves giving." Colin looked at Chris and added, "Not everyone is as generous as Chris Glandon. Others need Christmas to remind them to give."

Chris shrugged uncomfortably. "Umm…yeah, I guess my boss tries to do what he can."

"Mr. Bari—"Danielle began.

"Please, call me Colin."

"Okay…Colin, I know Ruby told you the rooms only included

breakfast, but we'd love for you to join us for Christmas dinner. In fact, for you to join us for all the festivities. We'll be having an open house party here on Christmas Eve, as well as having some friends over for Christmas dinner. And on Saturday, my friend Lily, who lives across the street, she and her husband are having a Christmas party. We'd love for you to join us."

"That's very generous of you. I'll be happy to share the Christmas festivities with you."

"I love having a full house this time of year," Danielle said.

Their conversation was interrupted a moment later when Owen walked into the room. Hunny started to stand up to greet him, but once again Walt silently told the dog to remain where she was.

I just want to say hello, Hunny conveyed to Walt.

Yes, but I told you, some people are intimidated by you. Let them come to you, Walt silently told the dog.

It is not fair. I can't help how I look. Hunny let out a little grunt, resting her head on her front paws.

"Did you have a nice walk?" Danielle asked Owen when he walked into the room.

"I forgot how miserable cold it can be up here," Owen said with a shiver.

"How would you like a cup of hot coffee or tea to warm you up? Maybe hot cocoa?" Danielle asked.

"I would kill for a cup of hot coffee," Owen said.

"You don't need to go to those extremes," Danielle said with a laugh as she stood up. She glanced around the room and asked, "Would anyone else like something?"

A moment later, after taking requests, Danielle left the room with Owen, who offered to help her bring back the warm beverages. Just as the pair stepped into the hallway, Colin asked Chris, "What's your dog's name again?"

"Hunny."

Colin looked at the dog and smiled. He reached out and said in a gentle voice, "Come here, Hunny."

As if seeking permission, Hunny peeked up at Walt.

Go ahead, Walt silently conveyed.

The pit bull jumped up and ran to Colin, who sat in one of the chairs across from the sofa. Her body practically folded in two as she excitedly wagged her stub tail, pressing up against his legs as she tried to kiss his hands, which now scratched behind her ears.

"She is a sweet dog," Colin noted.

"Unfortunately, that breed can be intimidating for some people. I know Danielle's next-door neighbor loathes her," Chris said.

"I doubt she actually loathes Hunny," Colin argued. "She is simply afraid. What looks like hate is often rooted in fear."

When Danielle and Owen returned to the living room carrying a tray with hot beverages and chocolate drop cookies, they found Hunny now sleeping by Colin's feet.

"I see Hunny has made a new friend," Danielle said as she set her tray on the coffee table.

After Danielle distributed the beverages, she said, "I was just telling Owen we would love for him to join us for our Christmas festivities."

"I appreciate the offer," Owen said, sitting in the rocking chair Lily normally used when visiting with Connor. "But I'm not sure I'll be staying through Christmas."

"Are you planning to go home and spend Christmas with your family?" Colin asked.

Warming his hands with his mug of coffee, Owen didn't answer immediately. Instead he sat quietly, staring into the coffee cup. "I don't think so."

"I take it you're not married?" Colin asked.

Owen looked up and gave a little shrug. "I suppose technically I am. I'm separated. But I imagine by this time next year, I'll be officially divorced."

The room grew quiet. Owen looked up and smiled. "Sorry. I didn't mean to sound like a drama queen."

"I don't think any of us thought that," Danielle said in a gentle voice. "I can understand how this time of year might be a little rough for anyone facing a divorce."

EIGHTEEN

Monday's afternoon sun pushed aside the drizzling clouds, revealing a portion of blue. The change of weather coaxed Chris and Noah outside with Hunny. They took the dog across the street, where they intended to pick up Sadie, Lily and Ian's golden retriever, to let the dogs play some ball and run along the beach. Chris had learned to grab the Oregon sunshine at any opportunity, even if it only lasted fifteen minutes.

Back at Marlow House, Walt had agreed to a game of chess with Colin, while Owen sat on the sofa, reading a book. Flames crackled in the nearby fireplace, and Max slept under the bottom limbs of the noble fir Christmas tree. Danielle was just heading to the closet on the second floor when Marie appeared, following her upstairs.

"That was sweet of you babysitting Connor," Danielle told Marie as she continued up the staircase, holding onto the handrail.

"It was a joy. But that Heather..." Marie chuckled instead of finishing her sentence.

"What about Heather?" Danielle asked.

"Heather had gone on and on about how all she wanted to do was read her book and relax. But once we were across the street, that girl could not keep her hands off Connor!"

Danielle paused a moment and looked at Marie. "Really?"

"He had just woken up from a nap and was ready to play.

Heather spent most of her time on the floor with him in the nursery on a quilt, the two of them playing peekaboo. Goodness, you should have heard those two giggling! I wish I had a camera. Of course, when it was time for a diaper change…"

"I guess you did that?" Danielle asked, continuing back up the stairs.

"I didn't really mind."

"I think Lily enjoyed her little break. Connor's usually pretty good when she takes him out, but still…"

"So what are you up to today?" Marie asked.

"I'm going to grab some things I bought and take them down to the parlor so I can wrap them later. I shoved the packages in the hall closet up here after we got home from Astoria. I'm trying to figure out how many gift boxes I'm going to need to pick up."

When they reached the second floor, Danielle paused a moment and looked at Marie. "There is something I have been meaning to ask you." Danielle glanced down the staircase and then realized she probably should not be standing there seemingly talking to herself. One of her guests could walk out of the living room and see her. She motioned for Marie to follow her, and they walked down the hallway so as not to be seen.

"What is it?" Marie asked.

"I'd like you to help me make your divinity. I know Adam tried last year, but we both know how hard it is to make. I've never been able to do it—not like yours."

"Oh, Danielle, that is so sweet. Especially coming from someone like you who is an excellent baker—and me, who hated anything to do with the kitchen. Gardening is what I enjoyed."

"But you did make killer divinity and peanut brittle," Danielle reminded her.

"Yes, but only at Christmas." Marie smiled.

"So will you help me this year with the divinity? I'd like to give it to Adam as one of his Christmas gifts—from both of us."

If Marie's eyes could make tears, they would be swimming in them. "Oh yes. I will teach you how to make it."

A few minutes later, when Danielle retrieved the bags of Christmas gifts from the closet, Marie offered to levitate them downstairs.

"You could fall carrying those," Marie said as Danielle headed to the first floor with several full bags of gifts in her arms.

"I don't think our guests would understand if they walked out of the living room and saw these floating down the stairs."

"I suppose you're right. But if you trip, I'll catch you," Marie said, now keeping a close eye on Danielle's feet. "Although I don't know why you brought them upstairs in the first place."

"I was going to wrap them in one of the upstairs bedrooms, but that was before we got guests."

When they reached the parlor, Danielle piled the packages on the desk just as her cellphone began to ring. She pulled it from her back pocket and looked to see who was calling. It was Joanne.

Danielle answered the call. A moment later she placed her hand over the phone and whispered to Marie, "I'll be right back."

OWEN CLOSED the book he had been reading and set it on the coffee table. He stood up, stretched, and then glanced over to the game table, where Walt and Colin quietly played chess.

"Excuse me," Owen said.

Walt and Colin looked his way.

"I was wondering, would you have some writing paper I could have? A scratch pad would work," Owen asked Walt.

"Certainly," Walt said. "There are several pads of paper sitting on the desk in the parlor. Help yourself. And if you need a pen, you'll find one in the desk drawer."

"Parlor?" Owen frowned.

"It's the small sitting room just inside the front door," Walt explained.

"Oh…" Owen chuckled. "I didn't know people still called rooms parlors anymore. I think I've only heard that used in old movies."

ALONE IN THE PARLOR, Marie eyed the shopping bags Danielle had brought down from upstairs. Sticking out from the bottom of the pile was the wrinkled corner of a blue-green sack. She stared at the packages, and the next moment they appeared to rearrange themselves; the blue-green bag moved to the top of the pile, revealing a mermaid image printed on one side in black ink.

In the next moment the mermaid bag floated up from the desk. Marie reached inside and pulled out the framed picture of her father and another man. As the bag fell back to the pile, the remaining item it held—the Christmas shoe—started to fall out, yet remained half in the paper sack when it landed on the desk.

Ignoring the shoe, Marie studied the photograph and smiled, thinking how much she missed her parents and wondering if she should move on so she could see them again. But then she dismissed the idea, telling herself she wasn't finished on this plane yet. She still needed to see Adam happily married. Then there was Connor, whom she wanted to watch grow up, and she had to meet Walt and Danielle's children—surely they would start a family soon.

So engrossed with her thoughts, Marie failed to hear the parlor door open. It wasn't until Owen stepped into the room did she realize she was no longer alone. The framed photograph fell abruptly to the desk. By Owen's frown, Marie suspected he had noticed the motion.

Wearing a puzzled expression, Owen walked over to the desk.

"What are you doing in here?" Marie asked. She knew he could not hear her and did not expect an answer.

She watched as Owen reached down to the desk, as if he was looking for something. He froze. Marie noted his curious expression. His right hand trembled as it reached down. He took hold of the tip of the Christmas shoe and gradually pulled it from the bag. When it was completely removed, she heard him let out an audible gasp.

Now holding the shoe with both hands, he stared at it as if in a trance. After a moment he took one finger and moved it over the fake gemstones—at least, Marie assumed they were fake. He turned the shoe over in his hand, revealing its sole covered in Christmas paper. He frowned. Turning the shoe slightly, he ran a finger over the rough glue-soaked paper.

Noise came from the doorway, and Owen looked up abruptly, as if jolted from a trance. He shoved the shoe back in the paper sack. Danielle walked into the parlor.

"I was looking for a notepad," Owen explained quickly. "Walt said I could find one in here."

"Certainly," Danielle said with a smile as she approached the desk.

Marie remained quiet, observing Owen.

Danielle pulled a notepad from under the pile and handed it to

Owen. He accepted it nervously and glanced down at the desk. She noticed the picture frame was out of the bag, sitting in clear view. She picked it up.

"I took it out of the bag," Marie quickly explained.

Danielle glanced over to Owen, who remained standing by the desk, notepad in hand. She picked up the picture frame and shoved it back in the bag with the shoe.

"That bag, it has a mermaid on it," Owen said. "Umm...looks familiar, can I ask what store it's from?"

"Mermaid Curio, a little gift shop in Astoria. Do you know it?" she asked.

Owen shook his head. "No, I just thought the logo was familiar."

"I picked up some silly items there for the white elephant gift exchange. So don't peek!" Danielle said with a laugh.

Owen gave Danielle a half-hearted smile, thanked her for the paper, and then left the room.

"He was awful interested in that shoe," Marie told Danielle when he left the room.

"What do you mean?" Danielle asked with a frown.

"I was looking at the picture of my father when he walked in the room. I don't think he saw it floating over the desk. But when he saw the shoe sticking out of that sack, he took it out and looked at it."

Danielle shrugged. "So? He was probably trying to figure out what it was."

Marie shook her head. "No. It was how he was looking at it. It was intense."

"Intense?" Danielle snorted. "How does one look intensely at a gaudy shoe?"

"Like Walt looks at your double fudge chocolate cake."

"Oh my, you don't think he has a shoe fetish, do you?" Danielle teased.

"Oh hush," Marie snapped. "You aren't taking me seriously. There is something off about that young man."

"He seems perfectly nice to me. From what he said, it sounds like he recently separated from his wife. So if he is acting a little standoffish, I think that might be why."

"I didn't say he was standoffish. He certainly wasn't with that shoe. I swear, I thought for a moment he was going to take it. Then you walked in, and he about jumped out of his skin."

"I don't know what you expect me to do," Danielle said.

"For one thing, do you really know who he is?" Marie asked.

"He says his name is Owen Gardener."

"Have you seen his ID? He would not be your first guest who lied about who he was."

"No. I have not seen his ID."

"Then you should ask him to see it," Marie insisted.

"Marie, I am not going to ask to see his driver's license just because he was checking out that silly shoe."

When Danielle left the room a few minutes later, Marie muttered, "If you won't, I will."

NINETEEN

M arie found Owen upstairs in the bedroom Danielle had assigned him. She sat on the edge of his mattress and watched him, wondering how she could get ahold of his driver's license for a quick look. As if he had somehow heard her thoughts, he pulled his wallet from a pocket, along with some change, and tossed it all on the dresser with his cellphone. He headed for the bathroom. When he was out of the room, Marie looked at the wallet and smiled.

"That was easy," Marie said, moving to the dresser. She looked down at the wallet and watched it open. The next moment his driver's license slipped out of the card holder and floated up so she could have a better look. She stood there a moment reading and rereading the information on the identification.

"Well, imagine that. Your name really is Owen Gardener." She turned the driver's license over, looking at it from all sides. It looked real enough. The license floated down to the wallet, retucking itself in the leather fold. Still not convinced, she looked at the other cards in the wallet. There were several credit cards, a Costco membership card, and a medical insurance card, all under the same name that was on the driver's license.

With a sigh she returned all the cards to his wallet before leaving the room in search of Danielle. She found her in the kitchen, making chili.

"Dinner?" Marie asked when she entered the room.

"Yes. Not sure Owen or Colin will want to join us, but I'm going to make a big pot, and everyone can help themselves."

"I just thought I'd tell you, you were right, his name is Owen Gardener."

Danielle stopped chopping onions and looked at Marie. "What did you do?"

"I didn't do anything bad," Marie said defensively. I simply took a quick peek in his wallet. He left it sitting on the dresser when he went to the bathroom, so it only took a moment."

"Well, maybe now you will stop worrying," Danielle said, resuming her chopping.

"But then I got to thinking, just because he gave you his real name, it doesn't mean he isn't dangerous."

"Dangerous? Just because you saw him looking at that ugly shoe?" Danielle asked.

"It is just a feeling I have, that he is not who he says he is."

"I thought you just proved he is exactly who he said he is," Danielle reminded her as she scooped up the diced onions and tossed them into a frying pan.

"It will only take you a couple of minutes to check him out. Considering some of the problems you've had in the past, I would think you would want to do that," Marie insisted.

Danielle let out a sigh. "And exactly how? Ask the chief to run a background check on him? I really can't be running down the chief and asking him to look into someone because he showed interest in a homemade Christmas decoration."

"That face thing all you kids do. Can't you look there?" Marie asked.

"You mean Facebook?" Danielle asked.

"Yes! See what you can find out about him there."

"I adore you, Marie, but I really need to finish this chili."

ACCORDING TO THE DERMATOLOGIST, the brown spots along her belly weren't dangerous, just ugly. Heather stood in her kitchen with the hem of her blouse pulled up, inspecting the discolored skin. Wrinkling her nose at the sight, she ran one finger over the brown rough spots. Perhaps there was no one to look at her belly—not with her current love life—and bathing suit season was months away, but Heather didn't like the ugly marks. The snotty medical assistant at the dermatologist's office had said something about them being age spots—which was obviously her way of telling Heather she was old. *I'm barely in my thirties. That's not old,* Heather told herself. *And younger than that stupid medical assistant!*

She hadn't asked if they could remove the spots. They had burned a precancerous growth off her face once, and that had been both painful and expensive. Heather knew exactly what she needed to do to get rid of them. She would have done it earlier, but she thought it best they first be checked out by her doctor.

Opening the kitchen cabinet, she removed a bottle of pure coconut oil and gave it a little shake to determine how much oil it contained. It was less than a quarter full. Removing its lid, she set it on the counter. Next, she searched her essential oil reserve for her frankincense oil. Once she found it, she carefully removed its lid, intending to add a few drops to the coconut oil, which she would then apply to her unwanted brown marks.

Just as she started to add several drops, a booming, "Heather, you need to help me!" filled her ears as Marie suddenly appeared next to her. Startled, Heather dropped the bottle of oil. It landed on the floor and rolled under the counter.

"Marie! Can't you knock?" Heather dropped to the floor and quickly retrieved the bottle, relieved it had not broken, nor had any oil spilled out—thanks to its plastic oil dropper cap.

Heather stood back up, the bottle of frankincense oil in hand, and looked around. Marie was nowhere in sight.

"Well, I guess I hurt her feelings," Heather muttered, preparing to complete her original task.

Just as she was about to add the frankincense to the coconut oil, a loud knock came from the overhead kitchen cabinet, and the next moment Marie appeared in the same spot she had been in a moment earlier.

"Is that better?" Marie asked.

Heather managed not to drop the jar of oil at Marie's second entrance.

"I could have broken this!" Heather said, waving the jar at Marie. "This little bottle cost me a hundred bucks!"

Marie's eyes widened. "For that tiny thing? Does that little bottle even hold an ounce?"

BOBBI HOLMES

Heather scowled at Marie and proceeded to add a few drops of the frankincense to the coconut oil.

"Well, you didn't break it. I don't know why you have to be so snippy," Marie said in a pout.

Heather set the tiny bottle of essential oil on the counter. "Seriously, Marie, when you were alive, wouldn't it have rattled your nerves for a ghost to just randomly pop in? You kinda scared the crap outa me."

"I didn't mean to scare you. I just figured you were used to ghosts popping in."

"I don't know if I will ever get used to it. What do you need?"

"I think there is something a little funny about one of Danielle's guests."

"I assume you're talking about one of the guys the Seahorse Motel sent over?" Heather recapped the bottle of frankincense oil.

"Yes. The younger one. I just think he acts...well, odd. I thought it would be a good idea to do a little checking on him. I'm not suggesting asking the police to run a background check, but look on the computer. You know, at that club where you all hang out."

"Club?" Heather frowned.

"Face friend thingy."

"You mean Facebook," Heather corrected.

"Yes. Will you do it for me? I know his name, and I have his address."

"Umm...why doesn't Danielle just check him out?"

"She's busy making chili," Marie said.

Heather studied Marie for a moment and then said, "You mean she doesn't want to stalk him?"

"Who said anything about stalking?" Marie asked

Heather chuckled. "That's sort of what it's called. Okay, let's go in the living room, and I'll get my laptop."

It didn't take long for Heather to find Owen's Facebook page. She showed Marie the profile picture to confirm it was the correct Owen Gardener.

"He doesn't have a beard," Marie mumbled, taking a closer look at Owen's profile picture.

"It doesn't mean it isn't him," Heather reminded her.

Marie studied the profile picture a few minutes. Finally she said, "That's him. The eyes. And the scar. The Owen Gardener staying

112

at Marlow House has a little scar over one eyebrow, just like the man in that picture."

Marie didn't understand how to go through his page. Her computer experience was limited to turning computers off and making random telepathic searches on Adam's computer. She left it to Heather to go through his Facebook posts and photos.

"Not much here. Not sure if he posts a lot and has his settings so we don't see anything, but he does have some posts that come up not set to private. In fact, some I would expect to be private. My guess, he is an infrequent Facebook user, and when he does post something, he doesn't set them to private," Heather explained.

"What have you found out about him?"

Heather shrugged. "He plays the guitar and likes to ride dirt bikes. Works for some manufacturing company. Looks like he and his wife are separated, at least that's my takeaway from some of the comments. It doesn't look like he has removed any of her pictures."

"How do you know those pictures are of his wife?" Marie asked. "Do they have the same last name?"

"No. But that doesn't mean anything. There is one of him and a woman posted a couple of years ago, and all the comments are saying happy anniversary. I just figure it must be his wife. And it is the same woman in most of the pictures. At least, up until six months ago. There are no pictures of her after that time. Pretty woman, but she looks rather high maintenance." Heather paused a moment and then said, "Hmmm…let me try something."

A moment later she pulled up another Facebook page, this one of the wife.

"She's not great about her privacy settings either." Heather laughed. "And I must say this Owen guy must be understanding."

"Why do you say that?" Marie asked.

"Because he is still Facebook friends with his wife. Or I assume…ex-wife, considering she has a ton of recent pictures on her page of her and another guy. I don't think this other dude is her brother, considering the poses. And according to one post, they're living together."

WHEN MARIE RETURNED to Marlow House, she found Danielle in the kitchen, finishing up dinner.

"Okay, you were right," Marie told her.

"Right about what?" Danielle asked.

"Your guest, Owen Gardener. I don't think he is a criminal."

Danielle chuckled. "I am very relieved. What changed your mind?"

Marie then went on to tell Danielle what she had learned at Heather's house.

"That poor guy," Danielle muttered.

"I don't think that's necessarily the case. According to Heather, they are still face friends, so he must be good with it."

"I assume you mean Facebook friends?"

Marie shrugged.

"From what he told us earlier, he and his wife are separated—not divorced. And I got the feeling he wasn't thrilled about the divorce idea," Danielle said.

"I do believe he should get used to it. After all, his wife is living with another man."

TWENTY

It felt like the old days of the B and B as guests gathered around the dining room table on Tuesday morning for breakfast. There were new acquaintances, like Colin and Owen, and friends who had once been guests at Marlow House B and B—when it was still in business—like Chris and his brother, Noah. Walt and Danielle sat at opposing ends of the table, chatting with their guests. Joanne brought an additional basket of warm muffins and cinnamon rolls to the table, and Chris helped refill coffee cups.

The current topic of conversation involved the careers of those sitting around the table. It began when someone asked Walt about his writing and shifted over to Chris's work at the foundation—leaving out the detail that he was actually the man behind the foundation, not just an employee. Danielle talked briefly about her marketing career and then the now defunct bed and breakfast. Noah shared several stories about his years teaching, and Owen touched briefly on his position at a manufacturing company as a purchasing manager and how this was a much needed break from work.

When the conversation got around to Colin, they were all surprised when he explained he was a retired priest.

"I didn't know priests retired," Owen said.

Colin shrugged, took a sip of his coffee, and then said, "I suppose one is always a priest—unless his faith has faltered."

"Has your faith faltered?" Danielle asked without thinking, instantly regretting her words.

Colin turned a smile in her direction and said, "No. I am happy to report my faith is probably stronger than ever. One reason I love Christmas, it can help renew faith that has been lost—or misplaced."

"I've always loved Christmas. There is something magical about this time of year," Danielle said with a sigh.

"I don't know. As I get older, it just seems like another day," Owen remarked as he picked up a slice of bacon from his plate.

"The Puritans who came to America—before this was a country —didn't believe in celebrating Christmas," Colin explained. "In fact, for a time celebrating Christmas was outlawed in Boston. It wasn't officially recognized as a federal holiday until 1870."

"Wow, that was the same year Frederickport was founded," Danielle noted.

"And just a year before this house was built," Walt added.

"While it wasn't an official holiday yet, both the North and the South celebrated Christmas during the Civil War," Colin continued.

They discussed Christmas traditions for another ten minutes when Owen said, "Christmas is for kids."

"I guess that makes me a big kid." Danielle glanced at her watch and then added, "I'm going to be leaving in about thirty minutes to go Christmas shopping with one of our neighbors."

"Lily?" Chris asked.

"No, with Heather. Lily is one of the people I'm shopping for. So, what are all of you planning to do today?" Danielle asked.

ELIZABETH SPARKS SLEPT in on Tuesday morning. Opening her eyes sleepily, she rolled over and looked at her alarm clock.

"It's almost ten thirty!" Elizabeth gasped, bolting upright in her bed. She rubbed sleep from her eyes and took a second look at her clock—just to be sure. It was indeed almost ten thirty. *When was the last time I slept so late?* she asked herself. But she was on Christmas break, and her parents wouldn't be arriving for a couple more days, so she told herself not to feel guilty. She deserved her rest.

She picked up her cellphone from the nightstand and checked her email. She then logged into Facebook and glanced through her friends' recent posts. One was from her boyfriend—her ex-boyfriend. They had broken up right before the beginning of Christmas break. It had been a mutual decision, without tears or drama. That was probably why they had decided to part ways. He was a great guy, an artist like herself, but whatever romance they had once imagined was no longer there—if it ever had been.

With a sigh, Elizabeth tossed her phone back on the nightstand and climbed out of bed. She walked to the window and began pulling her shades open. When they were about halfway open, she stopped abruptly and ducked behind the curtains and peeked outside.

"It's him," Elizabeth whispered to herself. The man she had seen parked in front of her house before—the one she kept running into around town—the man whose reflection she saw in the store window watching her—he was here again, sitting right outside her house.

From this angle, it was impossible to read the car's license plate. *Calling the police sounds a little extreme*, she thought. *What do I say? There is a guy sitting in his car by my house. Hardly against the law.*

The next moment the car drove away. Elizabeth let out a sigh of relief and went to get dressed. She had Christmas shopping to do.

DANIELLE AND HEATHER walked down main street together, each holding a bag carrying their purchases, when they ran into Elizabeth Sparks walking out of a store. After greeting each other, it was soon discovered they were all heading in the same direction—to Lucy's Diner to grab lunch. Danielle and Heather invited Elizabeth to join them, and she accepted their offer.

Fifteen minutes later they were seated at a table in Lucy's Diner. The server had already taken their order and brought their beverages. Picking up her glass of iced tea, Danielle paused a moment and looked over at Elizabeth and said, "Carla over at Pier Café told me about your stalker."

"You have a stalker?" Heather gasped.

"She told you about that?" Elizabeth asked. "Although, I am not surprised. I don't know, maybe that's why I told Carla."

"What do you mean?" Danielle asked.

Elizabeth shrugged. "I feel funny going to the police about this."

"What's going on?" Heather demanded.

Elizabeth recapped her encounters with the mysterious stranger.

"Did you think Carla would blab it to the cops, and then they would come ask you about it?" Heather asked after listening to what Elizabeth had to say. "Is that why you told her, because you felt funny going to the police yourself?"

"I didn't think that exactly…but maybe that was at the back of my mind…I don't know. And I was almost convinced it was my imagination, but then I saw him again. Parked in front of my house this morning."

"Do you have any idea who he is?" Danielle asked.

Elizabeth shook her head. "I have no idea. And I don't recognize his car other than it's a black sedan—sort of nondescript. I'm not a car person."

"Two door or four door?" Danielle asked.

Elizabeth cringed. "I don't know. I was looking at him."

"What does your boyfriend say?" Heather asked. "This lady I know, when she lived alone, this guy came up to her apartment door and knocked. The creep had his pants down. She yelled fire, and he ran away. They never caught him, but after that, her boyfriend stayed at her apartment every night until she moved."

"Fortunately whoever it is has kept his pants up. As for the boyfriend, we are no longer together," Elizabeth told them.

"I'm sorry to hear that," Danielle said.

Elizabeth shrugged. "Don't be. He's a nice guy, and we're still friends."

"When are your parents going to be here?" Danielle asked.

"They're coming Thursday."

"I imagine you'll feel better having them stay with you," Heather said. "Nice you get to spend Christmas with your parents. Danielle and I are orphans."

"Heather!" Danielle chastised. "That sounds so…so…"

"It's true." Heather looked at Elizabeth and smiled. "Chris is an orphan too. But he has a brother. Danielle and I don't have any siblings. Do you have any brothers or sisters?"

"I have an older brother," Elizabeth told her.

"Is he coming for Christmas? I'd think an older brother would be perfect for taking care of a stalker—especially one that police can't do anything about since technically he hasn't broken the law," Heather said.

"No. Mark is not coming for Christmas. In fact, it's been years since we spent Christmas together."

"You aren't close?" Heather asked.

Elizabeth shrugged. "We used to be. When we were kids. Back then, we had so much fun at this time of year."

"He helped you decorate the Christmas shoe, didn't he?" Danielle asked.

Heather looked at Danielle and frowned. "What is a Christmas shoe?"

Danielle cringed. "Dang. I should not have mentioned that. Forget I said anything about a shoe. You might get it in the white elephant exchange."

"One shoe?" Heather shrugged and said, "I guess that would make the perfect white elephant gift, a single shoe. Kinda useless."

Elizabeth flashed Danielle a smile. "Yes, he helped decorate it. But that was when we were both kids. He was a lot of fun back then and really got into Christmas. But when he got older, I almost think he resented the fact that Christmas had changed since we were kids. There was no longer a mountain of presents under the tree. My mother used to go a little crazy at Christmas."

"We never had a mountain of gifts under our tree," Heather muttered.

"One Christmas, when Mark was older, he got the Christmas shoe," Elizabeth began. "Actually, it was his wife who got it."

"I still don't know what that is," Heather said.

Elizabeth looked at Heather and explained. "It was a gag gift passed around in our family. Not the same shoe Danielle has."

While she didn't completely understand, Heather let Elizabeth continue without interrupting again.

"Mark had just gotten married, and it was the first Christmas his wife was spending with our family. Actually, it turned out to be the last Christmas too."

"Why?" Danielle asked.

"It was Mom's turn to pass on the shoe, and she decided it should go to her new daughter-in-law. Unfortunately, my sister-in-law did not think it was very funny."

Danielle cringed. "What happened?"

"The following Thanksgiving, I reminded my sister-in-law it was her turn to pass on the shoe. I figured she had gotten over her snit over getting the shoe and that she might have some fun passing it on. Heck, I thought it would be hilarious if she gave it to my brother."

"Did she do it?" Danielle asked.

Elizabeth shook her head. "No. She told me she didn't have the shoe anymore. That Mark had gotten rid of it when they had cleaned out their garage. I thought she was kidding at first, and then I realized she wasn't. When I got upset, she told me it really was none of my business what she did with the shoe, considering it had been given to her."

"Wow," Danielle said.

"When I asked my brother about it later, he told me the whole shoe thing was lame anyway, and he admitted getting rid of it."

"So that's what happened to the shoe," Danielle said.

"Yes. My brother and his wife never spent Christmas with me or my parents ever again."

"Because of the shoe?" Heather asked.

"It might have been because of something I said," Elizabeth confessed. "When Mark admitted he had gotten rid of the shoe, I just lit into him. We had a huge fight. And I said things I shouldn't have said about his wife. We never talked after that. And then they moved away."

"He hasn't kept in touch with your parents?" Danielle asked.

"No. It has broken my mother's heart, but she is convinced he will eventually reach out to us. He and Mom used to be so close. He was close to Dad too, but not like he was to Mom. I'm surprised he has kept away this long, but I think his wife was always jealous of our mother. And she never liked me."

"I know it is none of my business—but maybe you should try reaching out to him," Danielle suggested. "I say that as someone who, as Heather pointed out, has no parents—no siblings. I lost my cousin a few years ago. She was the last person in my family. While Cheryl and I had our issues, I would give anything to have her back in my life again. Unfortunately, I didn't realize that until after she died."

TWENTY-ONE

"I hope one of the neighbors doesn't notice our car," Forrest said as he drove down Beach Drive, Marcella in the passenger seat. "We keep cruising by here every few hours; someone is going to notice."

They spied two men walking down Marlow House's front walkway, the pit bull trailing behind them. When the men reached the sidewalk, one of them leaned down and snapped a leash on the dog.

"It looks like two of them are going, and they're taking the dog with them!" Marcella said excitedly.

"But I also saw someone in the living room," Forrest said as they neared the pier.

"This is going to be impossible getting in that house with all those people staying there," Marcella groaned.

When they reached the turnoff for the pier parking lot, Forrest kept driving.

"I thought we were going to get something to eat? We didn't have breakfast," Marcella complained.

"I don't want to eat at Pier Café again. The food is alright, but I want to go somewhere different."

"We could try one of those places Sam suggested. There is Beach Taco—" Marcella began.

"I don't feel like Mexican food."

"He said that place on the main street has the best burgers in town," she suggested.

"You mean Lucy's Diner?" he asked.
"Yes. I think that's the one."

DANIELLE, Heather and Elizabeth had just finished their lunch and ordered dessert when Marcella and Forrest entered Lucy's Diner. Heather and Danielle didn't notice the couple walking into the restaurant, but Elizabeth did.

"Wow, I'm surprised to see them in Frederickport," Elizabeth said in a low voice as she watched Marcella and Forrest walk to a table across the room and sit down.

Danielle and Heather glanced briefly in the couple's direction and then looked back to Elizabeth.

"Who's that?" Heather asked.

Leaning forward slightly across the table, her voice low so as not to carry across the room, Elizabeth said, "That's Forrest and Marcella Hooper." She looked at Danielle and added, "They're the couple who worked for Eloise Winterborne."

"Who is Eloise Winterborne?" Heather asked.

"She lived in Astoria—passed away about six months ago," Danielle explained. "Walt and I picked up some things from her estate at a curio shop the other day. I mentioned it to Elizabeth when I saw her at the museum. She was telling me a little about the woman."

"So who was she? Someone famous?" Heather asked.

Elizabeth shook her head. "No. Just a sweet little old lady with her share of quirks—a bit eccentric. The couple who just walked in, they worked for Eloise for about twenty years. After she passed away, they were pretty upset that she didn't even mention them in the will. Frankly, I can't say I blame them. But they did get pretty nasty with me at her funeral."

"Why would they get nasty with you?" Danielle asked.

"You know how I told you Eloise often took my craft classes?" Danielle nodded.

"When she died, she left her money to a variety of charities—including the one I started for the local arts. They accused me of taking advantage of her—manipulating her to leave the charity money. But it wasn't like I will see any of it. I don't even get paid for any of those classes."

"Why are you surprised to see them here? Astoria is not far from Frederickport," Heather asked.

Elizabeth glanced briefly over to the Hoopers' table again and then looked back to Heather. "After Eloise died, I heard the executor of the will asked them to stay on to help with the upcoming estate auction and to take care of the place. At the time, they assumed they were in the will. But they soon found out they hadn't even been mentioned."

"So they left?" Heather asked.

Elizabeth shook her head. "They really had nowhere to go. I don't think they're old enough to collect Social Security. They had no choice but to stay on or find another job. Staying to work for the estate gave them a roof over their head and a paycheck. But I heard they were recently told their services were no longer needed. I just assumed they would leave the area because Marcella Hooper made a scene after they were let go, said something about how she couldn't leave Oregon fast enough."

"It's hardly Oregon's fault," Heather said.

"I just think they were upset they'd devoted so many years to taking care of Eloise, and ended up with nothing. It left a bitter taste in their mouth, and they just wanted to leave—or so I thought."

"To be honest, I'm not sure how good they were at their job. Have you seen the Winterborne house? It looks as if it is ready to fall down," Danielle said.

"Not sure you can blame that on the Hoopers," Elizabeth told her. "I liked Eloise, but she was an odd little thing. She hated spending money. One reason she took my craft classes, they were the ones offered by the foundation; they didn't cost her anything. Just from what I overheard over the years, I don't think she would let them spend much on repairs. If Mr. Hooper couldn't fix it himself—without spending much money—it did not get fixed."

"That is certainly reflected in the current appearance of the property," Danielle said.

"And this Eloise, she had money?" Heather asked.

Elizabeth looked to Heather. "Yes. Her husband's family was very wealthy, and she ended up with everything. I've never been in her house, but I have driven by it when I was in Astoria, so I understand what Danielle is saying about it being run-down. I was rather shocked when I first saw it."

"So what did she do with all her money if she took free classes and never spent anything on her house?" Heather asked.

"She liked garage sales," Elizabeth said with a laugh.

The server brought their dessert, and they briefly stopped talking. After she left the table, their conversation returned to the subject of Elizabeth's stalker.

"Are you going to say anything to the chief about this guy you think is watching you?" Danielle asked.

"I don't know. What am I going to say? It's not like he has approached me. And it is not illegal to park in front of someone's house," Elizabeth said.

"At least give the chief his description," Heather said. "Maybe he can figure out who he is. If nothing else, tell us what he looks like. Maybe we have seen him."

Elizabeth set her dessert spoon on her plate and considered Heather's suggestion. "I guess he is tall—not like basketball-player tall, but respectably tall. Every time I've seen him, he is wearing a baseball cap and sunglasses. And he has a dark beard. Hard to tell his age. He could be twenty or sixty for all I know."

"Probably not sixty if he has a dark beard. Unless he dyes it," Heather noted.

"A lot of people have beards. In fact, two of our guests staying at Marlow House have beards," Danielle said.

"Exactly, which is one reason I feel funny going to the chief. Everyone wears sunglasses too—one time or another. And look around in the diner, I see a couple of guys wearing baseball caps— and a few beards," Elizabeth said.

Ten minutes later, after they finished their dessert and waited for their bill, Danielle asked Elizabeth what she had planned for the rest of the day.

"I need to stop at the museum. But I think I'll walk and come back for my car. It's nice outside."

"Do you want to do any more shopping?" Danielle asked Heather.

"Not really, unless you want to stop somewhere." Heather glanced at her watch.

"Would you mind if we stopped at Adam's office before we go home? It's just down the street," Danielle asked.

CHRIS AND NOAH chatted while they strolled down main street Frederickport, enjoying the brisk December afternoon while the sun shone brightly overhead. Each wore a heavy jacket to ward off the winter chill. Chris buried one hand in his coat pocket while his other hand held Hunny's leash. The pit bull walked on his left, looking at all the sights while careful not to tug on the lead.

Not once today had Chris needed to jerk the lead while issuing the command to heel. Chris glanced down at Hunny and smiled, proud of the well-behaved dog. Reluctantly he had to credit Walt for Hunny's training. It seemed being able to clearly communicate with a dog—especially one who wanted to please—made dog training a snap.

Just as they were about to pass Lucy's Diner, a man and woman stepped out from the restaurant, and without warning, Hunny lurched forward, jerking the lead from Chris's hand. The next moment the pit bull, now an uncontrollable mass of wiggles and whimpers, demanded attention from the woman, who, with her companion, stood speechless and frozen on the sidewalk, looking down at the dog.

"I am so sorry!" Chris shouted as he grabbed hold of Hunny's lead and attempted to tug her away. But the dog refused to budge and continued vying for the woman's attention.

"I think she likes you," Noah said, surprised at the pit bull's unexpected behavior.

"Oh my, umm…yes, I see that," the woman said nervously as she glanced over at the man at her side and then back to the dog, who now cried pitifully as Chris pulled her away.

"Can I pet her?" the woman asked hesitantly. "She seems friendly."

The man at her side remained speechless, but Chris loosened his hold, and Hunny happily returned to the woman, who now knelt before her, talking baby talk and accepting the dog kisses.

"GOOD LORD, I can't believe that just happened," Forrest told Marcella after the men and the pit bull left and were out of earshot. "That dog recognized you."

"Yes, she did. And thankfully she likes me," Marcella said. "While I'll admit, it was a little unnerving—after all, it is a pit bull—

I feel better about going back over there. And if we don't get the opportunity during the daytime, then I guess I'll have to sneak in when they are all sleeping, and make sure I take plenty of treats for my new friend. If we are lucky, they will put it by the tree."

"You keep saying that. But so far, we have not been lucky," Forrest snorted.

"Are you sure about that? Did you see how that dog just greeted me?"

DANIELLE AND HEATHER were just saying goodbye to Adam when Chris and his brother walked into the office with Hunny. The two women lingered a few minutes, listening to Chris tell them about the woman Hunny accosted, and how he was relieved she took it better than someone like Pearl might have. Danielle and Heather then said their goodbyes and headed out of the real estate office with their packages, en route to Danielle's car, which was parked down the street.

After they passed Lucy's Diner, Danielle glanced to the other side of the street and spied Owen Gardener sitting in his car. He wasn't getting out of the vehicle, and he appeared to be staring at something. Danielle paused a moment and glanced up the street. She noticed Elizabeth, who had just walked down from the museum and was now getting into her car.

"Why are you stopping?" Heather asked, no longer walking.

Danielle nodded to Owen. "That's one of our guests from the Seahorse Motel."

"You want to go say hi?" Heather asked.

Danielle glanced back to Elizabeth; she was now in her vehicle. The next moment she drove off in the opposite direction. Looking back to Owen, Danielle watched as he drove away from the curb and headed in the same direction Elizabeth had just gone.

"Owen has a black sedan," Danielle muttered.

TWENTY-TWO

Someone was walking on her belly, and she had a pretty good idea who it was. Danielle opened her eyes, lifted her head from the pillow, and looked down the bed. She watched as Max strolled up her body. He began to purr.

"Good morning to you too," Danielle whispered as she stroked the silky black fur along the cat's back. He settled on her chest, his nose just inches from hers. Danielle rubbed the fringe of white fur along his mostly black ears between two of her fingers.

His loud purr woke the other person in the bed. Walt rolled over to face Danielle and opened his eyes. "He is drooling all over you."

Max turned to Walt and stared at him for a moment.

"Well, you are," Walt told the cat.

The next moment Max abruptly leapt from Danielle and the bed. Walt looked over to the closed bedroom door and willed it to unlock and open. When it did, Max left the room. The door shut and relocked itself.

Danielle sat up in the bed and asked, "What did you say to Max? I didn't mind his morning snuggle, drools and all. He loves me."

Walt sat up. "Yes, he does. But he also wanted me to open the door so he could go out."

"So why not just wake you, why me?" Danielle asked as she reached over and kissed Walt and then climbed out of bed.

"He is a cat, love." Walt gave Danielle's backside a friendly swat as he followed her out of bed. "Cats do things in their own way. Haven't you learned that yet?"

Danielle shrugged and went to use the bathroom. When she returned minutes later, she picked up her brush and drew it through her hair as she looked into the dresser mirror. Walt took his turn in the bathroom, and when he came back into the room a few minutes later, Danielle said, "I keep thinking about Owen and how I briefly imagined he might be Elizabeth's stalker."

"I suppose anything is possible," Walt said as he sat on the side of the bed and pulled on his socks. "But as you remembered, Ruby said he didn't arrive in Frederickport until Saturday. And from what Elizabeth told you, her stalker first showed up on Friday."

"Maybe he was here Friday and Ruby just didn't know. But then again, Heather did go through his Facebook page for Marie, and she said he seemed like a rather boring—un-stalkerish—sort of guy. She thought it was amusing that I had jumped to that conclusion, especially when two black sedans drove by minutes later…But then, he was staring at Elizabeth…"

"Yes, and Elizabeth is a very beautiful young woman. And from what Owen told us, he is separated from his wife. It's not unusual for a married man to enjoy looking at a good-looking woman, much less a single man."

Danielle stopped brushing her hair and turned to Walt. She arched her brow and asked, "And just tell me, what beautiful young women have you been enjoying looking at?"

Walt grinned at his wife. "Love, I am a very lucky man—I seem to be surrounded by beautiful women, my wife included."

AFTER DRESSING ON WEDNESDAY MORNING, Danielle and Walt joined their guests downstairs for breakfast, which Joanne had prepared with the help of Chris and Noah. During breakfast, Chris asked Walt and Danielle if he could leave Hunny with them as he and Noah went on a little outing that day. The brothers wouldn't be returning until late that evening.

"Of course you can. I have no plans to leave today. Evan's coming over later, and we're decorating Christmas cookies," Danielle told them.

"Christmas cookies?" Colin perked up.

"Mostly sugar cookies. I have some wonderful Christmas cookie cutters. Nothing gets me into the spirit of the season like decorating Christmas cookies." Danielle grinned.

"But they don't taste as good as your chocolate drop cookies," Walt said.

"I already have some of those," Danielle reminded him. "Unless you have eaten them all."

Walt grinned mischievously.

"I always enjoyed decorating cookies. It's a wholesome tradition, one that the family can do together," Colin said.

"You are welcome to join us," Danielle offered. She then looked at Owen and added, "You too, Owen."

Owen smiled wistfully at the invitation and said, "I don't remember decorating cookies as a kid, but there was a cookie my mom made every year. I always thought that was what Christmas tasted like."

"Do you remember what kind of cookie it was?" Danielle asked.

"I don't remember what it was called. Not sure it had a name," Owen said with a shrug. "It wasn't a regular cookie batter. I remember Mom spread the ingredients in a pan—graham cracker crumbs, coconut, chocolate chips, and walnuts, some sort of canned milk and melted butter. It was all gooey, and I thought it tasted better than chocolate chip cookies."

"Ahhh, I bet you're talking about Magic Bar cookies," Danielle said with a grin. "Those are great to make when you don't have time to bake—but want a really delicious cookie."

"Magic Bar?" Colin asked.

"Yes. It's a recipe from the back of the Eagle Brand sweetened condensed milk can," Danielle told them.

"Hmm…not sure how I feel about learning what I thought was some secret family recipe came off the back of a can of milk," Owen said with a snort.

"Hey, don't knock recipes from the back of cans," Danielle teased. "Some of the most iconic recipes can be found there."

COLIN AND WALT resumed their game of chess while Owen drifted to the library to check out the collection of books. He was looking at the Bonnet reproductions—two life-sized oil paintings of Walt and Angela Marlow—when Danielle walked into the library.

"Your husband does bear an eerie resemblance to his distant cousin," Owen noted. "Actually, it is more than eerie. If I hadn't heard the story of these portraits, I would have assumed this one was of your husband."

"After we sold the originals to the Glandon Foundation for the museum, this spot was empty. We had so much more room in here without those portraits. But then Walt had to figure out what he wanted to do with his reproductions, and they naturally ended up here. I think this is where they belong—and I am rather glad they're back. Not that the originals are back, but you know what I mean."

"They do seem to belong," Owen agreed. "But they are big suckers."

Danielle laughed. "I think it was Lily who said it showed they had healthy egos—having life-size portraits made."

The two moved from where they stood looking at the paintings, with Danielle taking a seat on the sofa and Owen sitting on the chair facing her.

"Can I ask you a question?" Danielle asked.

"I suppose."

"Why did you come to Frederickport for Christmas?"

Owen considered the question for a moment. Finally he said, "I think I mentioned I'm separated from my wife."

Danielle nodded.

"I needed to get away—rethink my life. My choices."

"I'm sorry about your marriage," Danielle said. "I do understand how difficult it must be for you right now. I was married before Walt. My husband was killed in a car accident right before Christmas."

"Oh my god, that is horrible!"

Danielle smiled awkwardly. "With his lover."

Owen cringed. "Oh…"

"I wasn't sure if I should grieve for my husband or for my marriage. It was a confusing time. Happy to say I am at a much better place now. And I believe you will be in a better place one day too."

"I appreciate you saying that. But the truth is, I am not sad my marriage is over. What I regret is that it ever began."

Danielle was not sure how to respond, so she said nothing.

"In the beginning I thought I was madly in love with her. After all, she made me feel like the most important man in the world. For her devotion, she demanded all my attention, which I gladly gave to her. Until one day I realized the man I had been was no longer there—just the man she had turned me into. I don't know if that makes any sense. But I gave up a great deal to make her happy, and in turn lost everything that was important to me. When I could no longer be what she needed, she found someone else. And you know what I felt?"

"What?"

"Relief. Tremendous relief. Like I had been released from some prison I had locked myself into. But I can't go back and reclaim myself—reclaim what I lost. That's gone now. I suppose I came to Frederickport to say goodbye. I never said goodbye the first time."

Danielle frowned. "Goodbye? To who?"

Owen smiled. "Damn. I sound a bit dramatic. And I haven't even had anything to drink."

"That's okay."

"I guess I answered your question. Sort of. And if you will excuse me, I think I'll take a little drive."

COLIN MADE his chess move and then paused. He looked up. *Owen is leaving*, he thought. He looked at Walt and said, "How about we continue this game later? I'd really like to stretch my legs a bit."

AFTER WALT BID Colin a goodbye and watched the elderly man leave the living room, he moved over to the sofa and sat down. Hunny, who had been napping nearby, followed Walt. The pit bull sat by the sofa and looked up, vying for his attention.

Chris told us at breakfast that you met a new friend this morning, Walt conveyed to Hunny.

The dog continued to stare at Walt. She cocked her head.

Walt arched his brow. *What do you mean it wasn't a new friend?*

Hunny rested her head on Walt's knee, her eyes never leaving his.

The woman who smelled like bacon...are you sure?...she was with a man…what did he look like?…yes, yes, we all look pretty much alike, but we smell different…

"It looks like we are alone," Danielle announced when she walked in the living room a moment later. "Joanne just left, and I saw Colin leaving out the front door, and Owen left a few minutes ago." Danielle sat on the sofa next to Walt and set her cellphone she had been carrying on the coffee table.

"Hunny had another encounter with our intruder," Walt announced.

"Don't tell me she got in the house again?" Danielle groaned.

"No. Hunny saw her downtown. Remember the story Chris told us about Hunny going goofy over some woman they met downtown?"

"That was the woman?"

Walt nodded. "According to Hunny. Now that both Chris and Noah saw the woman, they should be able to help us ID her and track her down. Find out who she is, and why she broke into our house."

Danielle leaned over to the coffee table and picked up her cellphone. She dialed Chris. The call went to voicemail. She then tried Noah. Once again, the call went to voicemail.

"Drat," Danielle grumbled, tossing her phone on the table. "Neither Chris nor Noah are answering."

"Why didn't you leave them a message to call?" Walt asked.

"They'll see I called. I'm sure Chris will call me back. They're probably driving through an area with no service."

"Even if they don't, they'll be back tonight, and we can figure this out."

Danielle slumped back on the sofa while Hunny leaned against her legs. She reached down and scratched the dog's neck. "I think you need to have a long talk with this dog."

"What about?" Walt asked.

"The woman, whoever she is, broke into this house. I know Hunny does not have the heart of a guard dog, but sheesh. When she runs into someone she knows has broken into our house, I don't think the proper response is showering her with love."

TWENTY-THREE

Police Chief MacDonald arrived at Marlow House a little past noon on Wednesday, with his youngest son, Evan. Out on winter break, Evan and his older brother, Eddy, had been staying at their aunt Sissy's house during the day while their dad was at work. But today Eddy was off with his maternal grandmother, Christmas shopping for his brother and father, while Evan planned to spend the rest of the afternoon at Marlow House.

Marlow House and the mediums from Beach Drive held a special place in Evan's heart. Like them, he too could see ghosts. The only living member of Evan's family who knew his secret was his father, Police Chief MacDonald.

"Are you going to join us for lunch before you go back to work?" Danielle asked the chief as he walked into the entry hall with Evan.

"Am I invited?" the chief asked with a grin.

"Always. Thought it would be a good idea if we ate something healthy before starting on those cookies—to counter all that sugar," Danielle told him as they started toward the kitchen. Evan had already run ahead after seeing Hunny, and was currently petting the dog, who had submissively rolled over to enjoy belly rubs.

"You really need to do something about that ferocious dog," the chief teased.

Danielle stopped walking and looked at the chief. "Speaking of that, there is something I need to talk to you about." She looked over to Hunny and Evan and said, "Evan, I need to talk to your dad. You can go on to the kitchen. Walt is in there, and you can start lunch. But don't forget to wash your hands first!"

A few minutes later the chief and Danielle sat together in the parlor, the door closed.

"And you think that woman Hunny saw yesterday was the same one who broke in?" the chief asked after Danielle updated him on what had been going on.

"According to Hunny."

"Unfortunately, I can't use a dog's testimony to file breaking and entering charges against someone."

Danielle rolled her eyes. "Ya think?"

The chief grinned. "So who is she? We can at least find out who she is. Maybe figure out what she is looking for, keep an eye on her."

"I tried calling Chris's number again. They're still not answering. I left a message this time."

"Where did they go?" the chief asked.

"Noah wanted to take some photos along the coast. From what they said, they were heading down toward Seal Rocks Cove. The last time Walt and I drove that strip, we had spotty cell reception."

"And you have no idea who this woman might be? Hunny couldn't describe her?"

Danielle arched her brow at the chief. "Hunny is a dog."

The chief chuckled. "Yeah, you're right. Silly question—and the fact the dog is the one who told Walt about her in the first place, well, nothing silly or strange about that."

"Come on, Chief, you have to admit it makes our lives more interesting."

"I suppose." The chief stood up. "You promised to feed me?"

"Oh, one more thing. Not sure I should mention it, but I think you should know." Danielle went on to tell him what Elizabeth Sparks had told her about the possible stalker.

COLIN WAITED for the police chief to leave before coming downstairs. When he reached the bottom of the staircase and stepped onto the first-floor landing, he spied Walt coming out of the kitchen. When Walt noticed him, he paused a moment.

"There are some sandwiches left in the kitchen, if you're hungry," Walt told him.

"Thank you, but I'm still full from breakfast."

"I'm surprised, you barely ate anything," Walt said, not mentioning he had noticed Colin sneaking Hunny his bacon.

Colin shrugged. "You'll discover that when you get older, one of the things to go is your appetite."

"I don't see me ever losing my appetite for Danielle's double fudge chocolate cake," Walt said with a grin and then added, "Or Old Salts cinnamon rolls."

Colin chuckled and said, "We consume some things not to sate our hunger, but our desire."

"True," Walt agreed. "What are your plans today?"

"I thought I would take Danielle up on her offer to help decorate Christmas cookies. It's been years since I've done that. Sounds like fun."

"Considering how many sugar cookies she baked, she is going to need all the help she can get if she wants them all decorated. I think Heather and Lily are coming over later to help."

"You aren't going to decorate any?" Colin asked.

"No, I thought I would use this opportunity to work a little on my new book."

———

WHEN COLIN WALKED into the kitchen, he found Danielle sitting at the table with a young boy whom he knew to be Evan MacDonald, the police chief's eight-year-old son. On the table was a baking sheet filled with sugar cookies, some decorated with colored frosting and sprinkles, while the others waited their turn. Cookie shapes varied: Christmas trees, angels, stars, candy canes, and gingerbread-men-shaped cookies.

Danielle looked up to Colin and smiled. "Have you come to join us?"

"I have, if that's alright," Colin said, approaching the table.

"Certainly." She looked at Evan and added, "Evan, this is Mr. Bari, one of our guests staying with us through Christmas. Mr. Bari, this is Evan."

"Nice to meet you, Evan," Colin said, extending a hand to the young boy. "But please, you must call me Colin. I don't believe one should be so formal when decorating Christmas cookies."

Evan smiled up at the elderly man, shook his hand, and said, "Hello." When the handshake ended, Colin took a seat at the table.

"I thought Hunny would be in here waiting for something to fall on the floor," Colin said, glancing around for the dog.

"Walt told Hunny she had to stay out of the kitchen while we decorated cookies. Sugar is not good for her," Evan told him.

"Did he now? How obedient of Hunny to listen to Walt," Colin said with a chuckle.

Danielle and Evan exchanged quick glances, and Danielle changed the subject.

THEY HAD BEEN DECORATING cookies and chatting for about thirty minutes when Danielle received a phone call she needed to take. Telling Evan and Colin she would be back shortly, she left the kitchen.

"I imagine you are looking forward to Christmas," Colin asked Evan.

"Yes. But when I told Danielle I wish Christmas would just get here, she told me not to wish away the days. She said I should try to enjoy every day of Christmas week."

"Good advice. If you wished the time away, you wouldn't be decorating cookies now," Colin noted.

Evan grinned up at Colin. "Yes. And my grandma is going to take me shopping like she took my brother. And Danielle and Walt are having a Christmas Eve party, and Lily and Ian are having a party too! So I guess she was right. I would not want to miss all that."

"As you get older, Evan, you will notice how quickly time moves by. So tell me, what do you want Santa to bring you this year?"

"Santa?" Evan asked hesitantly.

In a whisper Colin said, "I understand some children stop believing in Santa as they grow up. Which in my opinion is just as foolish as wishing away your days."

"My older brother doesn't believe in Santa Claus anymore," Evan told him.

Colin arched his brow. "He doesn't?"

Evan shook his head.

"And what do you believe?"

"I haven't asked my dad about it…" Evan confessed.

"But what do you believe?"

Evan set the cookie he had been decorating down on a paper plate and looked up seriously to Colin. "There are other things my brother doesn't believe in—that I know are real. So I kinda think he could be wrong. What do you think?"

"Are you asking me if I believe in Santa Claus?" Colin asked.

Evan nodded.

"Between you and me—I know without a doubt there is a Santa Claus. Of course, just like other things some people believe in—like ghosts, for instance—"

Evan's eyes widened. "Ghosts?"

"Yes, ghosts. Some people believe in ghosts; some don't. Personally, I believe in ghosts. Yet I also know that some people who believe in them have it all wrong."

"All wrong how?"

Colin shrugged. "Take ghost stories, for example. The ghosts portrayed are often evil or scary. A ghost, in my opinion, is nothing more than the unleashed spirit of a person who has died, therefore will be no more evil or scary than the person was when alive."

"That's what I believe!" Evan said excitedly.

Colin smiled. "And then there are angels—"

"Angels?" Evan asked.

"Yes. I believe in angels. But unlike some people who believe in angels, I don't imagine they have wings or play the harp. I suppose some play the harp. Some might also play the guitar, but not all of them."

"My mother is an angel," Evan said.

"Your mother died?"

Evan nodded.

"I'm sorry. I bet she is an angel and looks after you and your brother," Colin suggested.

"That's what my dad says."

"So tell me, Evan, you never answered my question. What would you like Santa to bring you for Christmas?"

"What I really want for Christmas, I don't believe it's something Santa can bring me."

"Don't underestimate the magic of Christmas," Colin insisted.

"I'd like to spend Christmas with my mom, and my dad, and my brother. Just the four of us. Like when I was real little. I'd be happy if we could have just one more Christmas together."

"I don't see where that is out of the realm of possibility—not for Santa," Colin said.

"Maybe in a dream hop…" Evan muttered under his breath.

"Dream hop?" Colin asked.

Evan blushed. "Nothing. I am just being silly."

"No, please, explain this dream hop."

"It's when a spirit can visit you in your dreams. But Mom has moved on, and where she is now, it's harder for her to dream hop—especially to a dream where my brother and Dad are in—I mean really there."

Colin studied Evan and then smiled. "That is very interesting."

"But we all know Santa can't do stuff like that. He makes toys in the North Pole with his elves, but I don't think he can make a dream hop," Evan said.

"Ahh…that's what I was talking about earlier."

"What do you mean?" Evan asked.

"There is definitely a Santa Claus, but like every person from history, stories and legends about them can spring up—some which originate from a grain of truth, others pure fantasy. In the case of Santa Claus, those stories do no harm—in fact, they add to the magic of Christmas."

"I don't understand." Evan frowned.

"Do you know where the name Santa Claus comes from?" Colin asked.

Evan shook his head.

"I am sure you have heard of Saint Nicholas?" Colin asked.

"Yes. That's Santa's other name."

"Correct." Colin nodded. "The Dutch translation for Saint Nicholas is Sint Nikolass, which became the nickname Sinterklass. From that nickname came Santa Claus."

"Is Santa Dutch?" Evan asked.

"No. He isn't. Santa Claus is Greek."

"Santa is Greek?" Danielle asked when she walked back into the kitchen.

Colin smiled up at her as she walked to the table. "Yes, he is. Evan and I were just discussing Santa Claus and some of the misconceptions about him."

"Eddy doesn't believe in Santa anymore," Evan told Danielle as she sat back down at the table. "But Colin and I do."

Danielle flashed Colin a smile and then looked back at Evan. "I believe too."

"And what do you want Santa to bring you this year?" Colin asked Danielle.

"Me? Actually, I have about everything I have ever wanted."

"Surely there is one thing you would like?" Colin asked.

Danielle glanced to the window facing Pearl's house. "Maybe Santa could figure out some way to make our neighbor less cranky. It would be wonderful if she could soften up a little to Hunny and Max."

TWENTY-FOUR

D anielle was cookied out. She sat on the sofa in the living room, telling herself she didn't want to eat anything sugary for the rest of her life—or at least until tomorrow. Heather and Lily had come over to Marlow House not long after Danielle had told Colin her wish for Christmas. They had come to decorate cookies. Colin stuck around for about thirty more minutes before he excused himself and left the rest of the undecorated cookies to the women and Evan.

The chief had picked up Evan after work, and Lily and Heather had helped Danielle clean up the kitchen and put the cookies away. When they finished cleaning the kitchen, Ian came over to Marlow House with Connor, and they all decided to order pizza for dinner. They invited Colin and Owen to join them, but the men had other plans. Colin had invited Owen out to dinner at Pier Café.

Marie arrived around the same time as the pizza, and she spent her time playing with Connor on the baby blanket, which had been spread out on the floor near the Christmas tree, while the others ate pizza.

"It was fun today, but I ate entirely too many cookies," Danielle told them. Next to her on the sofa sat Walt, a paper plate with a slice of pizza on his lap.

"I ate too much frosting," Heather groaned.

"I imagine Evan is going to be bouncing off the walls tonight,"

Lily said with a chuckle. They all laughed.

"That Colin is sure a nice man," Heather said.

"Yes, he is," Danielle agreed. "But I heard him say something funny to Evan."

Marie looked up from where she sat with Connor on the baby blanket on the floor. "What's that?"

"I heard him tell Evan that Santa Claus was Greek."

"Greek? I always pictured Santa Scandinavian. Probably Norwegian," Heather said.

"Why Norwegian?" Lily asked.

"Think about it. Norway is close to the North Pole," Heather pointed out.

"Actually, Colin is right. Santa is Greek," Ian corrected.

Heather looked to Ian and frowned. "What are you talking about? That jolly man with the sparkling blue eyes, ruddy red cheeks and bowl of jelly belly is not Greek."

"I am talking about the real Santa Claus—Saint Nicholas. I suspect that's who Colin was referring to," Ian said.

"Ahh, Saint Nicholas who inspired the Santa Claus legend," Lily said.

"Yes," Ian said with a nod. "According to some historians, Saint Nicholas was Greek. He was born in a little port city on the Mediterranean Sea."

"That's where Colin said he was born!" Danielle interjected.

"Which might explain why he told Evan what he did. I imagine he's probably more familiar than most with the story of Saint Nicholas, considering he was born in the region," Ian pointed out. "I've read that historians often disagree about what is actually true in regard to the legend of Saint Nicholas. Much of the recorded history has been lost. So we rely on tales that have been passed down over time."

"The story I remember," Lily began, "Nicholas—before he was Saint Nicholas—inherited a fortune after his parents died, and he gave much of it—if not all of it—away to the poor. There was one story about three daughters. Their father couldn't afford a dowry, so it looked as if they were doomed to prostitution."

"Why in the world would that lead to prostitution?" Heather asked.

"Because in those days," Ian reminded her, "a woman couldn't easily get a respectable job to support herself. She needed to get married, and if her father couldn't afford to pay a dowry, then there was a chance she would remain unmarried, and when the father's money ran out, prostitution might be the only way she could survive."

"That's sick!" Heather gasped. "So what did Saint Nicholas do?"

"According to the legend, he gave the father money to pay the daughters' dowries. One story says he put the gold in the girls' stockings when they put them out to dry at night. Which is why we leave stockings on the fireplace for Santa to fill. Or so goes the legend," Lily explained.

"Saint Nicholas is also the patron saint of sailors," Walt added.

They all turned to him. "He is?" Danielle asked.

Walt nodded. "Yes, according to legend, he was traveling to the Holy Land when the ship was caught in a storm. Saint Nicholas supposedly admonished the storm, and it then subsided, saving everyone on board. It was considered a miracle. My grandfather told me that story."

"I think the most bizarre story I read about Saint Nicholas was how he resurrected the bodies of three children who had been butchered and pickled—to be sold off as ham," Ian said.

"Ewww! I could have gone forever without hearing that story," Heather cringed. "It is Christmastime, not Halloween!"

Ian shrugged. "Well, he did bring them back to life, so it had a good ending. And I will confess, I found that story on Wikipedia."

"What were you doing looking up Santa Claus on Wikipedia?" Danielle asked.

"I was looking for ideas for family Christmas traditions, and I ended up on Santa's Wikipedia page," Ian explained.

"For an article you're working on?" Heather asked.

"No." Ian shook his head. "But it is Connor's first Christmas, and I wanted to get some ideas. Some tradition we can start as a family this year."

"Did you find anything interesting?" Walt asked.

"I did, on another author's blog post. Her name is Bobbi Holmes. Not sure what she writes. But in one of her posts she talked about a Christmas family diary. On Christmas night, each member of her family writes a page that goes into the family Christmas diary. They write about what happened that year—the kids might just write about what they did for Christmas. When her children were small, they contributed drawings instead of writing anything. While Connor has a few years before he can draw a picture, much less write, I think this year his contribution might be hand prints and a photo."

"So you are going to do it?" Danielle asked.

"Yes. Lily and I plan to start a Christmas diary this year."

"THANKS FOR THE DINNER," Owen told Colin as the two men sat at a booth in Pier Café.

"Thanks for coming with me," Colin said as he toyed with his cup of coffee.

"But you didn't order anything," Owen said, "I feel funny letting you pay for my dinner."

Colin laughed. "I'm afraid I ate entirely too many cookies this afternoon. I'm not hungry. But I did think it would be nice to get out."

"So how did the cookie decorating go?" Owen asked.

"It was fun. You should have joined us."

Owen shrugged. "I just don't feel that Christmassy this year."

"Is it the pending divorce?" Colin asked.

Owen let out a sigh and sat back in the bench seat. "You have never been married, have you? I mean, priests can't marry, and I just assume you weren't married before you became a priest."

"No. I have never been married. But as a priest, I have counseled couples who had problems."

"Well, I don't really want—or need help with my marriage. Fact is, I know ending it is the best thing for me."

"And for your wife?" he asked.

Owen shrugged. "She is already living with someone else. In fact, she started seeing him before we ever separated."

"So what do you want to do now?" Colin asked.

"When I get home, I have to file for divorce. My wife hasn't yet. I think she is waiting for me to do it. And I will admit, I was waiting for her to serve me."

"Now that you are resigned to the fact your marriage is over, what do you want to do with your life?"

"I guess just move on. Go back to work when I get home. Like I have been doing since she walked out the door."

"Why are you here?" Colin asked.

Owen shifted uncomfortably in the seat. "You see…"

"Well, hello!" A woman's voice interrupted their conversation. Colin and Owen looked up from the table and found Marcella standing over them, her husband by her side.

"Hello," Owen said.

"We wondered how you were doing," Marcella said. "Do you mind if we sit down for a minute?" Not waiting for a reply, Marcella scooted into the booth next to Owen, pushing him to the end of the bench seat.

Colin glanced at Forrest, who stood in awkward silence. He then scooted over and motioned for Forrest to sit down.

"So tell us, how has it been staying at Marlow House?" Marcella asked.

"They are very nice over there. Beautiful home and the breakfasts have been great," Owen said.

"How much extra for breakfast?" Forrest asked.

Owen shrugged. "Nothing. Right, Colin?"

In response Colin gave Forrest a smile.

"I'm not sure what kind of deal Mrs. Crabtree worked out with the Marlows, but she said it wouldn't cost us anything, just what we were paying the motel. She told us breakfast would be included with the rooms, and so far, they have also invited us to join them for other meals," Owen explained.

"But not dinner tonight?" Forrest asked.

"We don't want to take advantage of them," Colin said. "After all, they are no longer running an inn. Owen and I thought we would have dinner here tonight, and let them visit with their friends."

"It's really nice over there," Owen said. "I have to say, it was a bit of good luck to have plumbing problems."

"I would love to go over and see what it looks like inside. I'm so disappointed it isn't a bed and breakfast anymore," Marcella said.

"There are lots of interior pictures of the house online," Colin pointed out.

Marcella forced a smile and then looked back at Owen and asked, "Are you two the only guests staying over there?"

"No. Their friend Chris Johnson and his brother are staying with them. Chris's house burned down."

"I did hear something about that," Marcella said. "So that's all?"

"Walt and Danielle, of course," Owen added.

"So what does everyone do all day? Just hang around the house? It must get kind of boring," she asked.

"Today Chris and his brother are out doing some sightseeing. Colin here helped decorate Christmas cookies."

"Oh, how fun." Marcella smiled sweetly.

"They're having a Christmas Eve party at Marlow House, and they are also hosting Christmas dinner there, which we have both been invited to."

"Isn't that nice…" Marcella glanced at her husband.

"Everyone is just hanging around Marlow House most of the time?" Forrest asked.

"Oh, their neighbors across the street are having a Christmas party Saturday evening—night before Christmas Eve. We've been invited to that."

"Are you going to go?" Marcella asked.

"Sure. Might as well," Owen said.

"Gee, I wish our plumbing broke. Sounds like you two are having a great time over there. Much more fun than a room at the Seahorse Motel."

TWENTY MINUTES later Marcella and Forrest sat alone in a booth at Pier Café.

"If all goes well, we will be out of here by Christmas Eve," Marcella told her husband.

"How do you figure that?" he asked.

"Didn't you hear what he said? Everyone is going to the neighbor's for a Christmas party on Saturday. When they are all over there, we can come through the alleyway, enter the kitchen door, and find what we are looking for," Marcella told Forrest.

"I just hope it's still there."

"Don't even say that," she admonished. "It is going to be there. You really need to be more positive."

"How can you say that?"

"Because you need to look on the bright side. I have a key to the house. The dog loves me. And they are all going to be across the street on Saturday."

TWENTY-FIVE

C hris finally returned Danielle's call on Wednesday evening, but she was in the bathroom and missed it. He left her a message telling her he and Noah were just going into a movie, and he would be turning his phone off, and they would not be home until after midnight. When initially leaving Chris a message to call her, Danielle had failed to tell him why she wanted to talk to him, so he assumed she had simply been checking to see when they would be home. Resigned to the fact she would not be able to ask Chris about the woman until the next morning, Danielle went to bed before midnight.

On Thursday morning, Noah and Chris slept in and missed breakfast. The moment Chris stepped out of his bedroom—wearing flannel pajama bottoms and no shirt—Danielle dragged him into the parlor and shut the door.

"Good morning to you too," Chris said as he found himself pushed into a chair facing the sofa. "I guess I missed breakfast?"

Before Danielle could respond, Walt walked into the parlor, shutting the door behind him. He curiously eyed Chris's bare chest and asked dryly, "You couldn't have let him get dressed first?"

Danielle shrugged. "He can get dressed later. After we talk to him." She then looked Chris's ridiculously ripped chest up and down. "Anyway, I'm enjoying the view." She glanced back to her husband and was met with a frown.

"What?" Danielle asked innocently. "Weren't you the one who said he enjoyed looking at beautiful women? I'm just looking too."

Walt rolled his eyes. "Fine. But no touching."

"Hey! I am sitting right here, you know," Chris grumbled. "You two are making me feel like a slab of meat. I feel so used!"

"Poor pretty boy," Walt said with a sigh as he sat on the sofa next to Danielle. He picked up the throw pillow and tossed it to Chris. "Here, you can cover up with this."

Chris grabbed the pillow and said, "Why did you drag me in here? I can't believe it is just to harass me."

"Sorry, Chris," Danielle said sheepishly. "I couldn't resist. But, we really do have something we need to ask you. In fact, that's why I called you yesterday."

Chris frowned. Before he could ask what it was, Walt said in a serious tone, "We know who the woman was who broke into Marlow House."

"Who?" Chris asked.

"The woman Hunny went crazy over downtown on Tuesday," Danielle explained.

With a look of confusion, Chris glanced from Walt to Danielle. "How do you know that?"

"Hunny told me," Walt said.

"I can't believe that," Chris said as he leaned back in his chair.

"Why not?" Danielle asked.

"Because of how Hunny responded to her. Like she was a long-lost friend. Not like she was an intruder who locked her in the hallway."

"Hunny wants to be loved," Walt told him. "And she always gets her feelings hurt when people respond negatively to how she looks—she is very self-conscious about it. It's obvious that when this woman broke in and found herself faced with a pit bull, she must have been soft-spoken with her—treated her in a way Hunny perceived as loving. She is not going to start snarling at her now."

"I originally got Hunny because I didn't want to hire a body-guard. I opted instead for a guard dog."

"You need to get over that idea. You don't have a guard dog. Although, if you were threatened, I don't doubt Hunny would rise to the occasion. She might want to be loved, but I imagine she would do whatever was necessary to protect you if she perceived real danger," Walt said.

"Really?" Danielle asked with a frown. "You honestly believe that? Have you seen how Bella can make her cower?"

Walt shrugged. "I'm trying to be optimistic."

Danielle looked back to Chris. "We need you to tell us everything you remember about that woman."

"Noah saw her too," Chris reminded them.

"Your brother hasn't come down this morning yet. I think he's still sleeping," Walt said.

"We got in pretty late last night."

"So what can you tell us?" Danielle urged. "Tell us everything you remember. Don't leave out any detail."

"Well…let me see…" Chris closed his eyes for a moment and tried to visualize the encounter. He opened his eyes and looked at Danielle. "She was probably in her late fifties. Maybe early sixties. Long gray hair. Past her shoulders. She was with a man. He had a mustache, wore glasses and a baseball cap—a green one. Umm… let's see…they had just walked out of Lucy's Diner."

"This was right before you came into Adam's office, right?" Danielle asked.

"Yeah. Just a couple of minutes before."

"I know who they are!" Danielle told them.

"Who?" Walt and Chris asked in unison.

"It's the couple who took care of Eloise Winterborne. Elizabeth pointed them out to us. She mentioned their names, but I can't remember what they were. Why in the world would she be breaking into Marlow House?"

"Who is Eloise Winterborne?" Chris asked.

"She was a wealthy woman from Astoria who passed away about six months ago. Walt and I purchased a few things from her estate when we were at Astoria the other day."

"Obviously they came here to get whatever you bought from the estate," Chris said.

Danielle frowned. "No. That can't be. We bought a couple of silly things for the white elephant gift exchange. Nothing valuable."

Chris arched a brow at Danielle. "Why else would she break into your house?"

"How would she even know we have them?" Danielle asked.

"Let's see these things you bought," Chris said.

With a sigh, Danielle reluctantly stood up and walked over to the desk. She picked up the blue-green bag with the mermaid logo and carried it to Chris. She handed him the sack and then returned to her seat with Walt on the sofa. They watched silently as Chris removed the items from the bag. First the shoe.

"Lovely," Chris said dryly, turning the Christmas shoe from side to side in his hand. "You were really going to give this to one of us?"

"If you were lucky, you'd be the one to get it," Walt teased.

Chris looked closer at the gemstones on the shoe. "These don't look real, so I don't think they're after this."

He set the shoe down and pulled out the framed picture.

"That we decided not to give at the white elephant party," Danielle told him. "The man holding the fish, that's Adam's great-grandfather. We're giving it to Adam."

"Nice. And you got this from the Winterborne estate?" Chris asked with a frown.

"I assume Eloise picked it up at a yard sale. From what we've been told, she frequented yard sales. Walt recognized Marie's father in the picture."

"I don't see anything worth breaking in for—unless I'm missing something," Chris said, reexamining the frame. "Unless…"

"What?" Danielle asked.

"Maybe something is hidden behind the picture. People hide things in frames. Maybe money, a stock certificate, some important document," Chris suggested.

"I really don't want to take the frame apart," Danielle said. "I'm afraid it might damage the photograph, considering it seems to be stuck to the glass along the edge."

"I can remove the back without disturbing the photograph or glass," Chris promised.

"Okay…I guess," Danielle said reluctantly. She and Walt sat quietly and watched as Chris lifted off the back of the frame.

A moment later Chris shook his head and said, "Nothing. Just the photograph." He reassembled the frame and then slipped it back in the sack with the shoe.

Danielle glanced at her watch. "I wonder if Mermaid Curio is open yet."

"Why?" Walt asked.

"I think I need to have a little chat with Bud Darrel."

"GOOD MORNING, Mermaid Curio, how can I help you?" came a man's voice on the other end of the phone.

"Can I speak to Bud Darrel?" Danielle asked.

"This is Bud speaking. How can I help you?"

"Hello, Bud, this is Danielle Marlow. My husband and I were in your shop on Saturday—"

"Of course! I remember. Have you reconsidered that antique trunk? It's still here."

"Umm…no. But I was wondering, do you have any more items from the Winterborne estate?"

"Like I told you, I only bid on the trunk."

"I was talking about the things that were in the trunk."

"I'm afraid those all went to the thrift store. I suppose they might still have them. Fact is, you were the only ones who showed any interest in those things, aside from the Hoopers."

"The Hoopers?" Danielle asked excitedly.

"Yes, they were the caretakers for Mrs. Winterborne. They stopped into the shop after you were here and wanted to pick up something for sentimental sake. I feel a little bad about it…"

"What do you mean?" Danielle asked.

"When they were here, I told them everything from the trunk was sitting on the counter, aside from what you bought. It wasn't until the next day I found a couple of things I had taken from the trunk and set in the rolling cart I use. Forgot all about that. The Hoopers didn't seem that interested in any of the remaining items. After I found the other things, I tried calling them. I was just going to give them the stuff if they wanted it, but they moved out of the room they were renting and left town. I don't have their phone number."

"Do you know what the other items were?" Danielle asked. "The things you took out of the trunk that we didn't see?"

"One of those puzzle boxes and an ugly statue. Also some pottery. I thought they might want the pottery. It had Mrs. Winterborne's initials on it. I think she made it. Figured that might be something they would want to keep for sentimental reasons."

"One more thing, did the Hoopers know we bought something from the estate?" Danielle asked.

"Yes. They asked who bought the missing items from the trunk. The card you had given me was sitting here. I gave it to them—I hope that was okay."

"That's fine..." Danielle looked over to Walt and Chris, who sat quietly, watching and listening.

"I just figured if they really wanted whatever you bought, they could contact you and offer to buy it. Didn't figure you were that invested in either item since you were buying them more for gag gifts."

"Did they say they might call and offer to buy them?" Danielle asked.

"No. In fact, after they saw what was on the counter from the trunk, they lost interest and just left. But they did take your card with them."

"Thank you. I appreciate your help."

"Is there some problem?" he asked.

"No. I just wondered if there were any items left from the trunk. Walt and I still need to pick up a few things for the white elephant gift exchange, and we were thinking of maybe driving over to Astoria," she lied. "One more thing, what thrift shop did you take the things to?"

WHEN DANIELLE GOT off the phone a few minutes later, she looked at Walt and Chris and said, "I didn't get their first names—but their last name is Hooper. And they did know we bought some items from the estate. But I don't think we have what they are looking for."

"Why do you say that?" Walt asked.

"I don't think anyone is going to break in to steal that shoe or picture of Adam's great-grandfather. I have a feeling whatever they are looking for was taken to the thrift store."

"Noah and I were planning to drive to Astoria today. Apparently my brother is a *Goonies* fan and wants to see the house. You want me to stop by the thrift store when we're over there? See if they know what came over from the gift shop from the Winterborne estate—see if any of it was sold. Buy what they have?"

"Like a treasure hunt?" Danielle asked.

TWENTY-SIX

Danielle stood on Elizabeth Sparks's front porch, holding a tin of cookies. She rang the doorbell. Several minutes later the door opened.

"Danielle, what a surprise!" Elizabeth greeted her.

"I'm really sorry to just barge in like this without calling first," Danielle said, holding out the tin. "But I thought maybe you'd forgive me for some chocolate drop cookies."

Elizabeth laughed and accepted the tin. "Hey, chocolate is my weakness. Please come in." Elizabeth opened the door wider. Just as Danielle stepped into the living room, she noticed an older man walking out from the kitchen.

"Danielle, this is my dad. My parents got here about fifteen minutes ago."

"Oh, gee, now I really am sorry for just barging in without calling first," Danielle said.

"No problem," Elizabeth assured her. She then looked at her father and said, "Dad, this is my friend Danielle Marlow. She owns Marlow House. Remember, I told you about her. She's the one who donated the rooms for the fundraiser."

"Nice to meet you, Mr. Sparks," Danielle said, extending her hand in greeting.

"Nice to meet any friend of my daughter's," he said, shaking her hand. "But please, call me Jim."

Several minutes later Mrs. Sparks walked into the room and there were more introductions. Ten minutes later, Danielle sat alone in the living room with Elizabeth while Mr. and Mrs. Sparks went to the guest bedroom to finish unpacking.

"Before my mother comes back, I wanted to ask, please don't say anything about the stalker," Elizabeth whispered.

"You haven't told her?" Danielle asked.

Elizabeth shook her head. "No. The more I think about it, I just overreacted. As far as I know, that man might have been visiting one of my neighbors when I saw him in front of the house. I know the people across the street have family for the holidays, and some of them are staying at a local motel. So maybe he's just some cousin of theirs that I happened to see when he is coming or going."

"I did say something to the chief about it when I saw him yesterday," Danielle said with a cringe.

"That's okay. He called me last night, asked me about it. We talked, and he agreed, it was probably nothing. After all, Frederickport is small, and if one of my neighbors has visiting relatives, it would not be unusual to run into them downtown."

"But I suppose it is always a good thing to be aware of what is going on around us," Danielle noted.

"So tell me, are you just delivering cookies, or did you want to talk to me about something?"

"I want to ask you about the Hoopers," Danielle whispered.

Elizabeth frowned. "Marcella and Forrest?"

"I guess that's their name." Danielle glanced to the hallway leading to the guest room and back to Elizabeth.

"What about them?"

"I'm going to tell you something and ask you, please don't tell anyone I told you."

Elizabeth's eyes widened. "Okay. What?"

"I can't tell you how I know, but Marcella Hooper broke into Marlow House. I think she might have broken in twice."

"Broke into your house? Why?"

"That's what I'm trying to find out," Danielle explained.

"Are you sure it was her? I know they got really snotty with me after they found out they hadn't been mentioned in the will, but I just can't imagine Marcella doing something like that. And why?"

"All I can tell you, someone—who for his own reasons does not want to come forward—saw her in our house."

"You say she broke in twice?" Elizabeth asked.

"The first time was when Chris's house was on fire. When we got home, we walked in and found the first floor of Marlow House ransacked. Someone had gone through all the rooms on the first floor. It was like they were looking for something. But we haven't noticed anything missing. In fact, there was some money sitting out, and it was not touched."

"And someone saw Marcella in the house then?" Elizabeth asked.

Danielle shook her head. "No. But then later, someone saw her going through some packages in our downstairs bedroom. They were recent purchases Heather had picked up for Chris. We think Chris's dog might have scared her off that time—but we know she was in the house."

"But why?"

"We think she was looking for what we bought from the estate when we were in Astoria. I talked to the shop owner, and he confirmed they had been in the shop wanting to look through the items, and they knew we had bought some things."

"That doesn't even make sense. Why would they want a deco-rated shoe?" Elizabeth asked.

"It was a shoe and a framed picture. But I don't think we have what they were looking for—I think they think we have it. But according to the shop owner, there were some items from the trunk he had forgotten about—that they didn't see when they were in the shop. I think they were there to get one of those items. I'm just trying to figure out what it is—and why they want it."

Elizabeth leaned back on the sofa and shook her head. "This is all kinds of bizarre."

"That's why I wanted to talk to you. Did Eloise have anything of value that the Hoopers might have wanted—something they would be willing to break in Marlow House to get?"

"Like I told you before, I never went into Eloise's house. But I know people who knew her, and they all said the same thing, she had a lot of useless junk. Oh, I guess some of the furniture was pretty nice—that all belonged to her husband's family—but nothing that someone could walk off with. Aside from some of the furniture, I don't think she had anything of real value. From what I heard, her husband's family was frugal—they didn't have nice silver or china. Of course, antique china is not really worth much these days. You can pick up anything on eBay for practically nothing."

"I heard she had a valuable engagement ring," Danielle said.

"Ahh, yes. I forgot about that. It was beautiful. Quite stunning, and I heard it was worth a fortune. Eloise always wore it, but then her arthritis got so bad that she couldn't wear it anymore. I think that is why she sold it."

"I heard she was afraid the Hoopers were going to steal it," Danielle said.

Elizabeth laughed. "That was not going to happen. Eloise had her attorney hire a firm that inventoried the house every year—just to make sure all her precious things were still there. Personally, I think the Hoopers were relieved when she sold that ring."

"Why do you say that?" Danielle asked.

"If she had lost it, she might have blamed them for taking it. But Eloise sold it, informed her attorney, told them to take it off the inventory list."

"And that was the only thing of value she had?" Danielle asked.

"Unless, of course, Eloise managed to pick up some priceless artifact at some yard sale. Something the Hoopers realized had value. I suppose that is always possible," Elizabeth suggested.

"If that was the case, then why not take it after she died, and before the executor came in to sell everything off?"

Elizabeth smiled at Danielle. "Eloise was a sweet little lady—but she had her peculiar quirks."

"Yes, you mentioned that."

"One was her obsessive need to inventory all her belongings. Each week, after returning from a yard sale, Eloise would have Marcella photograph all of her purchases and then fax them to the attorney to add to her inventory."

"Seriously?" Danielle asked.

"The Winterborne estate was worth a fortune, and her lawyer bent over backwards to keep her happy. So if she did pick up something at a yard sale, the Hoopers couldn't just walk off with it later. They would need to explain where it went."

"But after Eloise died, would the executor really care about all that junk she bought from yard sales?" Danielle asked.

"From what I heard, Eloise's executor went out of his way to follow her instructions down to the last detail. There was a lot of money involved—and the executor would be getting a hefty share for his work. If some long-lost relative showed up to claim a portion of the estate, he did not want anyone to raise doubts as to how he handled things. From what I understood, if the Hoopers wanted anything—even if it was a chipped coffee cup—they would have to bid for it at auction like everyone else."

The next moment Mrs. Sparks walked into the room carrying a plate of cookies. "I thought you and your friend might like a little snack." She set the plate on the coffee table.

Danielle looked down at the bar cookies and smiled. "Are those Magic Bar cookies?"

"They are," Elizabeth said, picking up the plate. She offered one to Danielle as her mother took a seat in a nearby chair.

"We were just talking about these yesterday," Danielle said as she took a cookie.

"You were?" Elizabeth asked as she took one for herself and then set the plate back on the table.

"Yes. We were decorating sugar cookies yesterday," Danielle explained. "In fact, after we were done, I swore I was never having anything sweet again." She then took a bite and said, "I lied."

"Magic Bar cookies are sort of our family's traditional Christmas cookie," Elizabeth explained. "It can't be Christmas if we don't have Magic Bar cookies."

"It's just because I'm not much of a baker," Mrs. Sparks said. "And these are easy to make."

OVER IN ASTORIA, Cindy Mae was helping her older sister, June, at the thrift store when two men walked in the front door.

"Oh my gawd, June," Cindy Mae gasped under her breath as she grabbed hold of her sister's wrist.

"What is it?" June frowned, glancing in the direction her sister was staring.

"Look what just walked in. Oh my gawd, who are they?" Cindy Mae groaned.

"Gorgeous, that's what they are. They have to be brothers," June said.

"One for each of us. I am taking the younger one," Cindy Mae said, finally releasing hold of her sister's wrist. The two women immediately stood up a little straighter, quickly combed their fingers through their hair in an attempt to neaten their appearance, and pasted smiles on their faces while readjusting their stances to best display their figures.

"Hello, may I help you?" Cindy Mae purred when the men reached the counter.

"Hi," the younger-looking one said with a smile, showing off straight white teeth. "I understand Mermaid Curio sent some stuff over here the other day—from the Winterborne estate auction?"

Cindy Mae leaned over the counter toward the men, propping her hands along the counter's edge as she attempted to reveal some cleavage. "Yeah. But it was a bunch of junk. We haven't put it out yet. I bet I can find you something else you would really like."

TWENTY-SEVEN

A tightly fitting black baseball cap replaced Pearl's favorite cloche hat. She felt it a more sensible choice for what she needed to do. It would better shield her from the afternoon sun while she made the necessary repairs. The cap would also prevent wisps of her shortly cut gray hair from straying into her eyes, something she found exceedingly annoying. She wore denim overalls and a black turtleneck sweater. She had intended to replace her tennis shoes for her work boots with the thick tread soles, but when she realized they were upstairs, she decided not to go up to fetch them —a decision she would come to regret.

Pearl dragged the ladder from the toolshed to the front of her house, grumbling all the way about the crook she had paid to hang her Christmas lights. She had called him about the drooping strand of lights, leaving a message on his machine. He had only called her back this morning, and that was to tell her it would cost her fifty bucks for him to come back to fix the lights. According to him, he couldn't be responsible for wind damage.

"There was no wind damage," Pearl said with a curse as she propped the ladder along the front of the house. "We haven't even had any wind! Stupid man just did a poor job the first time. If he thinks I'm going to pay him to fix his mistake, he's crazy!"

After steadying the ladder, Pearl returned to the toolshed to gather what she would need to make the necessary repairs. Several minutes later, she returned to the ladder and started up its rungs, making her way to the eaves along her two-storied house's roofline.

FLEECE SWEATPANTS and sweatshirts had been Heather's mode of attire during her Christmas break from work. Today she wore a quirky green pair adorned with reindeer that she had purchased online. They looked more like pajamas than street wear, but she didn't care, since she was only taking a short walk down her street to Marlow House. Before dressing that morning, she had pulled her raven-colored hair into two long braids; they fell past her shoulders and were still neat and tightly woven when she stepped out of the door that afternoon.

Heather carried a brown paper bag filled with freshly made tamales in one hand while she started down her front steps. Before reaching the sidewalk, she glanced back at her house and noticed her calico, Bella, sitting on the living room windowsill, looking outside. Turning back to the sidewalk, Heather continued up the street.

While passing Pearl's house, Heather noticed a ladder propped up against the front wall. She paused a moment and looked up at her neighbor's roofline. Using her free hand to shade her eyes from the late afternoon sun, she squinted, focusing on the woman standing atop the ladder.

"What are you doing up there?" Heather called out.

The sudden shout startled Pearl, who abruptly turned to Heather. The ladder swayed a moment, but the older woman managed to maintain her balance.

"Don't you have any better sense to know you shouldn't startle people when they are on a ladder!" Pearl shouted down at Heather.

"And don't you have any better sense to know a woman your age shouldn't be up on a ladder!" Heather returned.

"Go mind your own business!" Pearl yelled down before turning back to what she was doing.

With a shake of her head, Heather started back on her way up the street. A moment later she entered Marlow House property through the side gate and then headed to the back door into the kitchen. When she reached the door, she gave a perfunctory knock and was greeted by a, "Come in, door's unlocked."

When Heather walked into Marlow House's kitchen a moment later, she found Danielle at the kitchen table, dicing vegetables. Heather paused a moment and took a deep breath. She smelled the rich enticing aroma of a beef roast cooking.

"Smells wonderful," Heather said as she walked to the kitchen table.

"It's the roast for the shredded beef tacos. You are coming?" Danielle asked.

"Of course." Heather set the paper sack on the table. "I'm contributing homemade tamales for the dinner. Letty Cortez makes them every year with her mother and sisters. I bought a couple of dozen. What is Christmas without tamales?" Heather took a seat at the table.

Danielle peeked up at Heather and said, "Just as long as they aren't crabmeat."

Heather rolled her eyes. Several years earlier the local bank manager had been killed after eating crab tamales. It was not so much that the crabs had been lethal as the bank manager was allergic to shellfish.

"Speaking of killing people," Heather began. "I almost killed Pearl."

"What did she do now?" Danielle asked.

"No. I mean I almost killed her. For real."

Danielle frowned up at Heather.

"That crazy old woman was standing on a ladder, and I yelled at her. I must have startled her. She almost fell off the ladder. Would have snapped her neck."

"That's awful!" Danielle gasped.

Heather cocked her head slightly and asked dryly, "Would it have been? Really? Or did you mean that is awful that she didn't fall off the ladder?"

"Heather! That's horrible!"

Heather broke into a smile and shrugged. "Yeah. I guess it is. And you are right. It would be awful. Can you just imagine her crabby old ghost hanging around and haunting us?"

NOAH AND CHRIS returned to Marlow House about an hour before dinner. They found Danielle and Walt in the living room with Lily, Ian, and Heather. Chris unceremoniously dumped the items they had bought on the game table and then knelt down to greet Hunny.

After a moment Chris asked Lily and Ian, "Where's Connor and Sadie? Is Marie babysitting?"

"She might be over there, keeping an eye on Kelly," Lily said with a chuckle.

"Kelly's babysitting?" Chris asked.

"Joe has to work tonight, so she offered to watch Connor while we come over here. I just think she wanted to see her nephew," Ian said. "She and Joe are spending Christmas Day with Joe's family, and I think she's a little bummed that she won't be spending it with Connor on his first Christmas."

"Oh, she'll be with us at our Christmas party, and I know they are coming to the Christmas Eve here," Lily countered.

A few minutes later everyone gathered at the game table to check out the items Chris and Noah had brought back from the thrift store in Astoria.

"I recognize all this stuff. It was on the counter at the shop when we were there—except for the statue, puzzle box and pottery," Danielle said. "And that's what the owner of the shop claims wasn't on the counter."

"I don't think you'll find what they're looking for here. The statue was not only chipped, it was made in China. And not during the Ming dynasty," Chris told them.

"The puzzle box was also made in China," Noah said. "I took it apart, thinking maybe something was hidden inside, and I didn't find anything."

Chris looked at Danielle and asked, "Did you talk to the chief?"

"Yeah. I told him what we found out. He checked around. They're staying at the Seahorse Motel. They have reservations through Christmas," Danielle explained.

"What's he going to do?" Noah asked.

"What can he do?" Walt asked. "He can't very well go over there and say according to Chris's dog, you broke into Marlow House."

"If they had taken something, then maybe we could claim an anonymous tip said they saw them in the house and then get a search warrant. But as far as I know, they didn't take anything," Danielle said. "So there is nothing to find."

"That's everything?" Lily asked.

"Yes. According to the owner of the store, everything that was in the trunk was sent over to the thrift store—except for the two items we bought," Danielle explained.

"But maybe there was something else taken to the thrift store that wasn't included in what Chris and Noah brought back today," Lily suggested. "One of my mom's friends used to work at her church's thrift shop. I remember her telling us that all the really good stuff was often snatched up by the volunteers taking in the items."

"Only problem with that, the only items the shop owner mentioned the Hoopers hadn't seen were the statue, puzzle box and pottery—and the two we bought," Danielle reminded her.

"Plus, we have a copy of the receipt given to Mermaid Curio," Chris interrupted. He removed a piece of folded paper from his shirt pocket and handed it to Lily. "When the store owner from Mermaid Curio dropped that stuff off, they gave him a detailed receipt for tax purposes. This is a copy of it."

"How did you get this?" Lily asked.

Chris smiled. "The women at the thrift store were accommodating."

"If what that woman is looking for isn't on that table—then it must be one of the items you bought," Ian said. "The most logical place to look is in the frame. People hide things behind photographs."

"I already looked. Only thing in the frame was the photograph," Chris told him.

WHILE THE SHRUBBERY had broken her fall, it had also drenched her once dry clothes. The icy chill permeated Pearl Huckabee's bones. She could not recall ever before feeling this cold. Her ankle throbbed, but that was not her greatest problem. If someone didn't find her soon, she would at the very least die from pneumonia.

Her snotty neighbor's unwelcome shout was not to blame for the fall. That time Pearl had regained her balance. It was not until Heather Donovan had gone into Marlow House and Pearl had reached for one of the loose hooks holding up her Christmas lights that her tennis shoe slipped on the rung of the ladder. Unfortunately she was not able to catch herself, as she had when Heather had surprised her.

After falling to the ground, she had been knocked out—drifting in and out of consciousness. The sun was almost set before she was able to finally keep her eyes open. At first she had been confused, disoriented, trying to figure out where she was and how she had gotten there. Her clothes were wet, icy cold, and something hard was on top of her. She soon identified what that was—the ladder.

It took great effort to push the ladder aside, but finally she was free. Unfortunately, she had neither the strength to pull herself up nor an ankle able to hold her up if she managed to stand. She was fairly certain she had broken a bone. Whenever she tried to move her injured limb, excruciating pain ceased her. This was not how she wished to die. Moving even a few inches made her wince. She had shouted for help, but no one heard her. As the hours went by, her voice left her, as had all hope of being found.

Even if it was not almost dark and someone happened to walk by, they would not see the ladder. It was now hidden among the foliage along the front of her house—as was her injured and nearly freezing body. And if they did come by, they would not hear her shouting—the only sound she now made was a faint raspy plea for help.

Pearl closed her eyes and wrapped her arms around herself in an attempt to provide some warmth. She'd once heard freezing from death was relatively painless. But that was a lie. She ached in every cell. *Perhaps*, she thought hopefully, *that means I am not as close to death as I imagine.*

TWENTY-EIGHT

Danielle had arranged the food on the buffet in the dining room, with the help of her friends. At one end of the buffet were the large paper plates, napkins and silverware. Next were the tortilla warmers, one filled with warm corn tortillas, the other with warm flour tortillas. A large stainless steel pan held the corn tortillas Danielle had fried. Adjacent to the stainless steel pan were two slow cookers, one filled with shredded beef and the other with piping hot refried beans smothered in melted cheddar cheese. Assorted bowls filled the space between the slow cookers and pan with the tamales Heather had brought. They contained shredded cheese, diced onions, chopped tomatoes, shredded cabbage, chopped cilantro, sour cream, guacamole, and salsa.

Walt and Ian helped serve the beverages, which included cold beer, soda and iced tea. Colin and Owen joined them for dinner, and like the rest, they each made their own plate of food. Gathering around the dining room table, the group chatted while enjoying the meal.

"I think we should all share a Christmas story," Lily suggested while unwrapping a tamale.

"What kind of Christmas story?" Danielle asked.

"Something from one of our past Christmases," Lily said. "Something funny…maybe even embarrassing."

"I can tell one," Heather volunteered. Everyone looked her way before she continued. "When I was in fourth grade, I bragged to my entire class about the bike Santa had brought me for Christmas. They all started laughing at me. I wanted to die. I think that is the most embarrassed I have ever been in my entire life."

"Why did they laugh at you?" Lily asked.

Heather turned an *are-you-serious* look at Lily and said, "Because I still believed in Santa."

"They were the ones who were wrong, not you," Colin said. "Just because a person stops believing in Santa doesn't mean Santa's not real."

"I wish I had thought of that back then." Heather looked at Lily and said, "Okay, you must have one."

"Well, if it is something embarrassing, it would have to be the time my mother bought the entire family really dorky-looking matching Christmas pajamas. She made us all wear them to have a family portrait taken—which she used for our Christmas card that year."

Heather shrugged. "So? That doesn't sound embarrassing. Sounds cute."

"I was a sophomore in high school at the time," Lily told her.

They all laughed, and then Colin said, "I have a story."

"Embarrassing or funny?" Heather asked.

"Not really embarrassing or funny—perhaps just memorable," Colin said with a grin. "It was my first time visiting New York. I had some meetings scheduled, one was with a gentlemen who later became a friend. He was involved with the Episcopal church. Clem and I used to have some heated debates on theology. It was right before Christmas, and we decided to share a little Christmas cheer. We ended up writing a very snappy Christmas limerick. Although I will admit, Clem worked out most of the prose, I just gave him the idea of what to write. We were quite proud of ourselves." Colin laughed at the memory.

"Can you sing it?" Lily asked.

"That was a long, long time ago." Colin then looked at Owen and said, "Do you have a Christmas story to share?"

Owen set his half-eaten taco on his plate and looked up. "Christmas story?"

"Something funny or embarrassing from one of your past Christmases," Lily explained.

Owen took a deep breath and considered the question a

moment. "Mine isn't really embarrassing or funny either, but I remember the Christmas my sister and I saw Santa and his sleigh fly over our aunt's house on Christmas Eve."

Chris laughed. "Really?"

"It certainly looked like a sleigh and reindeer back then," Owen said with a grin. "For a long time that's what we believed. Although I don't remember us ever discussing it—I mean after we grew up and stopped believing. It was probably some lights from the airport or something, but in my memory, it sure looked like Santa and his reindeer."

"I rather love that story," Danielle said.

"So do you have one?" Owen asked Danielle.

"What comes to mind is the time my cousin Cheryl and I got tipsy on Christmas Eve. I think we were about twelve at the time."

"Dani!" Lily said with a laugh. "You never told me about that."

Danielle shrugged. "My parents were having their annual Christmas party. My mom and aunt always drank grasshoppers at the party. It was sort of a tradition."

"What is a grasshopper?" Owen asked.

"Sort of a creme de menthe milkshake-like cocktail—at least how Mom and my aunt used to make them. The only booze they have is creme de menthe and creme de cocoa. Anyway, they used to let us have a sip. But this one year Cheryl and I decided we wanted more than a sip, so under the pretense of helping bus dishes, we went around collecting any abandoned grasshopper cocktails—and finishing up what was left in the glasses."

Heather wrinkled her nose. "Yuck. Sounds gross. All those germs."

"Hey, we were twelve," Danielle said with a shrug. "Anyway, on Christmas morning I had my first hangover—at twelve years old," Danielle told them.

"Did you do it again the next year?" Walt asked.

"No. It was years before I had another grasshopper—or anything with alcohol."

WHEN ATTENDING CHURCH, Pearl lowered her head with the rest of the congregation during prayer. But instead of praying, Pearl typically used that time to think about what she planned to do for the rest of the day. After all, God didn't need her telling him what to do. As Pearl felt the darkness surround her, she thought about those times she had not prayed at church.

Lights were on next door at Marlow House. Pearl could see them if she lifted her head. It was dark out. She couldn't spend the night outside; as it was, she had already lost all feeling in her lower extremities. Pearl closed her eyes for a moment and then did something she had not done in years—she began to pray. First she recited the Lord's Prayer, followed by a prayer she had learned as a child. Her prayer turned into a plea until she was begging for his help.

Suddenly a thought came into her head. Pearl stopped pleading and felt around the ground for a rock. Once she found one, she held it tightly in her hand. The hand holding the rock reached to the nearby ladder, gently tapping it. Smiling and feeling hopeful, she tapped the rock against the ladder again, this time louder. It made a pinging sound. Excited, she again hit the rock against the aluminum ladder—and then again and again…

EVERYONE AT MARLOW HOUSE'S dining room table had finished dinner, but they all remained seated, telling Christmas stories. Colin was about to say something when he froze a moment and listened. No one else at the table heard what he had just heard, and none noticed his odd expression. They all continued to talk, oblivious to whatever had captured his attention.

Colin stood abruptly and looked to Danielle. "Do you mind if I help myself to some water in the kitchen?"

"I can get it for you." Danielle started to stand up.

"No, no. Sit down. I need to stretch my legs anyway. I always get a little stiff when I sit too long."

After giving Colin a soft smile, Danielle sat back down as he walked toward the kitchen. No one at the table noticed how he glanced down at Hunny, who had been sleeping by Chris's feet. Hunny woke up and looked at the elderly man. Their eyes met. Colin patted the side of his pant leg. Hunny stood up and followed him out of the room and to the kitchen.

A few minutes later Colin stood alone in the kitchen with the dog. He looked at the closed door leading to the backyard, Hunny watching him. Colin finally knelt down. Taking the pit bull's head between his hands, he looked into her eyes.

"Someone needs your help. This is your chance. You are going to have to dig under the side fence. She needs warmth first. And you can't tell them I sent you. But you have to let them know she is there. Do you understand?"

Hunny stared into the kind eyes. The next moment she turned and bolted from the kitchen, practically flying through the pet door into the backyard.

THE ROCK FELL from Pearl's hand. She could no longer hold it, much less hit the ladder. But then she heard something—it was coming from the fence separating her property from Marlow House. She tried to raise her head to see, but it was too dark to see anything. It sounded like frantic digging. But not the digging of a shovel—the digging of an animal. The next moment she heard something running in her direction—running and panting.

A moment later she found herself nose to nose with Chris Johnson's pit bull. She tried to scream, but it was impossible to make a sound. The dog stared at her, and then to her surprise it licked her face.

Oh my god, he is going to eat me! Pearl thought. *This is how it ends for me? A late night snack for my neighbor's dog?*

Instead of ripping the flesh from Pearl's bones, Hunny snuggled up close to the woman's side, resting her neck along Pearl's. The dog inched her furry warmth over Pearl's body without lying on her, sparing the older woman her full weight.

A desire for warmth replaced fear, and Pearl found herself wrapping her arms around the dog, soaking in its body's warmth. It felt so good, Pearl started to cry. Hunny lifted her head slightly and licked the tears from her face.

"Oh, please get help," Pearl whispered, never imagining the dog would really understand her plea. A moment later Hunny ran off.

HUNNY CHARGED into the dining room and started barking.

Everyone at the table stopped talking and looked at the dog. The next moment Hunny quieted and sat down. She stared at Walt.

Chris started to say something when Walt stood abruptly and said, "I think Hunny is trying to tell us something." Most of the people in the room understood Walt knew exactly what Hunny was trying to say, but they played along, as they all wanted to discover what Walt already knew.

As soon as they followed Walt outside, Hunny rushed to the side gate and dove into the tunnel she had dug between Marlow House and Pearl's yard. The dog disappeared. Instead of following Hunny, they all ran to the side gate and onto the sidewalk, heading over to Pearl's house.

Walt reached her first, yet only because Hunny had already told him where he could find her. As he knelt by Pearl's side, the dog was once again providing warmth as the injured woman wrapped her arms around the pit bull as if she were a lifeline.

Ian didn't have to be told what to do. He was the first on the cellphone, already calling 911 before Walt had a chance to check Pearl's vitals.

TWENTY-NINE

Absently chewing her lower lip, Danielle picked up the bottle of corn syrup from the kitchen counter and gave a frown. It was one of the items she had put on the grocery list for Joanne to pick up. "It's been a long time since I bought corn syrup," she told Marie, who was busy gathering the rest of the divinity ingredients from the pantry and setting them on the counter.

"You can't make divinity without corn syrup," Marie reminded her. "You do want to make it, don't you?"

"Yeah, I do. Your divinity tastes wonderful, and it is only once a year, so I suppose it won't kill us."

"Goodness, to even suggest my candy would ever kill anyone!"

Their conversation was interrupted when the kitchen door opened. In walked Lily from the side yard. She awkwardly held the door open while pushing a stroller into the kitchen. Sitting in the stroller was a happily alert Connor, who waved his hands excitedly while pounding on the table tray and drooling. Wisps of curly reddish blond hair covered his head while he excitedly looked around the room through bright green eyes, the same shade as his mother's.

"Good morning, Dani, Marie," Lily greeted them as she closed the door behind her.

"How did you know Marie was here?" Danielle asked, still standing by the counter.

"Because when I walked up and looked in the window, I saw a box of sugar floating across your kitchen, and I didn't see Walt around," Lily explained.

Danielle looked at Marie and cringed. "I suppose we should be more careful. After all, Colin and Owen are in the house."

"No, they're not. I just saw them walking down the street together, heading for the pier," Lily told her.

"If that's the case, let me take this little guy!" Marie said cheerfully as she reached for Connor.

"Marie wants to take Connor," Danielle told Lily. The next moment the baby seemingly floated up from the stroller and began floating around the kitchen while giggling.

"I came over to see if you know how Pearl is doing?" Lily asked as she sat at the table. Danielle poured two cups of coffee and then joined Lily, bringing her a cup.

"I spoke to the chief this morning. Since we aren't family, the hospital won't tell us anything if we call to check on her, even though we're the ones who called 911," Danielle began.

"Yeah, you mentioned that last night."

"According to the chief, she broke her ankle. They set it, and it doesn't look like she is going to require any surgery. But they are worried about pneumonia. She was outside for hours before we found her on that damp ground. It looks like she's going to be spending Christmas in the hospital."

"Pearl may not be my most favorite person, but I can't help but feel sorry for her. She must have been terrified yesterday, and now, having to spend Christmas all alone in the hospital," Lily said.

"I know. I feel sorry for her too."

"Did Walt ever figure out how Hunny knew Pearl had fallen?" Lily asked. "I just can't believe Hunny would dig under the fence like that."

"From what I understand, Pearl had lost her voice trying to scream for help. She started hitting the ladder with a rock, and Hunny heard the pinging sound. Apparently she sensed someone needed help and dug under the fence and found Pearl."

Lily furrowed her brows and looked blankly across the room.

"What?" Danielle asked.

"I'm just trying to picture Pearl having a Lassie and Timmy moment. You know, *Lassie, go get help. Timmy fell down the well!*" Lily said.

Danielle chuckled. "You still watching those old classic TV shows?"

Lily shrugged and then glanced over to check on her son, who appeared to be dancing across the room—some six feet above the floor. Lily shook her head and then looked back to Danielle. "Are you going to see her at the hospital?"

"They put her in intensive care last night, and the chief doesn't know how long she's going to be there. They only let family see intensive care patients."

"Is she that bad?" Lily asked.

"She's suffering from exposure. Heather saw her up on that ladder when she came over here yesterday. That was hours before we found her. According to the chief, she fell not long after Heather walked by her house."

"Do they think she's going to be okay?"

"From what the chief said, it sounded more precautionary, but I'm not sure."

"I guess as long as she's in intensive care, you won't go over there," Lily said.

"The chief promised he'd keep us updated on her progress and let me know when they move her to a regular hospital room. When they do, Walt and I plan to visit her. We thought we'd offer to keep an eye on her house, you know, like bring in her mail, or if she needs me to bring her something from home."

"That's nice of you, considering how she's treated you guys."

"She is our neighbor. And I do feel sorry for her, and she doesn't really have anyone," Danielle said.

"And it is Christmas," Lily added.

"True," Danielle agreed.

"Not to change the subject—but I am—last night, you never said what you guys are going to do about that lady who broke in here. Our conversation sort of ended when Colin and Owen came back," Lily said. "And then after finding Pearl, we never had time to discuss it again."

"I had one idea," Danielle said as she looked over at Marie. Lily looked too, and they both silently watched as the ghost played with the baby—Danielle actually seeing Marie, and Lily only seeing her son seemingly floating in midair.

Feeling the eyes on her and noticing the silence, Marie stopped making funny faces at Connor and looked to the kitchen table.

"What?" Marie asked.

"We know who broke in here. We know where they are staying. But what we don't know is why. We were hoping..." Danielle began.

"You want me to go undercover?" Marie asked.

"Yes. Hang out with the Hoopers, listen to their conversations. Hopefully they'll say something about breaking in here—and why. And if they plan to break in again," Danielle said.

Connor floated back to his stroller.

"Fine. But first, let's make Adam's divinity," Marie said. "And then I'll go down to the Seahorse Motel and see if I can find anything out."

MARIE DIDN'T BOTHER OPENING the door to the office of the Seahorse Motel. She simply moved through the wall. Once inside, she spied Sam sitting behind the counter, talking on the phone. He was the only one in the office.

She marched up to the counter and stood, listening to Sam's side of the phone conversation.

"That doesn't sound like a work call," Marie said.

She listened a few more minutes and then said, "Sam! Really? You should be ashamed of yourself? Who is she?...Oh, never mind. I don't want to know if she lets you talk to her like that!"

Sam let out a low laugh and then leaned one elbow against the desk behind the counter, the phone still by his ear. Marie folded her arms over her chest and shook her head in disgust. Sam lowered his voice as he continued to talk into the phone, his words barely audible as his eyes occasionally darted across the room as if he was on the lookout for someone coming into the office.

"Just how long are you going to be?" Marie said with a deep sigh. "I need to know what room the Hoopers are staying in, and I really can't look at the register with you standing there."

Sam laughed again and then leaned back in the chair.

Annoyed, Marie walked through the counter, looking for the register book. She found it sitting a few feet from Sam.

SAM LEANED back in the swivel chair and swung it around so that his back was to the counter. He glanced up to the wall clock to check on the time. "Come on, baby, I'll pick you up after I get off work, and we can try this all out for real."

He heard her giggle on the other side of the line. He smiled. Swinging the chair around again so that he was again facing the counter, his eyes widened when he spied the guest register was now open and its pages were slowly turning, as if someone was flipping through them looking for something. The only thing—no one else was in the office.

Sam bolted out of the chair, still holding the phone but no longer listening to the woman on the other side of the line. The pages stopped turning and slowly drifted down, falling back in place. He looked around anxiously and then waved his hand over the book, trying to feel for a draft—but there didn't seem to be one.

"THANKS," Marie said cheerfully as she turned from the counter and started to leave. Just as she reached the wall, she turned one last time to look at Sam. He was still standing over the registration book, wildly waving one hand over it, still looking for the elusive draft.

With a chuckle, Marie turned back around and walked through the wall. Several minutes later Marie found herself in Marcella and Forrest's motel room. Inside the room were two unmade queen-size beds separated by a nightstand. On one wall was a dresser under a large picture window facing the ocean. Next to the window was a wall-mounted flat-screen television facing two small recliners and a small table. Forrest sat on one of the recliners, watching television, while Marcella lounged on one of the beds, reading a magazine.

"This is exciting," Marie muttered. She took a seat on the empty recliner and waited. Forty-five minutes later she had finished watching a reality show with Forrest and had heard Marcella let out countless sighs while turning the pages of the magazine she read.

Tired of waiting, Marie looked at the television set. A moment later, the screen went black.

Forrest frowned and picked up the remote from the small table. He punched a button. When it did nothing, he punched it again.

"TV is broken," Forrest grumbled.

"It seems a lot of things break around this place," Marcella said as she closed her magazine and tossed it on the bed next to her.

"But I don't think they'll move us over to Marlow House for a broken television set."

Forrest pushed the remote's on button. The television turned back on. Before Marie had a chance to turn it off, Forrest beat her to it. He then tossed the remote back on the small table and said, "It's working. But I'm sick of watching television."

"This would have been a lot easier if we had run into Samuel Hayman before she died," Marcella said.

"True. But if we hadn't run into him at all, then we never would have discovered Eloise's little secret," Forrest reminded her.

"A lot of good it's doing us."

Forrest looked at his wife. "I thought I was the pessimist and you were the optimist?"

Marcella laughed. "You're right. I should just be grateful we did run into Hayman. Now we just have to get it."

"Get what?" Marie asked.

Forrest stood up and walked to the empty bed. "I'm going to take a nap."

Marcella picked up the magazine and opened it. She resumed her reading. Fifteen minutes later Forrest began to snore.

THIRTY

Residents and guests of Marlow House retired to the living room after breakfast on Saturday morning. Danielle sat on the sofa between Walt and Noah, while Chris and Owen occupied the chairs facing them, and Colin sat on the nearby rocking chair, with Hunny napping by his feet. Max stretched out under the Christmas tree on his back, occasionally swatting the gold ball hanging on the limb above him.

"Ever since I met you, I could swear we've met before," Noah told Colin. "But I just can't place where."

"I did have a brief career as a model," Colin said with a laugh. "Maybe you recognize me from one of the drawings."

"You were a model?" Danielle asked with surprise.

"I suppose that would be stretching it," Colin said. "It was hardly a career—I certainly didn't get paid. It was for an artist friend of mine from New York. I sat for him. But his drawings of me did become rather famous at the time."

"Really? Who was he?" Danielle asked.

"This was years ago, long before you were born," Colin told her. "Frankly, I never thought they looked that much like me. Tom made me considerably rounder and shorter than I really was. So now that I think about it, if I look familiar to you, I doubt it's from those drawings." Colin chuckled.

"As we all know, some people do have doppelgangers." Chris

snickered, looking to Walt.

"No kidding," Owen agreed. "That portrait in the library, I could swear that really was of Walt."

"It's because it is," Marie's spirit said when she burst into the room. Not everyone in the living room could see or hear her.

Danielle looked to Marie expectantly, curious to know what she had learned. She hadn't seen the spirit since they had finished making divinity the day before.

"I know a little," Marie said. "Why don't you excuse yourself, and I'll meet you in the parlor." Marie vanished.

———

MARIE WAS ALREADY WAITING in the parlor when Danielle walked in the room.

"What did you find out?" Danielle asked.

"Not as much as I had hoped I would. They spent most of the evening watching TV, reading or sleeping. They hardly ever talked with each other. I left them at the theater right before I got here; they're watching a double feature. So I doubt they'll be doing much plotting or chatting for the next few hours."

"But you said you know a little?"

"They are definitely looking for something that belonged to Eloise Winterborne. It was something they didn't know about until after she died."

"What is it?" Danielle asked.

"They never said. But, from what I gather, Samuel Hayman told them about it."

"Samuel?" Danielle frowned. "It must be jewelry."

"Maybe you need to take a closer look at that shoe. Perhaps that's not all paste," Marie suggested.

They were interrupted when Chris, Walt and Noah walked into the room.

"Colin went upstairs, and Owen went for a walk," Walt explained as he shut the door behind them.

"What did you find out?" Chris asked.

Marie repeated what she had told Danielle. When she finished, Walt said, "Let's look at that shoe again."

Danielle walked to the desk and pulled the decorated shoe from the mermaid bag. She handed it to Walt. He examined it and then passed it to Chris, who studied it, fingering the stones. When he was done, he passed it to Noah. When Noah was finished, he handed the shoe back to Danielle, who continued to examine the jewels affixed to the shoe while the men reached their verdict.

"I'm hardly an expert," Noah said. "I suppose they could be real. But even if they are, are there that many stones on that thing to risk getting arrested trying to steal it?"

"Two diamonds the same size don't necessarily have the same value," Chris reminded him.

"True. The color, the quality, the cut can all make a difference in value," Danielle agreed.

"You need to have someone look at this thing," Chris urged.

Danielle considered Chris's suggestion and then looked at Walt. "I know of only one person in Frederickport who could tell us if any of these stones are real. The only other option is to go out of town and find a jeweler."

"You're talking about Samuel Hayman?" Walt asked.

"We need to talk to him anyway. According to Marie, whatever the Hoopers are looking for, they are only looking for it because Sam told them about it," Danielle said.

"Sam Hayman, you're talking about the guy who used to own the jewelry store in town that closed before I moved here?" Chris asked. "The one who tried to steal the stones from the Missing Thorndike?"

"The very one," Danielle confirmed.

"What if he and the Hoopers are in this together?" Noah asked.

"That's what I was thinking," Walt said.

Marie shook her head. "No. I don't think so. From what I overheard, I got the distinct impression they've had no further communication with Sam Hayman. It sounded like they ran into him somewhere, and he inadvertently tipped them off to something that they are now following up on."

Danielle arched her brow. "Perhaps Eloise didn't sell her engagement ring to Samuel—maybe she traded it for something? She couldn't wear the ring anymore; maybe she wanted something else," Danielle suggested. "And now they're looking for it." Danielle glanced down at the shoe in her hand. "Maybe a bunch of loose stones so she could use them in one of her craft projects."

"That sounds a little crazy," Chris said.

Danielle shrugged. "Elizabeth did say the woman was a little quirky."

"Gluing valuable stones on an old shoe is more than quirky. It is nuts," Chris said.

"If this Sam Hayman guy tried to steal from you once, what makes you think you can trust him now to tell you the truth?" Noah asked.

"Because Sam served his time in prison, and he is trying to rebuild his life. The last time I saw him, he was riddled with guilt and regret. Anyway, it's not like I'm going to take him at his word if he says the stones are worthless, and then let him keep the shoe," Danielle reminded him. "And I think he would know that. He'd expect me to get a second opinion."

THIRTY MINUTES later Walt and Danielle were in the Packard, backing out of their garage, on the way to see Samuel Hayman at the house he now rented. Danielle had obtained his phone number from the chief and had called him up. Samuel agreed to meet her and Walt at his home.

"By the way, when I was talking to the chief, he told me they're moving Pearl to a regular hospital room today," Danielle told Walt as he paused a moment in the drive leading to the alleyway and used the remote to close the garage door.

"Do you want to stop over there after we talk to Hayman?" Walt asked.

"We might as well. We'll be out anyway." Danielle glanced down at the brown paper bag on her lap. She had put the decorated shoe in it before leaving the house.

Walt glanced over to Danielle and noticed her peculiar expression while staring down at the paper sack. "What are you thinking?"

Danielle glanced up to Walt and smiled as he pulled out into the alleyway. "Just remembering how Samuel tried to switch the diamonds and emeralds on the Missing Thorndike."

"Are you having second thoughts about having him look at the shoe?"

"Not really. But please be on your guard, just in case this thing turns out to be covered with priceless gems and he decides to hit us over the head, take it and skip town. After all, he practically did that once already."

Walt grinned. "True. Don't worry. If we discover he hasn't really mended his ways, I promise to levitate him to the ceiling and keep him there until the chief arrives."

Danielle chuckled. "Yeah, I can just see that now if Joe or Brian came instead of the chief."

SAMUEL LOOKED BETTER than the last time Danielle had seen him. He seemed more relaxed—rested. She noticed a touch of gray in his curly brown hair that had not been there the last time they had talked. The clothes he wore were just as outdated as what she had remembered him wearing when they had first met over three years earlier, and she suspected they were probably from the same wardrobe. One of his best features had always been, and still was, his straight white teeth, she thought.

Upon arriving at his house, she had introduced him to her husband, and like others who met Walt and were familiar with the portraits, he expressed his astonishment at how much he resembled his distant cousin. Together Walt and Danielle sat on a small sofa, which looked as if it had been picked up at a thrift store, while Samuel sat in a chair across from them, examining the shoe with a jeweler's loupe.

After a few minutes Samuel looked up and smiled sheepishly. He stood briefly and handed the shoe back to Danielle before sitting back down in his chair. "I'm really sorry to tell you this; none of them are real. My guess, they were taken from costume jewelry."

"Are you sure?" Danielle asked.

"Afraid so. Of course, you can get a second opinion."

"You have never seen this shoe before, have you?" Danielle asked, tucking the shoe back in the sack.

Samuel smiled. "No, I haven't. And it is…interesting. So tell me, why in the world did you imagine any of those were real?"

"Oh, it's not that we thought they were real," Danielle lied. "We picked this up at a yard sale to use for a white elephant gift, and then we got to thinking, maybe some of these jewels are real."

Samuel laughed. "That would be rather funny to give something like that away as a joke only to discover it was valuable. But no. I'm afraid it is just a shoe with artificial flowers and costume jewelry glued all over it. It would make a good white elephant gift."

"Can I ask you something else?" Danielle asked.

"Certainly."

"Do you know who Marcella and Forrest Hooper are?"

"Yes. They used to work for Eloise Winterborne. Did you know her?"

Danielle shook her head. "No. But I've heard of her."

"Funny you should mention the Hoopers. I ran into them about a month ago," he said.

"Did you?" Danielle glanced briefly to Walt and then back to Samuel.

"Yes, for some reason they were under the impression Eloise Winterborne had sold me her engagement ring. To be honest, I was a little concerned they were going to cause me problems, but I haven't heard from them again. So I assume they figured out what happened to it."

"You didn't buy it?" Danielle asked. "According to what Eloise told Emma Jackson, you did."

Samuel slumped back in his chair and groaned. "Is that why you're really here? Since I got out of prison I have done everything humanly possible to rebuild my life and regain trust. And now, now some fake story that I have no way of contesting since Eloise isn't here to confirm my story. This is going to ruin everything for me. I promise I did not take advantage of that woman!"

Startled by Samuel's outburst, Danielle furrowed her brow. "What woman?"

"Eloise Winterborne, of course."

"Perhaps you need to start at the beginning," Walt suggested.

"There is no beginning. At least, not really. But if there was a beginning, it might be the last time I saw Eloise, which was ages ago. She came into my shop to have her ring cleaned. She used to do that every six months."

"And you didn't buy it from her?" Danielle asked.

"No. I was already struggling back then. I didn't have the money to pay for that ring. I suppose had she mentioned something about selling it, I could have found her a buyer and earned a commission. But she never said anything to me about wanting to sell it."

"But she told people you had bought it," Danielle said.

"Yes. I didn't know anything about that until I ran into the

Hoopers, and they said something to me about always wondering what I had paid for Winterborne's engagement ring—implying I'd probably took advantage of her and didn't give her what it was worth. I told them I didn't know what they were talking about. I didn't have that kind of money back then. I thought they believed me. I certainly don't want them spreading that story. I don't need the IRS to come after me now for trying to hide an asset I never declared. I don't need that kind of trouble. But I swear, I haven't seen that ring since I cleaned it for her. That was over three years ago."

THIRTY-ONE

"I believe him," Danielle told Walt after they left Samuel's house and walked to the Packard.

"I believe he has never seen that shoe before, unless he is an excellent actor. And I don't think he was lying when he told us there were no valuable gems on it." Walt stopped by the passenger side of the Packard and opened the car door for Danielle.

Just before stepping into the vehicle, she paused and looked at Walt. "You don't believe him about Eloise's ring?"

"I'm not saying that," Walt began as Danielle climbed into the car. He shut the door behind her and then went to the driver's side of the vehicle.

"What are you saying?" Danielle asked when he climbed into the car.

"It could go either way. He was emotional when he talked about the ring. It could be because he was telling the truth and he was upset this could cause him trouble, or perhaps he did buy Eloise's ring for a fraction of its worth, and now he's afraid it's all going to come back and bite him. Remember, he supposedly bought that ring back before he tried to steal the Missing Thorndike, so it's not like that all took place when he was trying to turn over a new leaf." Walt closed his car door. Sitting in the driver's seat, he turned to face his wife.

"Maybe. But there are only three possible scenarios in all this," Danielle suggested.

Walt arched his brow. "Which are?"

"We know he didn't have the money to buy Eloise's ring for even close to its value, considering Samuel's money problems started long before he tried to steal the diamonds and emeralds from the Missing Thorndike. So the only three possibilities, he found a buyer for the ring, which we initially assumed. But if that is the case, I don't see why he would lie about it now. Why lie to cover up earning some commission?"

"The other two possibilities?" Walt asked.

"Another possibility, he is telling the truth. The last possibility— he did buy the ring from her, but paid a fraction of its worth. And if that is the case, then where is the ring now? From everything we've heard, he's struggled financially since his release from prison. Heck, his first job when he got out was washing dishes. And by the looks of that house he's renting, he is not much better off now. If he bought that ring, where is it? I would think that would have been a nice little nest egg to help rebuild his life when he got out of prison."

Before Walt had time to respond to Danielle's theory, her phone began to ring.

She picked up her cellphone and looked at it. "It's the chief."

Several minutes later, after chatting briefly with the chief and then saying goodbye to him, she looked at Walt and said, "Pearl was moved to a regular hospital room. How about we stop by and see her? I don't want to do it this afternoon, since we need to get ready for Lily and Ian's party."

BEFORE GOING TO THE HOSPITAL, Danielle and Walt stopped off and picked up a Christmas-themed floral arrangement to take to Pearl. Danielle figured they needed to take her something, and since it looked as if she was spending Christmas in the hospital, she thought the arrangement might help brighten the stay.

When they arrived outside Pearl's hospital room thirty minutes later, they found its door open to the hallway and Pearl sitting up in her bed, watching television. Before entering, Danielle knocked on the doorjamb, and she and Walt remained standing in the doorway, waiting for Pearl's acknowledgment.

A moment later Pearl looked their way. Showing no expression, but a slight flicker of recognition, she picked up the remote from her bed and turned off the television. Taking that as an invitation to enter, Danielle walked into the room, carrying the arrangement, followed by Walt.

"Hello, Mrs. Huckabee, how are you feeling?" Danielle asked when she reached the bedside.

Drawing her brow into a scowl, Pearl looked the pair up and down, her eyes glancing briefly at the floral arrangement before looking back into Danielle's face.

"I have a broken ankle. How do you think I feel? And I am getting a cold. I just hope it doesn't turn into pneumonia. Fortunately I had my shot, so hopefully I won't come down with some other strain."

"Umm...we brought you this." Danielle held up the floral arrangement. "Thought it might brighten your room a little. We heard you might be spending Christmas in here."

"I don't know how you heard that. The hospital staff had better not be sharing my personal medical records with strangers!" she snapped.

"No. But I asked the police chief how you were doing." Danielle glanced briefly over her shoulder at Walt, who returned a bemused smile.

"He shouldn't be sharing my private business either. But yes, looks like I'll be in this gawd-awful place through Christmas. You can go ahead and set it up there, I guess." Pearl pointed to the nearby dresser.

After Danielle set the flowers on the dresser, she turned to Pearl and asked, "We wondered if there was anything you might need us to do while you're in here. Perhaps bring your mail in, or maybe you need me to bring you something from your house?"

"I do not want a stranger looking through my mail or nosing around in my house. Just because you did the decent thing and called 911 when you found me—something I would hope anyone would do—don't imagine I have any desire to get chummy with people like you. Just leave my house and my mail alone, and don't think that just because I'm in here for a few days it gives you license to go poking around in my things. I have already hired someone to keep an eye on my house, and if I discover you have stepped onto my property in my absence, do not doubt I will call the police and press charges. Do you understand?"

Wide eyed and speechless, Danielle nodded. Finally she said, "Umm...no problem. I guess Walt and I will leave now and let you get back to your TV show."

Without another word, Walt and Danielle turned and headed for the door. Once they reached it, Pearl called out, "If you want to take those flowers with you, go ahead and take them."

Danielle paused at the door and looked back to Pearl. "No. It was a gift. Merry Christmas."

"WHAT A WITCH!" Lily said after Danielle recounted their visit with Pearl Huckabee. They sat with Walt and Ian in the Bartley living room while Connor napped in his bedroom, and Sadie continually nosed Walt for more attention.

"I'd like to know, what did she mean when she said *people like you*," Danielle asked.

"Nice people?" Ian snickered.

Danielle flashed Ian a grin. "Maybe. Who knows what her problem is. But obviously falling off her ladder did not improve her disposition."

"I don't think it usually does." Walt chuckled.

"At least I don't have to worry about Pearl calling the cops on our party tonight," Lily said with a giggle.

"By the way, looks like one of our white elephant gifts will be the shoe. So I don't need to do any more shopping. If you need me to help you do anything for tonight, I'm free," Danielle told Lily.

"What did you find out about the shoe?" Ian asked.

Walt then told them about their visit with Samuel and Danielle's theories.

"I have to agree with Danielle," Ian said when Walt finished his telling. "I doubt Samuel has it."

"So what happened to the ring?" Lily asked.

"According to what Elizabeth told us, the Hoopers had been hired by the estate to prepare for the auction. And from what Samuel said, it sounds like they found out Eloise hadn't really sold the ring not long before they were let go by the estate and had to move out," Danielle explained.

"By the time they talked to Samuel, they had already gone through most of her things," Walt said. "We assume they hadn't come across the ring—they didn't even know it might be in the house somewhere. But when they learned she hadn't gotten rid of it, they started searching for it, looking in places where it might have been hidden. For some reason, they focused their search on the items placed in that trunk."

"But you have all that stuff—don't you?" Lily asked.

"Walt and I don't think the ring was in it. We believe the Hoopers think it might be, because they obviously never found it anywhere else," Danielle told them. "But that ring might be shoved behind some loose board in that house. Maybe someone will find it someday like I found the Missing Thorndike."

"You didn't find the Missing Thorndike," Walt reminded her. "I showed you where I hid it."

SINCE HER DEATH, Marie had found herself less cognizant of the passage of time. Yet there were instances, like today, when she reminded herself she needed to pay attention. It would be easier if she could wear a watch. While she could conjure up the image of a watch for her wrist, it wouldn't keep time. So on days like today, this meant popping into the nearest building and looking for a clock.

The reason she needed to keep an eye on the time today was because she wanted to return to the theater before the end of the second feature. She wanted to be with the Hoopers when they left the movies, and hopefully they would be more talkative so she could learn why Marcella had broken into Marlow House.

Marie arrived at the theater about twenty minutes before the end of the second feature. She went directly to where she had left them, sitting near the aisle on row ten. But to her surprise, those seats were now empty. She noticed several noisy teenagers sitting near the aisle on row eleven. She then assumed the Hoopers had moved to other seats.

Standing in the aisle, Marie glanced around the theater and groaned. It was full and dark, and she didn't relish the thought of looking for them, so she decided it would be far easier to simply go to their car and wait for them there. She knew where they had parked. A few minutes later Marie stood in the parking lot of the theater and was surprised to find the Hoopers' car was no longer there.

"They already left!" Marie shouted before disappearing and going directly to the Seahorse Motel.

When Marie arrived in the motel parking lot, she was annoyed to discover the Hoopers' vehicle was nowhere in sight. Grumbling at losing the pair, she went into their motel room, intending to wait for them. The moment she stepped into the room, she found one of the motel maids changing the bedsheets. Looking around for somewhere to sit and stay out of the maid's way until the Hoopers returned, she discovered something else. The Hoopers' luggage was no longer in the room. In fact, none of their belongings were in the motel room.

A moment later Marie stood in the motel's front office. Sam was not behind the counter; instead there was a young woman busily surfing on her cellphone. Marie peeked behind the counter and found the registration book open. She took a look and her suspicions were confirmed. The Hoopers had checked out of the motel.

THIRTY-TWO

When Marie finally returned to Marlow House late Saturday afternoon, she found Danielle alone, wrapping packages in the parlor. Christmas carols played from a small Bluetooth speaker sitting on a nearby bookshelf, and a pine-scented candle burned in a brass candleholder on the coffee table, filling the room with the scent of Christmas.

"I'm so sorry. I've lost them. I can't find them anywhere!" Marie confessed after entering the parlor. She then plopped down on one of the nearby chairs as if exhausted.

Setting down her scissors, Danielle turned to face Marie. "You lost the Hoopers?"

"It appears they may have left town. Which I suppose is a good thing. But now you may never know why they broke in here."

"How do you know they left town?"

"I don't know," Marie admitted. "I just have to assume that's what they did. When I went to the theater, they were already gone, and the second movie was still playing. I went back to the motel, and they had checked out. I've been all over and can't find their car anywhere. I have to assume they left town. After all, I heard someone at the motel say all the rooms in Frederickport are full. So they obviously didn't move to another motel—at least not here."

Danielle considered Marie's words and then picked up the scissors. "I suppose that's entirely possible." She then went on to tell

Marie about their visit with Samuel, while wrapping one of her packages in shiny red gift wrap.

"Imagine that, Eloise lied to Emma about selling the ring," Marie said after Danielle finished updating her.

Danielle shrugged. "It seems that way. Not sure what Eloise ever did with that ring, but I know it wasn't in any of those things they put in the trunk, and it looks like the Hoopers must have come to that realization. Who knows, maybe they went back to Astoria to look through the Winterborne house."

"You mean break in?" Marie asked.

Danielle stopped wrapping a moment and turned to Marie. "They did break in here."

"I suppose you're right…should we do something?"

"Not sure what. I already talked to the chief about what Samuel told us. Aside from Mrs. Hooper breaking in here—which there is no way to prove—no laws have been broken. I suppose I could tell whoever is handling the estate that Eloise never sold that ring and they might want to look for it. But the fact is, maybe Eloise did something else with the ring. From what I understand, she had it removed from her inventory list a few years before she died. Do we really want to get involved at this point? It is a lot of speculation."

"Perhaps I should at least go over to the Winterborne house. Eva's been hanging out over there the last few days—oh, not the Winterborne house—but over at the film museum in Astoria. I wanted to stop and see Eva, I don't think she's coming to the party tonight, and while I'm over there, I might as well pop in at the Winterborne house and see if those two are poking around."

DANIELLE FILLED the large paper sack with the Christmas gifts she had wrapped. One was going under the tree—the gift for Adam. The rest she would be taking to the party across the street. Before picking up the bag, she grabbed her cellphone from the desk and tossed it in with the gifts. When she walked into the living room a few minutes later, she found Owen sitting on the sofa, staring blankly ahead, as if lost in thought.

"You ready for the party?" Danielle asked cheerfully as she set the filled paper sack by the tree. Kneeling down, she removed the gift for Adam and tucked it far under the branches of the Christmas tree.

"I don't think I'm going. It's really nice of you to invite me, but I have intruded enough on your Christmas," Owen told her.

Danielle stood up and walked to one of the chairs facing the sofa. She sat down and studied Owen for a moment. "You are more than welcome to come. The more the merrier."

Owen smiled sadly at Danielle yet said nothing.

After a moment of silence, Danielle asked, "Tell me what's really wrong."

"I never mentioned this before. But I used to live in Frederickport," he told her.

"You did?"

He nodded. "Yes. And I have a feeling I'll probably know some people at the party tonight. And even if I don't know anyone tonight, chances are I'll run into someone I know at your Christmas Eve open house. Which is why I should probably leave town before the party tonight."

"Why would it be a bad thing to run into someone you know?" Danielle asked.

Owen gave Danielle a shrug and leaned back in the sofa. "It's not like I have some criminal past—I don't want you to think that. It's just that I burned my bridges after I left town, and I doubt some people will be thrilled if they hear I'm back. Why ruin their Christmas?"

"You want to talk about it?" Danielle asked.

They sat in silence for a few minutes. Finally Owen said, "I don't know why I came back—no—that's wrong, I do. It's Christmastime, and something pulled me back here. It's been so long since I've really celebrated the holidays. So long since it felt like Christmas. I just wanted to see if I returned, would I feel it again?"

"Feel what?" Danielle asked.

"The Christmas spirit, maybe." Owen let out a deep breath, closed his eyes, and leaned back in the sofa.

"Who are you afraid of running into here?" Danielle asked. "Who wouldn't be happy to see you?"

Owen opened his eyes and looked at Danielle. "My old girlfriend, for one. We were planning on getting married when I met my wife. I know she never got married. I hope to hell it isn't because of me. But that was a long time ago. And then of course, there is my family…"

"You have family in Frederickport?" Danielle asked in surprise.

"Yes. But I don't imagine they will be thrilled to see me. Although, they might get some satisfaction in saying *I told you so*. They were always fond of my old girlfriend, and they were never thrilled with my wife. Looking back, I suppose they were right."

"When was the last time you saw your family?" Danielle asked.

Owen shrugged. "About sixteen years ago."

"Sixteen years?" Danielle gasped.

"After I got married, we stayed in Frederickport for about a year. But then some things happened—words were exchanged—and I figured if I wanted to make my marriage work, we needed to move away. What is it they say, three things that most often destroy a marriage—money problems, sex problems, and in-law issues. Ours was the in-laws. Well, her in-laws. She was estranged from her parents, so they were never in the picture. I guess in retrospect, that should have been a red flag for me."

"I understand sometimes we need to walk away from family. I have a close friend whose uncles actually plotted to kill him."

"Yikes." Owen cringed. "What happened?"

"They were arrested, sent to prison. One died in prison, the other is spending the rest of his life there. But my point—while I understand we sometimes need to walk away from family, that is not always the case. In fact, that is rarely the case, in my opinion. I know how precious family can be—how profound it is to be without them. But you—you have the chance to reconnect with your family again. But only you know if your relationship is something that's worth salvaging—or if it is something that was toxic. And if that is the case, then you probably shouldn't reopen that chapter of your life."

Owen considered her words a moment. Finally he shook his head and said, "No. It was never toxic. If anything was toxic, it was my marriage."

"Then come to the party tonight and think about what you should do. Instead of leaving today, maybe you'll want to stick around and see your family for Christmas."

THE SCENT of pine competed with the tempting aromas coming

from the Bartley kitchen. Lily and Ian greeted their guests while friendly chatter filled the house. Christmas carols played discretely in the background, and those not aware of Walt's gift in communicating with animals were impressed with how Hunny and Sadie sat obediently by the Christmas tree, neither dog jumping on people or trying to snag the appetizers that sat on decorative platters on a nearby table.

Ian's sister, Kelly, was busy holding her nephew, Connor, while her boyfriend, Joe Morelli, accepted a cocktail from Chris, who had volunteered as bartender while Ian greeted the guests. Danielle stood in the dining room chatting with Owen, whom she had talked into coming to the party, while Walt talked with the chief in the living room.

Danielle heard the doorbell ring and watched Lily leave the kitchen to answer it. A moment later Adam and Melony followed Lily into the dining room. Lily left Danielle to introduce Adam and Melony to Owen while she went to take some baked brie out of the oven.

"Adam and Melony, I would like you to meet—"

"Gardener?" Adam said in surprise.

Owen smiled and shook Adam's hand. "Hi, Nichols, it's been a long time."

"You two know each other?" Danielle asked, glancing from Owen to Adam.

"Yes. But it has been years. I almost didn't recognize you with that beard," Adam said.

They were interrupted a moment later when Colin tapped on Danielle's shoulder and asked if they could have a word in private.

"I hate to bother you," Colin said after pulling Danielle away from the others. "But I just realized I left my pillbox across the street in my room. I need to go get it. I have to take my heart medicine in about ten minutes, but I forgot my key. Can I borrow yours, please?"

"Certainly," Danielle said, digging her hand in one pocket. "Dang, I forgot..."

"You don't have your key?" he asked.

"No." Danielle pulled out her key and showed it to Colin. "I didn't want to take a purse, so I put the house key in my pocket, and my cellphone in the bag with the gifts I was going to bring over. But I just remembered, I forgot to bring the bag over. I need to run over and get those anyway. So if you want me to grab your pillbox when I'm over there, I will be happy to."

He shook his head. "No. To be honest, I'm not really sure where I set it. It would probably be better if I look for it myself. But I would be more than happy to bring the bag of gifts over for you."

Danielle flashed him a smile. "Thanks. But I should probably do it myself and make sure I have everything. We can both go over. You want to go now?"

THIRTY-THREE

T he branches arching over the alley driveway of one of the
houses on Beach Drive needed to be trimmed. Anyone parking
in that driveway risked scratching their vehicle, but the Hoopers
weren't concerned. The overgrown tree and nearby foliage helped
camouflage their car, making it practically unnoticeable to anyone
driving down the alleyway, especially during the dark cover of night.

Forrest and Marcella sat in their vehicle, going over their plans,
which had been inspired by the first movie they had watched earlier
that day at the Frederickport theater. They hadn't finished the
movie, but it had given Marcella an idea, and she had dragged
Forrest out of the theater to tell him. He had listened, and while
there were points of the plan he was not thrilled about—like
purchasing a gun—he had to agree it was probably their last shot at
retrieving the one item that could set them up for life. He didn't
want to spend his remaining years taking care of another eccentric
and aging senior citizen.

"I suppose we should have left that waitress with the purple hair
a better tip," Forrest said with a chuckle.

"She was a chatty little thing. Telling us all about how the people
who live in this house are gone for the holidays, and how that
neighbor of the Marlows is in the hospital," Marcella said as she
handed Forrest a ski mask.

"Do we really need to wear these things?" he asked.

"Yes, when we are in the house. Everyone might be across the street, but if someone comes back over for some reason and walks in on us, we don't want them to be able to identify us. Now, don't forget to put your gloves on."

A few minutes later, Marcella and Forrest climbed out of their vehicle and into the darkness, the evening's crescent moon obscured by the night clouds. Marcella turned on her flashlight and reached for one of her husband's gloved hands. Together they walked hand in hand down the alleyway toward Marlow House's back gate. When they reached it, they were surprised to discover it was locked.

"I don't believe this!" Marcella cursed. "They didn't have this locked before."

"They obviously know someone was in their house. They must have decided to do a better job at locking their gates. This just means we're going to have to go around and enter through the front door."

"This was going to be so perfect," Marcella groaned. "With that nosey neighbor in the hospital, there would be no one to see us."

"Calm down," he urged. "We're both dressed in black; there is practically no moon out; no one will see us when we go around to the front. Let's just get this done."

Marlow House's neighbor to the north had no fencing around their yard save for the Marlow House fence along the southern side of their property line. Fortunately for the Hoopers, that house was dark, and there didn't appear to be anyone home. Together Marcella and Forrest hurried through their yard, heading toward Beach Drive. When they reached the sidewalk, they looked across the street at what they had learned from the waitress was the Bartley house. Partygoers' cars lined both sides of the street, and the Bartley house was well lit.

Standing on the sidewalk and looking up the walkway to Marlow House's front door, Marcella smiled when she noticed one piece of luck—they had forgotten to turn the front porch light on. The area was almost pitch black. Marcella turned off her flashlight, not wanting anyone from the party to look over and notice a light moving up the Marlows' front walk. Strands of Christmas lights strung along the front of Marlow House helped illuminate their way as the Hoopers hurried up the walkway to the front door. When they reached the door, Marcella quickly unlocked it and went inside, leaving Forrest alone on the dark porch.

Reaching into her coat pocket for the dog treats she had put there earlier, Marcella waited for the pit bull to greet her. But there was no sound of paws running on the wood floor. She made a little whistle, but still no sign of the pit bull. Confident the dog was not in the house, she shoved the treats back into her pocket and pulled out her ski mask. She hadn't wanted to slip it on until she had the dog confined in a room, afraid the mask might scare the animal.

She then opened the front door and ushered her husband inside, locking and closing the door behind them. The house was dark inside. Like a couple of cat burglars dressed in black—which in essence they now were—the Hoopers stood in Marlow House, looking down the quiet hallway through the slits in the knit ski masks. Random night-lights plugged into electrical sockets helped break the darkness. From one of the open doorways down the hall came a colorful glow. Marcella nudged Forrest in that direction, telling him that was the living room. When they reached the doorway, they discovered the colorful glow came from the Christmas tree lights, the only lights on in the room.

Marcella hurried to the Christmas tree and leaned down, excited to find a paper bag filled with wrapped packages under its branches. "I bet it's here!"

She glanced up to the window, its blinds not all the way drawn, and wondered if someone from across the street looked over, would they notice the beam from her flashlight. Confident she had sufficient lighting from the glow of the Christmas tree lights, she turned off her flashlight and set it down. She pulled the large paper bag from under the tree and dumped its contents on the floor while Forrest stood over her, watching silently. The next moment a light in the hallway turned on, and they heard what sounded like the front door slam.

They both froze a moment, and then Forrest reached down and grabbed Marcella's hand and jerked her up, leaving her flashlight on the floor. They ran to the large picture window and took cover behind the curtains, crouching down close to the floor so furniture blocked their hiding spot.

The living room light went on.

AFTER TURNING on the living room light, Danielle looked back to

Colin, who stood behind her in the hallway. "I'll get the packages while you go up to your room and get your pills."

Colin smiled sheepishly and pulled one hand out of his coat pocket. It held a small pillbox. "I'm afraid I must be getting senile. I forgot to check my pocket. I had the pills with me all along."

"Then it is a good thing you didn't take up my offer to try finding them for you," Danielle teased as she turned back to the living room and headed toward the Christmas tree. Colin followed her into the room and took a seat on the sofa.

"That darn Max," Danielle cursed when she reached the tree.

"Max? Isn't he your cat?" Colin asked.

"Yes," Danielle said as she leaned down in front of the tree. "I guess batting glass balls isn't enough. He's now playing with the gifts." She started to pick up a package to put back in the paper bag when she noticed something else sitting on the floor by the tree. She reached for it.

Flashlight in hand, Danielle stood up and frowned. "I wonder who left this here." Shaking her head, she walked over to the coffee table and set the flashlight down. She then returned to the tree and began gathering up the packages and returning them to the paper sack. She spied her cellphone under one of the branches and then snatched it up, adding it to the bag.

Standing up, she said, "I think I have everything. Let's go."

Colin stood up, and Danielle started for the doorway with the bag of gifts when a female voice behind her said, "Stop right there."

Startled by the unexpected voice, Danielle twirled around and found herself facing two masked people, one pointing a revolver in her direction.

"Set the bag on the table with the flashlight, and no one will get hurt," the female voice ordered.

Danielle did what she was told and backed up, now standing next to Colin.

"Follow our directions, and no one will get hurt," a male voice instructed. "We are going to take you in the hallway and tie you up. I'm sure one of your friends will come looking for you soon, so I don't imagine you will be here long."

"You're taking that bag with you, aren't you?" Danielle asked, nodding to the table.

"You don't intend to risk your life over what's in that bag, do you?" the woman's voice asked.

"Of course not. I just have a favor to ask you," Danielle said.

"I'm the one holding the gun. I don't think you should be asking for favors," the woman snapped.

"We need to hurry up," the man said impatiently, glancing to the window. The next moment he drew the curtains completely closed.

"What did you do that for?" the woman holding the gun asked.

"Someone could drive by and see us," the man explained.

"Please, just one favor," Danielle asked sweetly.

"What?" the woman asked impatiently.

"My cellphone is in that sack. Can you please leave it? I doubt you want it anyway."

The woman glared at Danielle but made no attempt to look for the cellphone.

"Consider this. If you keep the cellphone, it will be easier for the police to track you when you leave here. You don't want that, do you?" Danielle asked.

"I can just throw it out the window," the woman told her.

"Why would you want to do that?" Danielle asked.

Colin began to chuckle. All eyes turned to him, curious to see what he found so amusing. Smiling broadly, Colin patted one of Danielle's hands. "I do find it rather endearing how you are pleading with our armed captors for the release of your cellphone. Perhaps young people of your generation really do have an unhealthy relationship with their cellphones."

Danielle looked to Colin and said, "It's just that it's such a pain to lose your cellphone. It wouldn't be the first time I'd lost one in similar circumstances."

The masked man rushed to the coffee table and dug through the packages. A moment later he pulled out a cellphone and then tossed it on a nearby chair. "There. We won't take your cellphone. Will you now go into the hallway so we can tie you up and get out of here?"

Danielle started to move toward the hallway when Colin reached out and grabbed her wrist, pulling her back. "No, Danielle. We can't let them take the packages."

Confused, Danielle looked to Colin and then back to the woman holding them at gunpoint.

"Yes we can. Seriously, we can," Danielle argued.

Colin shook his head and said calmly, "No we can't. I need one of them."

Danielle abruptly stepped back from Colin, her fear intensifying.

"Do you want me to shoot you?" the gun-toting woman shrieked, her hand now shaking.

"That is a rhetorical question, I assume," Colin said in an irritatingly calm voice.

"No one needs to get shot," Danielle pleaded.

"And no one will," Colin told her. He looked at Danielle and smiled reassuringly. "Don't be afraid, Danielle. It is all going to work out. I promise."

Danielle looked from Colin back to the woman, who was now standing next to her accomplice, the gun still pointed in her direction.

"Whatever anyone thinks is in that sack, you are all wrong. There is nothing of value in there. It's just a bunch of junk. Really. Just silly stuff we bought for a white elephant gift exchange. But if you guys want it, go ahead and take it, and I will let you tie me up while you make your getaway. But frankly, it's not there, whatever you think it might be," Danielle told them.

"Why don't you tell them what is in the bag," Colin suggested.

Danielle quickly listed off the items.

The woman's expression went blank, and she studied Danielle a moment. "What about the picture frame?"

"Picture frame?" Danielle asked.

"A picture of two men. One holding up a fish," the woman told her. "Where is it?"

"You want that?" Danielle asked in surprise.

"Where is it?" the woman demanded.

"It's under the tree—the gift tag is addressed to Adam," Danielle explained.

The woman nodded to her accomplice, who quickly ran to the tree and began searching for the package. He found one shoved far under the branches; it was addressed to *Adam*. Without pause, he stood up and ripped off the packaging, revealing the framed photograph.

"Now will you two move in the hallway so we can tie you up?" the woman asked. "Or do I have to shoot you both?"

"We aren't moving in the hallway, and you are not shooting anyone. But I am taking that gun," Colin told her as he took a step in her direction.

THIRTY-FOUR

D anielle watched in horror as the elderly man fearlessly walked to the intruders—or perhaps it was foolishly. She glanced around and thought this might be an excellent time for Marie to make an entrance. She would pray for Walt to come looking for her, but she wasn't certain he would be able to stop a bullet if the nervous woman holding the gun pressed that trigger a little tighter.

Each step Colin took toward the couple, they took one step back, the woman's gun hand growing increasingly unsteady.

"I don't want to shoot you," the woman pleaded, her voice shaking as much as the hand holding the pistol, her back now against the wall.

"I know you don't, Marcella," Colin said in a gentle voice. He reached out and, without incident, took hold of the gun and removed it from her grasp. She broke into tears and began to sob.

Colin stepped back from the couple, still holding the gun. He glanced to the sofa and said, "Forrest, why don't you help your wife to the sofa and you both sit down. She looks rather upset."

"How did you know she wouldn't shoot you?" Danielle demanded, visibly shaken.

Colin turned to Danielle and smiled. He showed her the contents of the gun's cylinder, it was empty. "Bullets are typically required before you actually shoot anyone." He casually slipped the gun into his coat pocket.

"How did you know it didn't have bullets?" Danielle asked, still standing. Behind her the couple had taken a seat on the sofa while the man attempted to calm his wife.

"For one thing, Marcella is no killer. She was never going to shoot anyone." Colin moved over to one of the chairs facing the sofa. He sat down and then motioned for Danielle to take a seat.

Anxious, but also curious, Danielle sat down on the empty chair and looked over to the intruders.

"Why don't you take off those masks. It must be hot," Colin said.

Forrest ripped the ski mask off his head, sending his eyeglasses and now sweat-soaked hair askew. Straightening his glasses, he looked at Colin and asked, "How did you know who we were?"

Colin sat back in the sofa and smiled. "There is a lot I know. But I think it only fair that we explain it to Danielle. After all, it's her home you broke into—three times now."

No longer crying, Marcella pulled off her ski mask, revealing damp gray hair and red-rimmed eyes.

"I already know who they are," Danielle said. "And I already know why they have been breaking in here. But it's not here."

Marcella stared at Danielle, clear confusion on her face.

"You are looking for Eloise Winterborne's engagement ring, aren't you?" Danielle asked.

Marcella frowned. "How did you know? Did you already find it?"

"No, I didn't find it. But someone saw you break into Marlow House," Danielle began.

"Who?" Marcella asked.

"That doesn't matter. But you were later identified as the care-takers to Eloise Winterborne. I talked to Samuel Hayman, and he told me he never bought Eloise's ring—and that he had recently told you that. And I know you were at the shop in Astoria when we bought the items from her trunk. You have been looking for her ring, and you thought it was hidden in one of the items put in the trunk. But it wasn't."

"That's where you are wrong," Colin said. They all turned to look at him.

"We've already gone through everything—the ring isn't here. It's probably hidden under some floorboard back at the Winterborne estate," Danielle explained.

Colin smiled and looked at Marcella and Forrest. "Shall you tell her, or do you want me to?"

Forrest looked at Colin and asked, "Who are you?"

"Don't you remember? We met at the Seahorse Motel. I had the room next to yours."

"I know that," Forrest snapped. "But how do you know about the ring? How do you know any of this?"

Colin let out a sigh and shook his head. "None of that is important, but we are wasting time. If you two want to get away from here without getting arrested and ruining your Christmas, then we need to clear up a few things."

"You are letting us go?" Marcella asked.

Danielle frowned and looked at Colin. "You are letting them go?"

"It's Christmastime, Danielle. When you hear everything, I believe you'll want to let them go too," Colin told her.

Danielle let out a sigh, crossed her arms across her chest, and slumped back in her chair.

"You just want us to tell you where it is hidden so you can take it," Marcella accused Colin. "You must have overheard us talking at the motel."

Colin let out a weary tsk, tsk, tsk and then said, "I already know where it is. It's in the picture frame. Of course, even if I hadn't already known about it, I would have figured that out a few minutes ago. If you will remember, your husband just unwrapped the frame after you demanded Danielle tell you where it was. You are definitely not cut out for a life of crime."

Danielle turned to Colin. "How can the ring be in the picture frame? Even if someone shoved it between the matting and the photograph, there would be a big lump. Anyway, we already took the back of the frame off. There was nothing there."

Colin stood up and walked to where Forrest had dropped the picture frame. He picked it up and walked back to Danielle. He handed it to her.

"Shake it," he told her.

Danielle frowned. "Shake it?"

"Yes. Give it a good shake. But hold it next to your ear, or you won't hear," Colin explained.

Danielle did as instructed. She heard a rattle sound and then looked from Colin to the couple sitting on her sofa.

"Marcella and Forrest here are not a hundred percent certain that rattle is Eloise's ring, but they are certain enough that they risked breaking in here." He then looked at the couple and said, "Now explain, why are you here?"

Marcella let out a deep breath and slumped back in the sofa. She looked to Danielle with a weary expression. "Eloise bought that frame from a neighbor's yard sale. The thick frame around the picture is not solid. The hole that's used to hang the picture is also a keyhole. The frame itself—the portion around the picture—has a hidden compartment that slides open when you use the key. She thought it was very clever and used to say if she had some treasure, that's where she would hide it."

"If you thought the ring was in the frame, why didn't you just take it?" Danielle asked.

"Because the frame had already been put with the rest of the items in the trunk and locked up. We made an excuse to look in the trunk again, and when I shook the frame, I heard it. There was something inside the hidden compartment. I knew then that had to be where she put the ring. But we couldn't take the frame, and I didn't have the key to open it."

"They wouldn't just give it to you?" Danielle asked. "After all, they didn't know what it held."

Forrest shook his head. "No. Eloise's instructions were very exact, and the executor of the will followed them to a tee. I think one reason, there were rumors that she had a codicil to the will made, using another attorney, and they were afraid if it was found, and distribution of the estate reviewed—or even contested—he didn't want to give anyone reason to accuse him of not following her instructions exactly. We just figured we would buy the frame and then break it open."

"So you don't have the key?" Danielle asked.

"If we had the key, we wouldn't be here now," Marcella confessed.

Danielle turned to Colin and asked, "What is your role in all this?"

"I don't want to see two good people ruin their lives by making a stupid mistake," Colin explained.

"You think we are good people?" Forrest asked.

Colin turned his smile to Forrest. "For years you and your wife cared for Eloise Winterborne. She was never easy—and while some caretakers can be cruel or harsh, you never were, even during those times when you had every reason to resent her."

"She was an odd woman, but she wasn't a bad person," Marcella said. "She was all alone. We felt sorry for her. And I know she accused us of taking things, but she used to accuse the neighbors of taking her newspaper too, and she didn't even have a subscription."

"But we did think she was going to remember us in her will. It's not like we expected to inherit her estate. We never once thought that—or even wanted it. We simply wanted some sort of retirement. Marcella and I aren't getting any younger. I don't know if we are up to being caretakers again, and I'm not sure what else we can do at our age. Was that really so wrong?"

"The only thing that was wrong was to break into Marlow House," Colin said.

The Hoopers lowered their heads. Danielle wasn't sure if it was in shame or because they were caught.

"What now?" Marcella asked, raising her head again and looking at Colin.

"I think you should both leave and go back to Astoria. I know the room you rented there is still available."

"Why would we do that?" Marcella asked.

"Considering it is Saturday, and Christmas is Monday, you will want to be there next week when they call you," Colin explained. "If you leave now and go somewhere else—like out of the state—you will just have to come back next week anyway. Why not go back to the community you know—where you have friends—and enjoy Christmas."

"Who is calling us?" Marcella asked.

Before Colin could answer the question, Marie burst into the room. Standing in front of Danielle, her back to the sofa, she asked, "Danielle, what are you doing over here?"

"Who is calling us?" Marcella repeated.

Marie twirled around and faced Forrest and Marcella. "They are here! I have been looking all over for them." She turned back to Danielle and said, "You will never guess what happened. I went to the Winterborne estate—what a mess. But apparently the Realtor must have talked the executor into doing some repairs. No way are they going to sell that—"

"Marie, please, not yet," Colin said. "And can you move over there so we can see Marcella and Forrest?"

Danielle and Marie jerked their heads to look at Colin.

"You can see me?" Marie muttered.

"Marie? What are you talking about?" Marcella asked. "You're not making any sense."

Colin smiled at Marie. Her eyes widened and she stepped back, no longer blocking the Hoopers from his view.

Colin looked back to the Hoopers and said, "I knew about the ring and the frame, didn't I?"

Marcella and Forrest nodded. Danielle and Marie listened.

"I also know Eloise had a codicil made to her will—one that takes care of you both," Colin said.

"It's true!" Marie exclaimed. "That's what I wanted to tell you," Marie told Danielle, ignoring Colin's glare. "There were contractors working at the estate when I got there, and they were doing some repairs in one of the rooms and found some papers that had been hidden behind some boards. One was a recent codicil to Eloise's will, including the Hoopers!"

THIRTY-FIVE

Danielle's cellphone began to ring. She stood in her living room with Colin and Marie. Picking up the phone, she saw it was Walt calling.

"Is everything okay?" he asked when she answered his call.

Danielle glanced to the doorway where Marcella and Forrest had rushed through a few minutes earlier—out of the living room, down the entry hall, and out the front door into the night.

"Yes. I'll explain everything later. But right now, I'm talking with Marie and Colin. I'll be over there as soon as I can."

"What do you mean you're talking with Marie *and* Colin?" Walt asked.

"Just that. I'll explain everything later." Danielle ended her call and set the cellphone on the table.

"Do you think they're going back to Astoria, like you suggested?" Marie asked.

Colin shrugged. "It doesn't really matter. It would simply be more convenient for them if they did. But next week when they get that phone call, which I'm sure they will, they'll be returning."

"What are you going to do with their gun?" Danielle asked.

"Gun? What gun?" Marie asked.

"The Hoopers came here with a gun—an unloaded one. Colin took it away from them."

"Tossing it off the end of the pier would probably be the best place for everyone. If we turn it over to the police, it will just cause unnecessary problems. And frankly, the Hoopers saved someone's Christmas by buying the gun today."

"In what way?" Danielle asked.

"People who illegally purchase firearms typically don't have good intentions," Colin said. "The Hoopers took this gun off the street, and the next person who would have bought it—if they hadn't—won't be able to find another one as quickly. Hopefully before they do, they will reconsider their life choices."

Danielle glanced over to the framed picture still sitting on the coffee table. "I suppose I need to get that back to the estate?"

"Absolutely not," Colin said as he sat back down in a chair and then motioned for Marie and Danielle to both sit down.

Marie took a seat on the sofa and asked, "And what do you think she should do with it?"

"I suppose whatever Danielle wants. She did buy it. It belongs to her," Colin said.

Danielle sat down next to Marie. "It just doesn't seem right."

"It's what Eloise wanted," Colin explained.

Danielle studied Colin a moment, tilting her head slightly as she did. "You knew Eloise Winterborne?"

Colin leaned back comfortably in the chair. He crossed his legs casually and smiled at Danielle. "I did. Eloise expressly requested the ring be removed from her inventory list. It was her way of declaring it was no longer part of her estate."

"Why would she do that?" Danielle asked.

"When Eloise could no longer wear the ring, she had no one to leave it to—and she felt if she left it to the estate, it would simply be sold anyway, by people who weren't particularly interested in the ring aside from its monetary value," Colin explained. "She rather liked the idea of putting it somewhere that it could be discovered— like a hidden treasure. She often wondered who might someday find it and what they would think. To her, the feeling she experienced imagining someone eventually discovering the ring was akin to what a person might feel when giving someone a special Christmas gift— that anticipation of them opening your gift. Of course, in her case, she could only imagine what it would be like."

"She was quirky," Marie scoffed.

"Did you know Eloise when she was alive—or was it Eloise's ghost who told you all that?" Danielle asked Colin.

He smiled at Danielle but did not answer.

"Have you always been a medium?" Danielle asked.

"Medium?" He frowned.

"Have you always been able to see ghosts?"

"Not always," he told her.

"You obviously know Marie is a ghost," Danielle pointed out.

Colin's smiled broadened. "Yes. She was rather hard to ignore."

"Who are you, really?" Marie asked.

"You don't believe I am who I say I am?" he asked.

Marie studied him through narrowed eyes. "I don't think you are. Is your name really Colin Bari?"

"Bari is more a place than an actual surname," he explained.

"And your first name?" Danielle asked.

"It's a variation of my real first name. This time of year I find it less confusing. Yet understand, my lack of transparency is not for nefarious purposes—no more than your friend using his mother's surname Johnson instead of his own, Glandon."

Danielle's eyes widened. "You know who Chris really is?"

He gave Danielle a nod. "Yes, certainly. Your friend embraces the spirit of Christmas every day of the year."

"You won't tell anyone?" Danielle asked.

"Of course not. His anonymity will be respected."

"I assume you followed the Hoopers here?" Danielle asked.

"No. I didn't. The Hoopers aren't the reason I came. But I knew why they were really here, and what they were up to. I seriously doubted they would be successful in their efforts—certainly not with spirits keeping watch on Marlow House. But I couldn't let them ruin their lives by such a foolish and misguided act."

"Then why did you come?" Marie asked.

Danielle sat up straighter and stared at Colin. "Wait a minute, earlier, when the Hoopers wanted to take that bag of gifts, you said we couldn't let them take it, that you needed something that was in the bag. What was it? What could you have possibly wanted?"

"The shoe, Danielle." He motioned to the paper sack. "Go—open it. See for yourself."

Wearing a frown of confusion, Danielle stood a moment and then retrieved the package containing the Christmas shoe. She unwrapped it and then sat back down on the sofa, still holding it.

"Why would this bring you here?" Danielle asked.

"Eloise picked that shoe up at a thrift store. The only thing she added was the gift paper glued on its sole. Peel the paper off, and you'll see," he instructed.

Danielle used the tips of her fingernails to help pry one edge of the gift wrap from the bottom of the shoe. After lifting one end, she was able to rip off the multilayers with one firm tug, revealing a small gold key glued under the paper.

Prying off the key, she looked up to Colin. "Is this the key to the frame?"

Colin nodded.

"This is what brought you here?" she asked.

"Heavens no! Something much more valuable than a key—or Eloise's ring. Read it, Danielle. Read what is written on the bottom of the shoe."

Danielle studied the shoe, holding it upside down so she could see the sole. She couldn't see the writing before, not covered with the decoupaged Christmas wrap, and she hadn't noticed it when first tearing off the paper, being more interested in the small gold key she had uncovered.

With a frown, she tilted the shoe slightly so she could better read what someone had written on the bottom of the shoe in felt-tip marker: *The Gardener-Sparks Christmas shoe—the gift with sole.*

Danielle stared at the shoe. "Sparks? This couldn't be Elizabeth Sparks's family's Christmas shoe...could it?"

"It is," Colin told her. "The shoe ended up in a thrift shop, where Eloise found it. It never occurred to her the shoe had been the one her art teacher had told her about. She always called Elizabeth, *Elizabeth the Artist*; the surname Sparks never meant anything to her."

"How do you know all this?" Danielle asked.

"It's very complicated," Colin said.

She looked back to the shoe and murmured, "I wonder who Gardener is?"

"It's Elizabeth's older brother's last name. Elizabeth's mother's first husband died when she was pregnant with her first child—a boy. She remarried a few years later and had Elizabeth. The older brother always went by his real father's surname, although his mother's second husband was every bit a father to him," Colin explained.

"Gardener...that's Owen's last name," Danielle murmured.

"That's because Owen is Elizabeth's older brother," Colin explained.

Danielle shook her head. "No. Elizabeth told me her brother's name was Mark."

"His real name is Owen Mark Gardener. Before he was married, he went by his middle name," Colin explained.

"His middle name is Mark!" Marie said. "I saw it on his driver's license."

"Owen is Elizabeth's older brother?" Danielle asked.

"Yes, the same one who carelessly threw out the Christmas shoe —and his family," Colin explained.

"That's why he was looking at the shoe like that," Marie said.

"Yes. He knew you had the shoe. He told me all about it when I took him for dinner the other night. Of course, I already knew," Colin explained.

"How?" Danielle asked.

"That's not important right now. What is important, you need to make sure Owen gets that shoe tonight during the gift exchange. It's the nudge he needs to do what he desperately wants to do, but hasn't yet found the courage."

"Reunite with his family?" Danielle asked.

"Yes. He carelessly threw away his family when he left Frederick-port—just as he carelessly tossed out the Christmas shoe. When most people look at that shoe, they see nothing more than a tacky collection of fake gems and artificial flowers glued onto an absurd canvas. But for some, it represents something precious and priceless —family with its unique traditions, shared stories, and private jokes, which can only really be appreciated by the family members."

"Can't I just give this to him?" Danielle asked. "Do we really need to make it part of the white elephant game?"

"Yes, you can just give it to him. And now that I think about it, it really would be out of place in a white elephant gift exchange, considering its value is priceless," Colin said.

Marie reached over and picked up the gold key and asked Danielle. "Are you going to open the hidden compartment?"

Danielle looked over to Colin and asked, "Why did Eloise hide the key on the shoe? If she wanted someone to find the treasure in the frame after she died, wouldn't she have taped the key on the back of the frame? She couldn't have imagined the shoe and frame would end up at the same place. I know they did, but she certainly didn't know that."

"No." Colin shook his head. "She only hid the key there in case she wanted to open the frame's hidden compartment. And she would never have taped it on the back of the frame for fear someone would find it before she died. Eloise never imagined that the eventual owner of the frame would also have the key. She just assumed someone would realize it had a hidden compartment and pry it open."

"That might never have happened," Danielle said. "I certainly would never have guessed that frame had a hidden compartment."

"I'm just explaining what Eloise thought," Colin said.

"And Eloise told you all that?" Marie asked.

"Some of it. Some of it I figured out on my own," Colin explained. "But now that Danielle has the key, it won't be necessary to break the frame to free the prize."

Danielle studied the key for a moment while she considered Eloise's wishes for the ring.

"What are you thinking, Danielle?" Marie asked after a prolonged silence.

"I was just thinking how Eloise put the ring in the frame because she liked the idea of someone finding the hidden compartment—and she imagined their excitement at getting it open and discovering something was hidden inside—something valuable beyond their wildest dreams. She liked thinking of how excited that person might be," Danielle explained.

"Very true," Colin agreed.

"But if I open the frame now, none of that will happen," Danielle said.

"What do you mean?" Marie asked.

Danielle looked to Marie. "For one thing, I already know what's in the hidden compartment. Sorta like knowing what's in a wrapped Christmas gift before opening it. That element of surprise—which is part of the fun—is gone. And another thing, I am really the last person I know who would be remotely excited to find a valuable piece of jewelry. Do I really want something else to lock up in my safety deposit box? And if I sell it, that is really no different than the estate selling it, which, according to Colin, Eloise wanted to avoid."

"But if someone else finds the ring, chances are they would sell it too," Marie argued.

"Yes, but they will experience the excitement of finding it—and then the excitement of selling it so they can buy something they really want. I won't experience any of that."

THIRTY-SIX

D anielle's cellphone rang again. She peeked at it and cringed.
The next moment she answered the call. "I promise I will be
there in ten minutes. I have to rewrap a couple of gifts. But I
promise I will be there in a few minutes."

"What is going on over there?" Walt asked.

"I'll explain later. But everything is fine."

When Danielle got off the phone, she went to the parlor and
sorted through the items Chris had picked up from the Astoria thrift
shop. She selected the puzzle box and then hastily wrapped it.

"What are you doing?" Marie asked. The ghost stood at the
parlor doorway with Colin.

"I need to substitute something for the shoe. I'm going to use the
puzzle box Chris picked up." When she was finished wrapping the
white elephant gift, she grabbed a Christmas gift bag and some
tissue paper from a basket sitting under the desk.

"What's that for?" Marie asked.

"It's for the shoe."

THE SOUND of lively chatter and laughter blended with Christmas
music hit Danielle the moment she opened the door to the Bartleys'
home. It didn't appear anyone, save Walt, had particularly noticed

her absence the last forty minutes, considering everyone seemed enthralled with whatever conversation he or she was currently engaged in.

Walt greeted her the moment she walked into the house, giving her a quick kiss and taking the large bag of gifts she carried. Marie flashed him a smile and walked to the living room, while Colin followed her.

"I was getting worried about you," Walt whispered in her ear as they walked into the kitchen. "What were you doing?"

"Dani? Where have you been," Lily demanded. She stood in the kitchen with Kelly, while holding Connor on one hip.

"I forgot my white elephant gifts," Danielle told her. "And then I had to rewrap one."

"Why?" Lily asked.

Danielle glanced from Lily to Kelly and then looked back to Lily. "Max got into the packages and ripped one," she lied.

Lily frowned. "That doesn't sound like Max."

"Max is a cat, isn't he?" Kelly asked. "Cats always do stuff like that."

"Where should I put these?" Walt asked, holding up the bag slightly.

"You can set it on the counter," Lily told him.

After Walt set the bag on the counter, Danielle walked over to it and pulled out the gift bag holding the Christmas shoe.

"What's that?" Lily asked.

"Something I have to give Owen," Danielle explained.

"What is it?" Lily asked.

"It's the shoe," Danielle said with a smile.

Lily frowned. "I thought that was for the white elephant game?"

Danielle shook her head. "No. It's too valuable for that."

Danielle flashed Lily and Kelly a grin and then turned from the counter, holding the gift bag, while a confused Walt followed his wife from the kitchen.

"What is going on?" Walt asked.

"I can't explain it all now. But I need to give this to Owen."

"Did you know he is Elizabeth Sparks's brother?" Walt asked when they stepped out of the kitchen.

Danielle paused for a moment and turned to Walt. "How did you know?"

"Adam told us. Apparently they have been estranged for years," Walt explained.

"Where is Owen?" she asked.

"I saw him going down the hall right before you got here. I assume he was going to the bathroom," Walt told her.

"I need to give this to him," Danielle said. When she stepped into the hallway a few moments later, the door to the guest bathroom opened and out walked Owen.

"Owen," Danielle called out, "I need to give you something."

When she reached Owen, she handed him the gift bag. Confused, he looked down at the bag and reluctantly accepted it.

"I don't understand. Lily said we were doing the gift game in an hour," Owen asked.

"This isn't a white elephant gift. It's for you," Danielle explained while Walt stood silently behind her. The three stood in the hallway outside the guest bathroom door while the sounds of the party drifted in.

He shook his head and started to hand the gift bag back. "No, you shouldn't be getting me anything. I feel funny as it is that you wouldn't let me get the gift for the game."

"This belongs to you," Danielle explained. "I'm simply returning it to its rightful owner—at least, to one of them."

Confused, Owen reached into the bag and pulled out the white tissue paper and then looked inside. He let out a gasp.

"Merry Christmas," Danielle said softly.

Reverently, Owen dipped his hand in the gift bag and pulled out the Christmas shoe. "How did you know?"

"Read the bottom. It has your name."

Owen turned the shoe over and looked at the inscription. A smile curled his lips. "When I saw it at your house, the bottom was covered with Christmas paper. I was sure it was the same shoe. I mean seriously, how could there be two almost exactly the same?" He let out a laugh.

"Eloise Winterborne bought this at a thrift shop. While your sister had told her about your family's Christmas shoe, Eloise didn't remember Elizabeth's last name, and she had no idea it was the same shoe. I doubt she even knew your sister no longer had it. Eloise is the one who covered the sole with gift wrap."

"How did you know Elizabeth is my sister—or that Eloise was the one who added the Christmas wrap?" Owen asked.

"I would like to know that myself," Walt said under his breath.

"I have my ways. Anyway, after I removed the Christmas paper from the bottom of the shoe, I saw the name Sparks. Elizabeth had told me about the Christmas shoe. I knew it had to be the same one. And your last name is Gardener. You told me you used to live in Frederickport, that you were estranged from your family—and Elizabeth implied she was estranged from her brother. Plus, I saw you downtown watching Elizabeth. At the time, I didn't realize she was your sister." It wasn't exactly the truth, Danielle thought. But close enough.

Danielle took the now empty gift bag and tissue paper from Owen while he continued to hold the shoe—studying it.

"I remember when we made this," Owen said, his voice barely a whisper. "I think I was my grandpa's favorite—oh, not that he didn't adore Elizabeth. But I was the firstborn, and those first few years of my life, before Mom remarried, Grandpa was always around. I was his boy. He never had a son." Owen paused a moment and took a deep breath, wiping a tear from the corner of his eye.

"Elizabeth mentioned something about your grandfather being sick when you made this," Danielle said.

"He died a few months before the next Christmas. His last Christmas, he was pretty sick, and we were over there a lot, helping Grandma. I just remember how he really loved the idea of us making the Christmas shoe." Owen glanced up and asked, "Did Elizabeth tell you about the bridal shoes?"

Danielle nodded. "She did."

"I think Grandpa was a little annoyed when my uncle got rid of the bridal shoes. I heard him say once that my uncle didn't have much of a sense of humor. Anyway, Grandpa didn't glue anything on the Christmas shoe, but he kept giving us suggestions, telling us we needed to add more stuff. And then when my aunt and uncle opened it up on Christmas morning—well, Grandpa laughed like hell. It was good to hear him laugh; he was sick so much of the time."

"And then the shoe was passed around?" Danielle asked.

"I know it probably seems silly, but it really was fun each Christmas, as every family member wondered if they would be the one to get it that year. Even my uncle thought it was pretty funny. Once my cousin wrapped the shoe in an enormous box filled with a couple of

THE GHOST AND THE CHRISTMAS SPIRIT

bricks and gave it to his brother, who was completely fooled." Owen smiled at the memory.

"So why did you get rid of it?" Danielle asked.

Owen let out a deep breath. "We hadn't been married long. My wife knew about the Christmas shoe, but she didn't get it. Thought it was stupid. Of course, at the time she didn't tell my family that. And then Mom gave it to her on our first Christmas as a married couple. In retrospect, I understand it was Mom's way of welcoming her into the family—in spite of the fact we all knew my parents had adored my old girlfriend."

"And your wife didn't appreciate the gesture?" Danielle asked.

Owen laughed dryly. "That is an understatement. She took it as an insult. Like they were mocking her. Making fun of her. She was pretty upset, because she had heard how Mom had given my old girlfriend a pair of expensive earrings during our last Christmas together. And the shoe was the only thing Mom gave her that year. Oh, Mom and Dad gave us a Christmas gift, something for the both of us—but nothing just for her. Nothing but the shoe."

"But why did you have to get rid of it?" Danielle asked.

Owen shrugged. "If I hadn't, it would have looked to her like I sided against her. Like I said, she just didn't understand the whole Christmas shoe thing—thought it was stupid. I suppose that should have been a red flag. I imagine if Grandpa had still been alive, he would have doubted more than her lack of humor."

Danielle handed the bag and tissue paper back to Owen. He accepted it and then returned the shoe to the bag.

"So, are you going to take this to your family?" Danielle asked.

"I want to see them…but…I don't know if it's too late."

"Come on, Owen, if being reunited with your family's Christmas shoe isn't a clear sign you need to go to them, then I doubt even Santa arriving in his sleigh to escort you there will convince you."

IT WAS ALMOST MIDNIGHT. Connor had been asleep for hours in his nursery. Lily and Ian had said goodbye to most of their guests. The only ones remaining were Walt, Danielle, Heather, Chris and Noah. Colin and Owen had returned to Marlow House, with Marie going with them. Before following the pair back to Marlow House,

Marie expressed her concern to Danielle. "He already admitted he is not who he said he was. I need to keep an eye on him."

When those remaining at the Bartleys' drifted back to the living room, Danielle told Lily, "Your party was a success. Everyone seemed to have a great time."

"Now will you explain what happened after you left earlier?" Walt asked.

"Let's see…first Colin and I were held at gunpoint by two people wearing ski masks," Danielle said calmly.

Chris rolled his eyes, and Walt said, "I am serious, Danielle."

"So am I," she said calmly. The room went silent and everyone stared at her. She smiled at her friends and then proceeded to explain what had happened when she had returned to Marlow House to retrieve the white elephant gifts.

When Danielle finished recounting the events from earlier that evening, everyone remained silent. Finally, Walt asked, "Why do you think Colin is a medium?"

"It's pretty obvious, isn't it?" Danielle asked. "He could see and hear Marie."

"You told us he didn't flinch when he took the gun from that woman. Even if he was confident she would not intentionally shoot him, that doesn't mean she wouldn't have panicked and pulled the trigger."

"You are suggesting he was a little too calm for a living man?" Chris asked.

Walt looked to Chris and said, "Yes, if he did indeed react the way Danielle said."

"He did," Danielle insisted.

"You think he is a ghost? But we could all see him?" Ian asked.

"It wouldn't be the first time more than just the mediums saw a ghost—especially at Christmastime," Walt reminded them.

THIRTY-SEVEN

D anielle woke on Christmas Eve morning to the sound of rain
falling on the rooftop. Joanne would not be coming in to help
with this morning's breakfast. But Danielle was not concerned
because she knew Walt and Chris would help her. She rolled over in
bed to Walt's side and found it empty. Rubbing her eyes, she sat up
and glanced around the room. There was no sign of Walt, and she
didn't hear any sounds coming from the adjoining bathroom.

"Good morning, sleepyhead," Walt greeted her when he walked
into the bedroom a moment later, carrying two cups of coffee. He
was already dressed for the day.

Danielle glanced at the clock. "Wow, I slept in."

"You had a busy night last night," Walt said, handing her one of
the cups. "Being held up at gunpoint and all that."

Danielle accepted the cup and chuckled, "No kidding." She took
a sip.

Walt sat down on a nearby chair with his coffee. "I thought you
might want to get up. Owen is downstairs waiting to say goodbye.
He was hoping to see you before he leaves."

"Owen is leaving?" Danielle asked.

"Yes. He's going over to his sister's house to see her and his
parents. He's hoping to make amends," Walt explained before
taking a drink of his coffee.

DANIELLE MADE it downstairs within fifteen minutes to say goodbye to Owen. She had first washed her face and combed her hair, but didn't bother applying any makeup. She slipped on dark blue leggings and an oversized powder blue Christmas sweater decorated with snowflakes, before pulling on her boots. She found Owen standing in the entry hall with his suitcases, talking to Chris and Noah. Marie stood with them, but Owen was unaware of the ghost's presence.

"We tried to talk him into breakfast before he leaves," Chris told Danielle when she reached them.

"I'm too nervous to eat," Owen said. "But I did have a cup of coffee."

"So you're going to see your family?" Danielle stood in front of Owen, Walt now by her side.

"I hope they want to see me," Owen said. "And I just realized, I haven't even bought any Christmas gifts."

"Just give them the Christmas shoe. I have a feeling that will be enough," Danielle said before giving Owen a parting hug.

"I want to thank all of you. You've been so nice." Owen glanced around and said, "I wanted to say goodbye to Colin, but I haven't seen him this morning."

"I'm afraid he got up early," Chris told him. "He left right after I got up. Told me not to expect him back until later this afternoon."

Owen let out a sigh and picked up his suitcases. "Well, tell him thanks, would you. He is a good listener."

Ten minutes later, after Owen finished his farewells and went out to his car, Danielle and the rest stood at the living room window, looking outside, watching him drive off.

"I would love to be a fly in the corner," Danielle said.

"What do you mean?" Chris asked.

"I wish I could see how the reunion goes."

"I guess I could be a fly," Marie said cheerfully. "I'll be back later to report how it all went." In the next moment Marie vanished.

ELIZABETH SPARKS WAS JUST OPENING her blinds when she spied him drive up. She immediately ducked behind the curtain and then peeked out again. It was him, the man with the beard and sunglasses. He parked his car. Like the other times, he sat in the vehicle and didn't seem to be making any attempt to get out. He just sat there, staring up at her house.

"What are you looking at?" Mrs. Sparks asked when she walked into the living room.

"There is a man parked in front of the house," Elizabeth said in a whisper, still peeking outside.

"I doubt he can hear you," Mrs. Sparks said with a laugh, approaching the window.

"He's getting out of the car!" Elizabeth blurted, moving completely from the window's view.

"Elizabeth, why are you getting so jumpy?" Mrs. Sparks intended to look out the window but was yanked to one side by her daughter.

"Don't let him see you!"

"Who is it?" Mrs. Sparks asked, making no more attempt to look outside.

"I don't know. But I have seen him a few times—parked in front of my house. And I have run into him around town, watching me," Elizabeth told her.

"Why didn't you ever mention this before?" her mother asked.

The next minute the doorbell rang.

"That's him!" Elizabeth said, holding onto her mother.

The two women stood quietly in the living room, not looking out the window, waiting for whoever was ringing the bell to go away. The doorbell rang again.

"Isn't anyone going to get that?" Mr. Sparks asked when he walked into the room. He didn't wait for their response but walked straight to the door and opened it.

The women stood silently, waiting and watching as Mr. Sparks stood at the open doorway looking out onto the front porch, saying nothing.

After a few moments of silence, Mr. Sparks said, "Mark?"

"Hi, Dad," came a male voice.

"Mark?" Elizabeth and her mother said in unison. The women rushed to the doorway and found Owen Mark standing on the front porch, holding a Christmas gift bag in one hand and his sunglasses in the other.

"Oh my god…it is you. The beard, I didn't even recognize you!" Elizabeth said. "You've been here for a few days, haven't you?"

"I didn't know if you would want to see me…" he said in a small voice.

WHEN MARIE RETURNED to Marlow House, she found Walt and Danielle sitting at the breakfast table with Chris, Noah, Lily, Ian, and Heather, eating biscuits and gravy with scrambled eggs and sausage. Connor sat in a nearby baby seat on the floor, with Hunny and Sadie standing guard. The moment Marie appeared in the room, Danielle asked her about the reunion.

"He didn't even have an opportunity to give them the shoe," Marie said when she took a seat at the table.

"They didn't want to see him?" Danielle asked.

"Are you kidding? That boy was greeted like the returning warrior. I meant he didn't get an opportunity to give them the shoe when he first arrived. There was so much hugging and crying. Goodness, I swear I was going to cry myself, and then I realized ghosts don't cry."

"I don't know about that," Danielle said. "I seem to recall a lot of sobbing when Cheryl realized she was dead."

"Not the same thing, dear. But it was quite lovely. They were so busy catching up that he didn't even get a chance to give them the shoe until he had been there a good hour. And then there was another wave of tears. I do believe everyone over at that house got their Christmas wish this year."

"That's the best kind of Christmas wish," Danielle said as she snatched another biscuit from the basket on the table.

"So tell me, what is everyone wishing for this Christmas?" Ian asked his friends.

"I got my Christmas wish," Noah said. "I'm spending Christmas with my baby brother again this year."

Chris smiled at his brother and said, "Spending Christmas with family and friends is on the top of my list. But I realize I will be getting something I have wanted for a while."

"What's that?" Lily asked.

"I never mentioned it before, but I have often thought about how I'd love to design my own house. But there just aren't any empty lots available—at least not right on the ocean in Frederick-port, where I want to live."

"There is now," Lily reminded him.

Chris flashed her a grin. "Exactly. While I didn't burn my house down intentionally—"

"I hope not," Heather interjected.

"I now have the opportunity to build the house of my dreams—on the street I want to live on," Chris said.

"That's because we are such wonderful neighbors," Heather teased.

"True," Chris conceded. He then looked at Walt and Danielle and asked, "What's your Christmas wish?"

"Considering all my blessings since—since my second chance—I think I'm good for quite a few Christmases," Walt said.

Chris looked from Walt to Danielle and asked, "What about you?"

"I would have really liked Pearl Huckabee's attitude toward Hunny to change. It makes me nervous, I worry that if Hunny were to get out when Pearl is home and we aren't, that she might do something to hurt her," Danielle said.

"I imagine Pearl will have a different attitude, considering Hunny is the one who practically saved her," Noah suggested.

"I wouldn't be so sure of that," Walt said. "Danielle and I stopped at the hospital to see her, and Pearl made it a point to tell us nothing has changed between us."

"That woman has a serious problem," Heather muttered.

"So what about you?" Chris asked Heather.

"Are you asking if I have a serious problem?" Heather frowned.

With a laugh, Chris said, "No. What is your Christmas wish, you goof."

"Oh...that," Heather said sheepishly. "I don't know. I haven't really thought about it. But things are kind of good right now. Probably the best they have been in a long time for me. If I had a Christmas wish, I think it would be that things keep going the way they are."

"I agree!" Lily said. "I am at a really good place. Lots of blessings to be grateful for."

Marie glanced down at Connor, who had just fallen asleep. "I agree with you there."

"Last night the chief was telling me what Evan wanted for Christmas," Ian said.

"A puppy?" Heather asked.

"No. He wants a dream hop with his mother—actually he wants a dream hop with his mother, father and brother. He wants them to spend Christmas together," Ian explained.

"I wish I knew how to do that for Evan." Marie looked at Walt. "You did that with Danielle—how did you manage to get her family together for the Christmas dream hop? Maybe if I knew, I could do the same thing for Evan. It would mean so much to him."

"I'm afraid I don't know," Walt told her. "So much I've forgotten since coming back over to this side."

"Don't know what?" Lily asked with a frown, since she was unable to see or hear Marie.

"How to dream hop," Danielle explained.

"Maybe Eva would know how," Heather suggested.

"Where is Eva, by the way? She hasn't been around all week," Danielle asked.

"Eva feels rather social this time of year—off visiting her old haunts," Marie said.

"Pun intended?" Chris asked.

The next moment red and green glitter began falling from the ceiling above the table, disappearing before it reached the tabletop. The mediums stopped talking and looked up to the ceiling.

"Eva? Is that you?" Walt asked.

"Is Eva here?" Lily asked.

The glitter began to swirl, turning from red and green to pure white, forming a miniature tornado, and from its core emerged a vision of a woman dressed in a green gown and a festive hat decorated in gold and red for the season.

"Did someone call my name?" Eva asked with outstretched arms as she slowly descended from the ceiling, the toes of her shoes almost touching the table—and about to enter the bowl of gravy.

"Look out for the gravy!" Danielle called out.

The next moment all traces of glitter vanished, and Eva's vision disappeared and then reappeared, standing next to the table.

"It's not as if my shoes are real," Eva reminded her. "Although shoes in the gravy—even if they are only an illusion, not very appetizing."

"Merry Christmas, Eva," Danielle greeted her. "We are happy to see you."

"I'm not too late for your party, am I?" Eva asked.

"That's not until tonight," Walt told her.

They were interrupted when Colin walked into the dining room.

"Colin, hello," Danielle greeted him. "There is plenty of food left over, if you are hungry."

Eva, whose back had been to the new arrival, turned around to see who had just walked into the room. When she saw who it was, she said, "Nicholas, is that you?"

"Eva," Colin returned, "I wondered when I would be seeing you."

THIRTY-EIGHT

L ily was dying of curiosity to know what was going on, but since she could neither see nor hear Eva and Marie, the one-sided conversation was driving her insane. Adding to the intrigue, it seemed Colin was now talking to Eva, and it sounded as if he knew her. She wanted to ask questions, but Connor woke up from his brief nap and began to fuss. He needed to be changed and fed. Since she and Ian had just finished breakfast, they said goodbye minutes after Colin's arrival and left Marlow House to the ghosts and mediums. Danielle would have to fill her in later.

"You know each other?" Danielle asked Eva.

"Yes. Nicholas and I are old friends," Eva said as she sat down on the chair Lily had abandoned.

"I thought your name was Colin?" Noah asked.

"Colin is a French variation of Nicholas, didn't you know that?" Eva asked. "This time of year he prefers to go by Colin to go unnoticed." She looked to Chris and said, "Like you do, when you go by your mother's maiden name instead of your legal surname."

"How do you know each other?" Walt asked, looking from Eva to Colin.

"I first met him a few years back," Eva began. "When Colin was going through Salem, and I was visiting a cemetery there. It was at Christmastime, and you know how unusual it is for someone like me to find anyone new to talk to—someone who can see and hear me.

Newly departed spirits who haven't yet crossed over don't count. They tend to be rather self-absorbed, only wanting to talk about themselves and their new predicament. But not Nicholas, he has always been interested in other people. Although technically, I suppose I am no longer a person."

"I will confess, when we first met, I wasn't sure you were a spirit, or perhaps some lovely actress dressed in a period costume for some Christmas play," Colin told her with a smile.

"I understand going by a nickname, but I don't understand what Eva means when she said you wish to go unnoticed at this time of year. You mentioned something similar to me yesterday when Marie asked if you were who you claimed to be," Danielle told Colin.

"Isn't it obvious?" Eva asked with a laugh. "An older gentleman with a white beard at this time of year, whose name is Nicholas?"

"Are you suggesting children might confuse him for Santa Claus?" Chris asked.

"It is Christmastime. And in all those Christmas movies I see people watching this time of year, the character who turns out to be Santa Claus is typically named Nick or Nicholas," Eva reminded them.

"I don't know," Heather argued. "He obviously doesn't have the belly for the part."

"Ahh, the rumor of Saint Nicholas's girth is greatly exaggerated," Eva said.

"Perhaps. But would it really be so bad if kids thought you were Santa?" Danielle asked.

"It could be annoying," Heather suggested.

"That's not the reason," Colin corrected. "Sinter Klaas prefers a sense of anonymity."

"Sinter Klaas is a Dutch nickname for Saint Nicholas," Noah noted.

"If he really wanted anonymity, then he shouldn't have run around dressed in bright red, hung out with elves, and driven around in a flying sleigh," Heather snarked.

"Speaking of Santa Claus, I tried to get Walt to dress up to play Santa for our party tonight, but even when he had a beard, I don't think he could pass for the jolly old fellow," Danielle said.

"What about Nicholas?" Eva asked, turning to look at Colin.

Colin stroked his white beard and said, "While I have the beard, as Heather pointed out, my stature might not be convincing in the part. But I could give it a shot."

"Would you really be willing to do it?" Danielle asked.

———

PEARL HUCKABEE SAT ALONE in her hospital room, looking up at the television from the bed as she rapidly punched the remote, looking for something to watch. It was mostly reruns and stale Christmas movies. *It's a Wonderful Life* was playing on one channel, but the last thing she wanted to do was watch a movie about angels. Perhaps Clarence wasn't the main character, but she found the premise absurd, even for Christmas. She told herself she was beyond the age of embracing the notion of Christmas magic and angels. Real life was about falling off ladders when fixing your Christmas lights. It was not about some angel arriving to save the day.

Disgusted with the television programming, she turned off the set and leaned back in the bed. Perhaps she could take a nap and sleep her time away so she could get home faster. A knock came at her doorway. She looked to see who it was.

"Merry Christmas, Mrs. Huckabee," an elderly bearded man said from the open doorway.

"Who are you?" she snapped.

He gave her a smile. "I'm a volunteer at the hospital, may I come in?"

"Do I know you? You look familiar," Pearl said.

"I don't think we have met before."

"Are you some sort of geriatric candy striper?" she asked.

He chuckled and walked into her room. "Something like that. I just wanted to see how you are doing, and if there is anything I can get you to make you more comfortable. I know it is never fun to be in the hospital, and especially during Christmas."

"The only thing that would make me more comfortable is if I could get home in my own bed. I'm trying to listen to my doctor's advice, but frankly, I don't know why I can't go home. My ankle is not going to heal any faster in this bed than mine at home—and at least I will be more comfortable there."

"When you go home, is your bedroom on the first floor, or will you have to use stairs?"

Pearl frowned. "My bedroom is upstairs. But I do have a guest room downstairs I could stay in. Even that would be better than here."

"You do look healthy and not like someone who needs to stay in a bed all day. Perhaps your doctor will decide it would be alright for you to go home a little early, in time for Christmas."

"I don't see that happening," she grumbled.

"You never know," he said with a smile. "Merry Christmas, Mrs. Huckabee."

He turned and left the room. Pearl sat there a moment, frowning at the now empty doorway.

"I guess I should've asked him to bring me some cookies," she muttered. Picking up the remote, she looked back to the television, deciding to give it another try.

"Merry Christmas, Mrs. Huckabee," came another voice from the open doorway. Instead of turning on the television, Pearl set the remote down on the bed and looked to see who had just walked in her room.

"Doctor, I didn't expect to see you today," she greeted him.

"I have good news," he said cheerfully, walking up to her bedside with clipboard in hand.

"The only good news I want to hear is that I'm going home."

"If you will promise to use that spare bedroom you told me about, and not use your stairs until your ankle heals, then you can go home today," the doctor told her.

She sat up straighter in the bed. "I can?" She looked to the doorway and then back to the doctor. "Did that volunteer talk to you?"

The doctor frowned. "What volunteer?"

"The one who was just in here. An older man, white beard."

"I don't know of any volunteer with that description. Did you say older man—white beard?"

"Yes, he was just in here not five minutes ago."

"I honestly don't know who you are talking about," the doctor said. "Perhaps he was visiting someone else on this floor. Why did you think he had talked to me?"

Pearl considered his question a moment and then shook her head. "It was nothing. But you say I get to go home, today? Really?"

"Yes. I have arranged for a nurse to go home with you, help you get situated. She won't be spending the night, but will be there to get you settled in."

"How much is that going to cost me?"

"Don't worry about it. What your insurance doesn't pay, I have already arranged for our Benevolent Fund to cover. It's a fund the Glandon Foundation started last year for the hospital, to help cover these types of expenses."

When the doctor left the room, Pearl remembered where she had seen the bearded man who claimed to be a volunteer. He was one of the guests staying at Marlow House. The one who had arrived in a taxi.

DANIELLE no longer felt uncomfortable wearing the Missing Thorndike while in Eva's presence. Eva, the necklace's owner before Walt had taken it, had once told Danielle her time for diamonds and emeralds had ended with her life, and the necklace was where it belonged.

Walt had convinced Danielle not to sell it, and while she normally kept it locked in her safety deposit box at the bank, she took it out to wear on special occasions, like their Christmas Eve open house. The antique diamond and emerald neckless looked stunning with the floor-length red dress Danielle had chosen for the party.

Standing in the entry hall with a cocktail in hand, Danielle had minutes earlier welcomed several new guests to the gathering. They had just walked away with Walt to get a cocktail from the bar set up in the living room. She stood alone a moment, surveying the wide open area, decorated festively for the holiday, while Christmas music played in the background.

Across the entry hall, sitting on a wingback chair—one they had brought out from the library—near the first-floor landing by the staircase was Colin, wearing a green suit and bright red jacket, reminding her of one of those vintage Santa Clauses she had seen on Victorian Christmas postcards.

He sat talking to the children who had come to the open house, all convinced he really was Santa Claus, in spite of the fact he lacked the generous belly. Heather stood at his side and helped direct the children. Danielle smiled at the sight, remembering how

Heather had said something earlier about kids being annoying, yet she didn't seem to be bothered by them at the moment. Danielle had also overheard Heather telling one of the children that Santa was cutting back on Christmas cookies and was watching his weight —which was the reason for the more slender version.

Danielle chuckled at the thought and then looked around at the other guests who were drifting from room to room, chatting with friends they encountered along the way. Smiling, she felt a wave of the Christmas spirit rush over her. The years she had been married to her first husband, Lucas, she had enjoyed Christmas, but she hadn't felt the same Christmas spirit that she had experienced as a child. She knew it was because she had missed her parents.

The Christmas spirit she remembered from her youth had returned the first Christmas with Walt. He had given it back to her, by way of a dream hop with her deceased family. While she enjoyed the next Christmas, it wasn't the same, and they had been dealing with Marie's recent death. Marie's spirit had stuck around, but Danielle had hated seeing Adam grieve his grandmother.

The next Christmas—their last one—might have been special, considering Chris was reunited with his brother. But she was unable to think about that Christmas without also remembering Chris's uncles, who had plotted to kill her and Chris. Those unpleasant events tended to tarnish the Christmas memory.

Danielle then thought about the Hoopers and how they had held her at gunpoint just yesterday. Yet for some reason that memory, in spite of the fact it had happened less than twenty-four hours earlier, didn't give her chills of terror—if anything, it felt more like an inevitable event that had helped bring them to a better day.

As if on cue, the doorbell rang. Danielle watched as Lily answered the front door. In walked Elizabeth Sparks, with her parents and her brother. Owen had shaved off the beard. When the brother and sister looked in her direction, Danielle suddenly realized why she thought Owen had looked familiar when they had first met. Brother and sister had the same eyes. When Danielle walked over to greet the new arrivals a moment later, a fresh new wave of the Christmas spirit overwhelmed her.

"I love Christmas," she whispered before welcoming Elizabeth with a hug.

THIRTY-NINE

"I won't tell them you aren't really Santa," Evan whispered to Colin as he sat on his knee, taking his turn giving Santa his Christmas wish while Heather snapped his picture.

"How do you know I'm not?" Colin asked.

Evan grinned. "Because we decorated Christmas cookies together, and I know you are really Mr. Bari."

"Do you know who Saint Nicholas is?" Colin asked.

"Sure, another name for Santa Claus."

"A long, long time ago, Saint Nicholas was also known as Nicholas of Bari," Colin explained. "And you remember what my first name is?"

Evan nodded. "Yes. It's Colin."

"And Colin is a French variation of Nicholas," Colin explained.

Evan frowned. "What is a variation?"

"It's just another way to say it—like a nickname. Your brother is called Eddy, but his real name is Edward, right?"

"So you're saying your first name is really Nicholas?" Evan asked.

"Yes." Colin smiled at Evan.

"Are you saying you really are Santa Claus?" Evan asked.

"You did tell me you believed in the possibility, didn't you?"

"But you don't look like Santa Claus, except for the beard," Evan argued.

"True. But legends and stories often grow up around people, and can sometimes take on a life of their own," Colin explain.

"Santa doesn't have a big belly?"

"When drawing my picture, my friend Thomas thought he should depict me slightly more rounded. Artist interpretation. It took him a while to decide on my wardrobe."

"Who is Thomas?"

"Thomas Nast. He was a cartoonist who lived from the mid-1800s to the early 1900s. His drawings of Santa Claus influenced how many people today imagine Santa might look," Colin explained.

"And you knew him?"

"Yes. I met him on one of my visits to New York. I sat for him when he did some drawings—but as a cartoonist, he didn't always draw the world as a photograph might see it."

"Are you saying you're the real Santa Claus?" Evan asked in a whisper.

"You can figure that out yourself—on Christmas morning."

"How would I do that?" Evan asked.

"When we decorated Christmas cookies, you told me what you wanted for Christmas. If you get it—then I suppose you will have your answer, won't you?" Colin's eyes twinkled.

THE CARS PARKED along both sides of Beach Drive could not damper Pearl's enthusiasm for being home. The Marlows' house was lit up like a Christmas tree, she thought, which was perhaps fitting considering it was Christmas Eve. It was obvious to her they were having a Christmas party next door, and it looked as if most of Frederickport was in attendance, considering the number of cars parked on their street.

Pearl managed to hobble inside using crutches, while the nurse accompanied her. Once in her living room, Pearl sat on her recliner while the nurse busily prepared the guest bedroom and moved some of Pearl's personal belongings downstairs. While Pearl would normally resent a stranger sorting through her things, she was simply grateful she was able to come home.

When the nurse finished preparing the guest bedroom, she went over some final instructions from the doctor, when Pearl's doorbell rang. The nurse went to answer the door while Pearl stayed in the living room on her recliner. When the nurse returned a few minutes later, she was carrying a large box.

"What is that?" Pearl asked.

"A man from next door came over and brought you this," the nurse said, setting the box on the table next to Pearl so she could see.

"What man?"

"He didn't give his name. An older gentleman with a white beard. Said he was from next door, and they heard you had come home. So they wanted to send this over for you." The nurse lifted off the lid so they could both look inside the box.

"Oh, yummy! It's all kinds of food—looks like maybe pumpkin bread, some sliced turkey and ham, a couple of tamales, some salads, and cookies—and pie! They have just about everything in here for a Christmas feast! Would you like me to fix you a plate before I leave? Or should I just put this in your refrigerator?"

Wearing a frown, Pearl leaned back on the chair. "A man with a white beard, you say?"

"Just like Santa!"

ALL THE GUESTS had gone home and Danielle was alone in the kitchen, putting away the food while Walt, Chris and Noah helped straighten up the rest of the house, bringing in any stray glassware and dishes. Joanne had left a few minutes earlier after offering to help, but Danielle had insisted she go home, as she had visiting family, who had also come to the open house.

"I wanted to say goodbye before I left," Colin said when he walked into the kitchen a moment later.

"Goodbye?" Danielle asked, closing the refrigerator and turning to face Colin.

"Yes, it's time for me to go. I wanted to thank you for your generous hospitality, and for letting me take your neighbor some food."

"How did you know Pearl had gotten back?" Danielle asked.

"I might have overheard your friend the police chief mentioning it," he said.

"Hmm...funny, he never said anything to me. But why are you leaving now? It's Christmas Eve. You know you are invited to join us for Christmas."

"And I appreciate your invitation. But I have to leave because it is Christmas Eve," he explained.

"I don't understand," Danielle said.

"Christmas Eve is a busy night for Santa," he reminded her. The next moment he vanished.

EDWARD MACDONALD PULLED the covers up over his youngest son, Evan, who snuggled down in his bedding, looking up at his father.

"Did you have fun tonight?" Edward asked as he sat down on the edge of the mattress.

"I think Mr. Bari is really Santa Claus," Evan whispered.

"Mr. Bari? You mean the older man staying at Marlow House, the one who played Santa tonight?"

Evan nodded. "I know lots of people don't believe in Santa. Eddy doesn't anymore. But Eddy doesn't believe in ghosts either."

"And just why do you think he is Santa?" Edward asked.

"I'm not really sure yet. But I will know in the morning."

Edward arched his brow. "Really? Well, why don't you just try to get some sleep. It is late and we have a big day tomorrow."

MORNING SUNSHINE STREAMED through his bedroom window, waking Evan. He looked around his room and felt a pang of disappointment. Everything in his bedroom seemed the same— just as he remembered it from the previous day. The comic books he had piled on his desk before going to the party at Marlow House were there. The jacket he had worn was abandoned on his desk chair. He had slept through the night and hadn't had a single dream —at least not one that he could remember.

"Get up. It's Christmas morning!" Eddy said excitedly as he burst into Evan's bedroom.

Reluctantly Evan got out of bed and put on his slippers. He

followed his older brother out of his room and into the hallway. Once he reached the living room the aroma of freshly baked bread assaulted his senses, bringing him to a complete stop. His father did not bake bread, but he could remember his mother baking bread on Christmas morning. It smelled like Christmas.

"What are you waiting for?" a woman's voice called out from the doorway leading from the living room to the kitchen. Evan turned abruptly to the sound of the voice—a vaguely familiar one that he could barely remember. And there she was, the mother who had been taken from them when he was far too young to lose a mother.

Evan raced to her arms; they were now open, welcoming him, as she knelt down to receive his hug. He dived into her embrace, his face buried along her neck. He breathed in her scent—he had never completely forgotten how she smelled, how she looked, how she felt. Tears began to slide down his cheeks.

She held him tighter and whispered, "Don't cry, love, you might wake up."

With a sniffle, Evan blinked away the tears and looked up into his mother's eyes. They were just inches from him.

"Why are you acting like such a baby?" Eddy asked.

Evan had forgotten all about his older brother, who had walked into the living room with him. He looked over to Eddy, who now stood with their father. Neither one seemed surprised to find Evan with his mother. Evan looked back to his mother and whispered, "Are they really here?"

"Yes, but they don't know it isn't real. They won't until they wake up," she told him.

"This isn't real?" Evan said with disappointment.

She kissed his nose. "No, silly. I'm here. But the rest...well, you know."

"I would like a little of that loving," Edward said good-naturedly as he approached his wife and youngest son. Cindy MacDonald released Evan and stood up, opening her arms to give her husband a hug. Evan stood next to his parents and smiled, watching the pair embrace.

"Why does it feel like it has been ages since I held you like this?" Evan overheard his father whisper into his mother's ear.

"I love you, Ed. I want you to always remember that. You are such a wonderful father to our boys."

"Come on, stop getting all mushy. I want to open presents," Eddy said from the sidelines.

Cindy released her husband and then looked down at Eddy. "Okay. But I want a Christmas hug from you too."

Eddy gave his mother a wide grin and then ran to her, jumping into her arms and giving her a tight hug. "I love you, Mom."

THEY OPENED THEIR CHRISTMAS GIFTS, but Evan couldn't seem to comprehend what was in any of the packages—but he didn't really care. He just loved hearing his mother's laughter and witnessing his father's happiness. He couldn't recall the last time his father looked so serene. Even Eddy seemed unusually good humored.

After breakfast, the boys sat on the sofa with their mom while she read them Christmas stories and their father built a fire in the fireplace. When the stories were done, the four gathered at the kitchen table to play games. And when the afternoon grew late, they sat down as a family to enjoy Christmas dinner.

When it was time to go to bed, Cindy and Edward tucked their sons in, starting first with Eddy. When it was Evan's turn, he waited silently in his bed, looking up at his parents, saying nothing about the reality of the moment, not wanting to spoil it for his father.

"Did you have a good Christmas?" Edward asked his son after dropping a kiss on his forehead. Cindy stood close by his side, looking down at her youngest son.

"This was the best Christmas ever," Evan told them.

EVAN'S EYES FLEW OPEN. It was pitch dark in his bedroom. He looked over at his alarm clock on the nightstand; the digital numbers lit up brightly. It was 2 a.m. on Christmas morning. Evan thought the dream had felt much longer. He climbed out of bed and walked to his bedroom window, pulling open the curtains. Overhead a half-moon lit up the night sky. Resting his elbows on the windowsill, he dropped his chin on balled fists and looked up at the moon.

The sound of bells broke the silence, and the next moment he saw what appeared to be a silhouette of a tiny sleigh pulled by reindeer dart across the half-moon and then disappear.

Eyes wide, Evan just stared. Finally he whispered, "Thank you, Santa. It really was the best Christmas ever."

FORTY

Walt, Chris, and Noah sat in the living room, drinking coffee, waiting for Danielle to join them on Christmas morning. They had already decided to have cinnamon rolls and coffee by the tree before opening their Christmas stockings and some of their gifts. Chris and Noah sat on the chairs facing Walt, who took a seat on the sofa. Max was already in the room when they arrived, napping under the Christmas tree. No one had gotten dressed for the day, each wearing a robe over flannel pajama bottoms and a shirt.

The men had been chatting for about fifteen minutes when Danielle arrived, carrying a tray with more coffee and fresh cinnamon rolls, while Hunny trailed behind her. She, like the men, wore flannel pajama bottoms and a T-shirt. But unlike them, she wasn't wearing a robe. Danielle set the tray on the coffee table and said, "I just talked to the chief on the phone. It seems Evan got his Christmas wish. In fact, it sounds as if everyone over at the MacDonald house had the perfect Christmas." She took a seat on the sofa next to Walt and drew her stocking feet up on the cushion next to her.

"Are you saying Evan had a Christmas dream hop?" Chris asked.

"It appears so and with Eddy and his father. Of course, at the

239

time the chief had no idea it was a dream—or a dream hop. It all seemed real to him."

"How does he know it wasn't just a dream?" Noah asked.

"He said he woke up to this sense of euphoria. But then he realized it had all been a dream—and for a brief moment he felt profound sadness. And then Evan came into the room and, well, seems they had the same dream. Evan knew all along it was a dream hop. As for the chief, knowing his wife had really visited him and it wasn't just a dream, it made his Christmas."

"What about Eddy?" Walt asked.

"He woke up this morning and told his father about the dream he'd had of his mother, and how it had felt so real, like she had really been there. They didn't say anything to him about having the same dream. The chief didn't want to confuse him. But he did tell Eddy he believed it was possible for our departed loved ones to visit us in a dream. That seemed to make Eddy happy."

Danielle then went on to tell them what Evan had told his father about Colin being Santa.

When Danielle finished recounting the tale, they all sat in silence for a moment.

Finally Chris said, "Last night after Colin did his disappearing act on you, we all decided without a doubt he was a ghost."

"Yes, I sort of figured that one out when he vanished," Danielle said before taking another sip of coffee.

"But is he the ghost of Saint Nicholas?" Chris asked.

"You are talking about the real Saint Nicholas?" Danielle asked.

"According to what Evan told his father, Colin eluded to being Santa Claus. And he did tell Evan about his friend Thomas Nast—and I recall him mentioning something about modeling for a friend name Tom. Could it be possible that the spirit of the real Saint Nicholas inspired Thomas Nast's drawings?" Walt asked.

"I remember now why he is familiar," Noah said excitedly. "I saw him once, when I was a child. It was after our mother died. It was a Christmas party at the group home I had been sent to."

Walt looked at Noah. "Christmas party—that's it. That's why he is familiar to me too. It was a Christmas party during the war."

Danielle picked up her cellphone, which she had set on the tray earlier. She started doing an internet search.

"What are you looking up?" Chris asked.

"I just remembered something else Colin told us. He mentioned another friend from New York. One he wrote a Christmas limerick with. I think he said his name was Clem..." Danielle focused her attention on her search, and when she found what she was looking for, she began to silently read. After a moment she began to laugh.

"What?" Walt asked.

"Clement Clark Moore wrote *The Night Before Christmas*—he was also from New York, and according to this wiki page, he was involved with the Episcopal church, like Colin's friend Clem."

"Are you suggesting the spirit of the real Saint Nicholas helped Moore write *The Night Before Christmas*?" Chris asked.

"I am not suggesting anything. I'm just repeating what Colin told us when he was here."

THE BARTLEY FAMILY, along with Heather, Adam and Melony, joined the current residents of Marlow House for Christmas dinner. Also present were the spirits Eva and Marie. Danielle wanted to ask Eva about Colin, but she arrived after Adam and Melony showed up, making it impossible to have a conversation with the spirit.

When dinner was finished, everyone pitched in to clean the kitchen and then met in the living room to open more Christmas gifts.

Adam and Melony sat next to each other on the floor by the Christmas tree, where Adam watched baby Connor, who was nearby on a baby blanket, smiling and cooing happily. Adam was impressed at how well behaved Connor had been all afternoon, never once fussing or crying, and now he seemed quite content to be alone on his baby blanket, staring up at the tree and making gurgling sounds. Yet what Adam failed to see was his Grandma Marie, who had spent the evening keeping the baby entertained.

Danielle passed out presents, and Adam was surprised when Danielle handed him two from her and Walt. He tore the gift paper off the heaviest package, and when he lifted off the box's lid, his eyes lit up. "Please tell me this is Grandma's recipe," he asked, looking down at the box of divinity.

"You tell me. Taste it," Danielle urged.

Before Adam had a chance to take a piece, Melony reached over and snatched a square and quickly popped it in her mouth. The next moment she shouted, "Oh, it is! This is Marie's divinity!"

When she tried to grab a second piece, Adam swatted her hand away and grabbed a piece for himself. Instead of wrestling him for more divinity, Melony sat back and watched as Adam took a bite of the candy. He closed his eyes and moaned.

"I think he likes it." Melony laughed.

Adam looked at Danielle. "How did you do it? It tastes just like Grandma's."

Danielle shrugged smugly and said, "I like to think Marie's spirit guided me." She gave Marie a wink.

"Guided you, my foot," Marie chortled. "I made it while you sat there and ate cookies."

Heather and the other mediums suppressed their amusement over Marie's comment and Danielle said, "Adam, consider the gift from me and your grandma."

Adam smiled up at Danielle. "Thanks. This was the best gift. You didn't have to give me anything else."

"Oh, go ahead and open the other one. It's just something Walt and I picked up—thought you would like it."

Adam quickly opened the second gift while everyone watched. A moment later he held the framed picture in his hand, studying it. "Is this Grandma's father?"

"Yep." Danielle nodded. "We picked it up in Astoria. It came from the Winterborne estate. I assume Eloise bought it at a yard sale. We were going to use it as one of the white elephant gifts, but after we got it home, we thought there was something familiar about one of the men in the photograph. I started looking through some of the pictures I got from the museum—the ones that belonged to Walt Marlow," Danielle lied. "And I realized the man in the picture is your great-grandfather."

"Wow, this is really cool," Adam said.

"Oh, there is one other thing." Danielle pulled a small gold key out of her pocket and handed it to Adam.

"What's this?" Adam asked with a frown, taking the key.

"We picked up this key from the estate too." It wasn't exactly a lie. "And then I remembered seeing a frame like this in a catalog of my mother's. It has a hidden compartment. The key seems to fit, but I didn't open it. I thought it might be more fun if you open it, see what is inside. It may be empty, but when I shake it, sounds like something might be in there. Who knows, maybe you will find a hidden treasure."

Adam stared at the key a moment. "I seriously doubt I will find a treasure like you have a habit of doing. I don't imagine there is anything in here, but a frame with a secret compartment is kinda cool." Adam shoved the key in the small hole in the back of the frame while they all watched. Not sure how the secret compartment was supposed to open, he gave it a little wiggle, pushing it to and fro.

"It doesn't seem to work. Just my luck," Adam said with a laugh. The next moment the hidden compartment flew open, sending a glittering ring from its hiding place—landing in Melony's lap.

PEARL OPENED her front door and looked outside into the Christmas night. Earlier that evening she had spied her neighbor Heather walking over to the Marlows' house, and then the Bartleys from across the street walking over. There was just one car parked in front of Marlow House. While they obviously had company, the street was significantly quieter than it had been on Christmas Eve.

Draped over her shoulder was her afghan, which she intended to use to keep warm. It was cold outside, but there were no clouds in the sky, and the near half-moon cast light on her front porch. She had made herself a turkey sandwich and intended to eat it under the stars. Awkwardly she made her way outside on her crutches while holding onto the sandwich. Once on the front porch, she sat down on a patio chair and wrapped herself in the afghan.

Pearl sat quietly in the chair for a good fifteen minutes, holding her uneaten sandwich and looking up at the moon. While she was grateful to be home, a wave of loneliness washed over her. It was then she heard a scratching sound. Looking toward the fence separating her property from the Marlows', she watched as the head of a pit bull popped up from the tunnel the dog had dug under the fence on the day of her fall.

She watched as the dog wiggled its way to her side of the yard and then stood there a moment, just looking at her, as if debating what to do next.

"It's you," Pearl said to the dog. "I understand your name is Hunny."

Hunny cocked her head slightly at the sound of her name. She continued to watch Pearl.

With a sigh, Pearl slapped the side of her good leg and said,

"Come here, Hunny."

Hunny trotted to Pearl, her butt wiggling with the stump of her tail wagging. When she reached Pearl's side, she rested her chin on Pearl's knee as she looked up into her eyes.

"I suppose I owe you a thank-you," Pearl said, stroking the dog's head. "You are kind of a big baby, aren't you?"

Hunny licked Pearl's hand.

Pearl laughed. "Okay. This will be our secret. Do you like turkey?"

"I THINK ADAM IS IN SHOCK," Chris said after Adam and Melony went home on Christmas night. Minutes earlier they had all walked the couple to the door and had since returned to the living room.

"He almost accidentally proposed to Mel," Heather said with a laugh.

"Almost accidentally?" Chris repeated with a laugh.

"He's really going to be in shock when he gets that thing appraised," Danielle said. "He has no idea it is the Winterborne engagement ring."

They all laughed.

"If you'll excuse me, I have a few more stops to make," Eva said as she stood up.

"Before you go, I have something to ask you," Danielle said. "I couldn't with Adam and Mel here."

"What is that?" Eva asked.

"Colin—we now know he is a ghost—"

Eva arched her brows. "You do?"

"But what we want to know—is he really the ghost of Saint Nicholas? I mean the real Saint Nicholas?" Danielle asked.

"If you are asking if the man you know as Colin was Saint Nicholas—also known as Nicholas of Bari—who was born over seventeen hundred years ago—the generous priest and philanthropist who inspired what we know as Santa Claus—yes. But if you are asking if he is his ghost, no."

"What do you mean he isn't his ghost?" Danielle asked.

Eva smiled at Danielle and, before disappearing, said, "Nicholas is an angel, not a ghost."

THE GHOST AND THE SILVER SCREAM

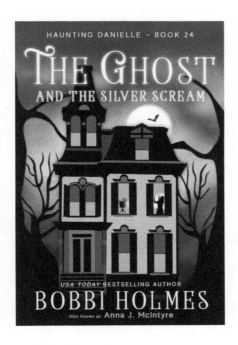

RETURN TO MARLOW HOUSE IN

THE GHOST AND THE SILVER SCREAM

HAUNTING DANIELLE, BOOK 24

Hollywood descends on Marlow House in preproduction for the movie adaptation of Walt's bestselling novel, *Moon Runners*. Hoping for inspiration, they found death instead.

There's a murderer loose, and as the body count increases, secrets are revealed—and it starts to get a little crowded with all these new ghosts hanging around.

NON-FICTION BY
BOBBI ANN JOHNSON HOLMES

Havasu Palms, A Hostile Takeover
Where the Road Ends, Recipes & Remembrances
Motherhood, a book of poetry
The Story of the Christmas Village

BOOKS BY ANNA J. MCINTYRE

COULSON'S WIFE

COULSON'S CRUCIBLE

COULSON'S LESSONS

COULSON'S SECRET

COULSON'S RECKONING

UNLOCKED 🔒 HEARTS

SUNDERED HEARTS

AFTER SUNDOWN

WHILE SNOWBOUND

SUGAR RUSH

CPSIA information can be obtained
at www.ICGtesting.com
Printed in the USA
LVHW031637170220
647192LV00005B/1175